Beautiful MONSTER

USA Today Bestselling Authors

J.L. BECK & S. RENA

Copyright © 2022 by Bleeding Heart Press

Cover Design: C. Hallman

All rights reserved.

No part of this book may be reproduced in any form or by any electronic or mechanical means, including information storage and retrieval systems, without written permission from the author, except for the use of brief quotations in a book review.

BLURB

I thought I knew the truth.

I thought he was my savior.

I'd spent my entire life running from him, only to become trapped in his web.

He says I'll become his wife, that I'll provide him an heir.

I'll do both of those things under one condition.

His father must die.

PROLOGUE - CHRISTIAN

Eavesdropping is never an acceptable act. At least, that's what my father has always told me. But what am I supposed to do when he doesn't tell me anything?

All the secrets. The whispers and conversations that end the moment I enter a room.

If I want to know something around here, this is the only way to make that happen. I lurk in the distance, listening in on every discussion. He says I'm not ready, that I'll need to prove that I can handle what it means to be a Russo before he lets me in on things. Yet I'm months past my fourteenth birthday, and he still treats me like a kid.

I'm not a fucking kid, and one day, I will make sure he knows it.

"E sei sicuro che questa sia la strada che vuoi intraprendere?" *And you're sure this is the route you want to take?* my father says while tugging his pants legs up and then sitting behind his desk.

I stand in the hall on the other side of the door, watching him through the slit between the wall and the hinges. It's late, and most of the staff have retreated to their quarters. The lights are out except for what shines in from the moon and many lamp posts around the property.

From this angle, I can't see who is in my father's office, but by the soft timbre of her voice, I know it's a woman.

"Marco ha chiesto questo," she says. *Marco asked for this.* When she inches a little to the right, I can finally see who it is.

My father stares at her for a moment, contemplating her offer. I observe his features and can sense that he's interested. I should be surprised, but Samuele Russo is a greedy man, and we've been at war with the Guilianis for as long as I can remember.

I didn't catch the entirety of the conversation, just the end, and apparently, we're joining forces. What does that mean for our families? Why isn't Marco here to make this deal?

"Va bene. Ma chiariamo una cosa." *All right. But let's get one thing clear.* Samuele leans forward, resting his elbows on the desk and boring his sight into the woman.

She's nervous if the stiff roll of her shoulders is any indication. Something is off about this, but I can't quite put my finger on it. Why now, after all these years, is my father entertaining this?

"Non si torna indietro. Ottengo ogni centimetro di territorio. E prova ad attraversarmi, e farò in modo che ognuno di voi desideri non essere mai nato." *There's no turning back. I get every inch of territory. And try to cross me, and I'll make every last one of you wish you'd never been born.*

"Finché manterrai la tua parte dell'accordo, non avremo nulla di cui preoccuparci." *As long as you keep your end of the deal, we won't have anything to worry about.*

"E la ragazza?" *And the girl?*

"Dipenderà da te." *That'll be up to you.* The woman grabs her purse from the corner of the desk and slowly turns toward the door.

My father is up on his feet and rounding his desk a second later. "Piacere di fare affari con lei, signora Giuliani. Devo dire che questa offerta non poteva arrivare in un momento migliore." *Pleasure doing* business with you, Mrs. Guiliani. I must say, this offer couldn't have come at a better time.

She shrugs. "Meglio tardi che mai. Sono sicuro che il mio amato marito avrà molto da dire." *Better late than never. I'm sure my beloved husband will have a lot to say.*

Samuele laughs, his thick bravado echoing through the hall. The two inch toward the exit, and I scurry away so as not to be seen. Curiosity stirs inside me, and I find myself needing to make sense of what's going on.

Our families have hated each other for ages, yet Marco sent his wife here in the middle of the night. For what—a truce?

As they leave the office and head toward the front of the house, I hide around the corner, peeking around the wall until she's gone. My father stands with his back against the floor-to-ceiling door and digs his phone from his pocket. After undoubtedly punching in the number to Carlo, his underboss, he brings the receiver to his ear.

"Carlo, riunite tutti. Dobbiamo parlare. Dopotutto, sembra che stiamo ottenendo lo scambio di Guiliani." *Carlo, gather everyone. We need to talk. It looks like we're getting the Guiliani trade after all.*

Something about the deal intrigued me. It's been days since that woman left our estate, and I haven't been able to get the whole ordeal out of my mind. I also knew that asking my father to fill me in would be pointless. Besides, that would let him know I was snooping.

Instead, I decided to figure out for myself what it's all about. My father thinks I'm too young to understand, too naïve, but the truth is, I see and know more than he thinks. After years of watching in the distance, I can recite every plan of attack or pinpoint the flaws in the plans he's too proud to admit he has.

For the last week, I've snuck out at night, stealing one of my father's many cars and parked it at the top of the hill just yards away from the Guiliani residence. Like I have every night, I kill the lights and roll the car into park, careful not to slam the door as I exit.

The trek down the short path between a row of trees is uneven. So I take my time to ensure I don't slip down the small mountain and plummet to my death at the bottom. It's close enough to the property that I can't hear anything that goes on inside, but it does sit at the perfect angle for me to see inside. And with a pair of binoculars and thanks to the wall of windows, I get more than a glimpse of the things that happen in the Guiliani's household.

You would think that as a man of his status, with enemies near and far, he'd want more privacy, as opposed to giving the world a full view of his life. Windows cover every inch of the back half of the house, the half that faces the woods. Maybe that's why he did it, thinking that no one would possibly dare to spy on them or that the trees and mountains would shield him and his secrets.

But that's the thing about secrets. Nothing can ever really keep them under wraps. No matter what you do or how many people you kill, nothing stays hidden forever. And at only fourteen years old, I learned that early on.

Pulling my binoculars from my backpack, I squat low to the ground and settle into my spot. Coming here has become one of my favorite things to do. Not because of what happens in that house but because I know everything there is to know about this family while they are none the wiser to my presence.

It's addicting.

Adjusting my vision, I search through the house. The interesting thing about people is that they are creatures of habit. They'll do the same thing over and over, despite the consequences. It's a comfort, I guess, or selfishness, maybe. In one room, there's the woman who visited my father. She's sitting on her bed, her legs spread wide with her hand between her thighs. My body reacts, my dick twitching at the sight of her touching herself.

I let my gaze linger for a moment before breaking my concentration and searching the rest of the house. It appears quiet. There are no other lights on, at least not until I reach the end. My movement is quick, and I miss it at first, but double back.

There they are. Marco and a woman who is not his wife are locked away in another room. And just on the opposite side of that is a little girl.

She sits on the floor, playing with her dolls without a care in the world, oblivious to the things happening around her. Just next door, her father is betraying her mother and is balls deep in the cunt of one of his workers.

This isn't the first time, and if I had to guess, he enjoys being with her more than he does the woman he's married to. In the short time I've watched them, he's touched his wife maybe once, while just about every other night, sometimes two and three times, he's with this woman. She's his favorite.

And while this happens—while the adults betray each other—this little girl is in her own world. So innocent. So pure. Observing her is probably the best part of all. And not in any creepy way. She's a child. But maybe that's what I like about her.

She reminds me that I've never had this. A loving home where I could be a kid and play with toys until I couldn't keep my eyes open. It's as if I get to live vicariously through her. I get to be a kid again until it's time for me to pack up and return to my world. And at the end of each night, I'm reminded of just how different our lives are.

Our fathers may both be ruthless, cutthroat criminals who lie, kill, and cheat, but none of that touches her. Like now, she's a ball of joy and doesn't even know that things are haywire around her.

She's everything I've never been. She's happy and loved, which is why this whole thing doesn't make any sense to me. Why would Marco agree to give up everything he worked for to my father? It's supposed to be a truce, but I know Samuele better than anyone, and that'll never happen. Once my father gets what he wants, he'll surely put a bullet between Marco's eyes, and the world this precious little girl knows will be over.

A car pulls up, the sound of tires over the pavement breaking my thoughts. A man gets out, slamming the door and racing toward the house. A second later, I see him through the window moving through the bottom level of the home. Even though I can't hear what's happening, his hasty movements tell me that something is about to go down.

When I refocus on the upstairs areas, I notice that Marco and his mistress have finished their rendezvous, but I couldn't pinpoint when since I've been so focused on the girl. Now, he's rushing through the halls, meeting the man at the top of the stairs. He wears a frown on his face as he listens to the man.

Whatever it is, it pisses him off because his face is now a bright shade of red, and his fists are clenched at his side. Needing to make sense of it all, I adjust the focus again, but it only does so much. The ability to read lips would come in handy right about now.

The only thing I do know for sure is that he's yelling. Shouting is more like it. From the corner of my eye, I catch a glimpse of the girl standing with her Barbie in hand. The mistress is at her side, covering up both of the child's ears with her palms. And once again, I'm reminded of how different we are. Even from her father's rants, the girl is shielded —protected.

Marco throws something, shattering it against the wall outside the child's room. She and the mistress jump, then the woman kneels in front of her, saying something to her. By the encouraging head nods and the gentle rubs on the girl's arms, something tells me she's trying to relax. And when the little girl joins in, I know that I'm right. They're singing or at the least saying the same thing again and again until Marco and the man leave the second floor, and things seem to calm down. The mistress kisses the girl's forehead and mouths what looks like the words: andrà tutto bene. *It's going to be okay.*

∽

By the time I make it home and sneak my father's car back into the garage, the driveway is full of cars. Every member of the organization is here, causing a frown to form on my face. The only time everyone is in the same place at the same time is when shit is about to get crazy.

No one hears me come in or sees me watching from the entrance of the great room. My father is in the center, his nostrils flared and gun in hand. Carlo and the others crowd around him, some staring at the floor, others at him, while the rest carry blank expressions.

"Come cazzo ha fatto a scoprirlo?" *How the fuck did he find out?*

Carlo shrugs. "Forse la puttana ha parlato." *Maybe the bitch talked.*

Samuele shakes his head, pointing his gun in Carlo's direction. It never fails to surprise me how unfazed they are about having guns drawn and pointed in their faces.

"Nessuno mi sfida. Li voglio morti. Ognuno di loro, e il territorio di Marco sarà mio in un modo o nell'altro." *No one defies me. I want them dead. Every last one of them, and Marco's territory will be mine one way or another.*

Carlos nods. "E il bambino?" *What about the kid?*

My sense perks up at the mention of the little girl. The hairs on my neck rise as I dread my father's response.

"Sembra che me ne frega un cazzo? Uccidila. Meglio ancora, prendila. Probabilmente prenderò un bel soldo per la figlia di Marco Guiliani." *Does it look like I give a shit? Kill her. Better yet, take her. I'll probably get a good penny for the daughter of Marco Guiliani.* He laughs and the others join him.

"No," I yell without thinking.

The crowd parts, making way for my father to finally spot me standing in the entryway.

"Vattene da qui, ragazzo." *Get the fuck out of here, boy.*

"No. Lascia che lo faccia io." *No. Let me do it.*

My father scratches his brow. "E cosa potrebbe essere?" *And what might that be?*

I step forward, shoulders back and head held high. "Parli sempre della necessità di mettermi alla prova. Questa è la mia occasione." *You're always talking about needing to prove myself. This is my chance.*

He stares at me for a moment. They all do.

"Vuoi il territorio di Marco. Bene. Allora mi assicurerò che tu lo prenda, ma anch'io voglio qualcosa." *You want Marco's territory. Fine. Then I'll make sure you get it, but I want something too.*

"Vai avanti." *Go on.*

"Lo faccio per te. Ucciderò Marco e non potrai più trattarmi come un bambino. Mi lasci lavorare, rivendica un posto negli affari." *I do this for you. I'll kill Marco, and you can't treat me like a kid anymore. You let me work, claim a place in the business.*

"Non sei pronto." *You're not ready.*

"Lo sono e lo dimostrerò. Non più nascondermi le cose, ma voglio qualcos'altro." *I am, and I'll prove it. No more keeping things from me, but I want something else.*

"Sì?" *Yeah?*

"La ragazza. Lei è mia. Non le faremo del male." *The girl. She's mine. We won't hurt her.*

"Perché non dovremmo? Cosa diavolo dovrei fare con una bambina di dieci anni?" *Why wouldn't we? What in the hell am I supposed to do with a ten-year-old girl?*

"La tata. Può crescerla e, quando sarà abbastanza grande, la rivendicherò," I blurt out, my chest heaving with adrenaline. *The nanny. She can raise her, and when she's old enough, I will claim her.*

Samuele looks back and forth between Carlo and me for several minutes. It's so long that I begin to grow restless. And just when I think he isn't going to give in, he smiles.

"Bene. Uccidi Marco, dimostra il tuo valore e ti darò la ragazza." *Fine. Kill Marco, prove your worth, and I'll give you the girl.*

All I can do is nod. Not in a million years did I think that would work, but it did. He caved. He's going to let me prove myself, something I've wanted for a very long time, and at the same time, I'll keep her safe.

"Conosco la sua routine," I admit. *I know his routine.*

"Come lo sapresti?" *How would you know that?*

"Li ho guardati." *I've been watching them.*

"Hmph." Samuele smirks. "Sono impressionato." *I'm impressed.*

"Lo faremo domani sera. Dovrebbe essere solo lui e la sua famiglia, nessuno dei suoi uomini." *We'll do it tomorrow night. It should be just him and his family, none of his men.*

"Bene. Domani allora." *Okay. Tomorrow then.*

I tip my chin at him and turn to leave the room.

"E Christian," he calls out, finishing when I glance at him from over my shoulder. "Fai un casino e la ucciderò proprio di fronte a te." *And Christian. Screw this up, and I'll kill her right in front of you.*

"Non lo farò," I deadpan and leave the room without another word. *I won't.*

I don't get very far when I hear my father say, "Mentre sta uccidendo Marco, ti assicuri che tutti gli altri siano morti... specialmente la ragazza." *While he's killing Marco, you make sure everyone else is dead... especially the girl.*

I freeze in place, fighting the urge to run back in there. Instead, I gather my emotions and decide right here and now that I'll have to find another way to keep her safe.

MONSTER

1

SIÂN

*W*hat the hell happened to me?

My head is so heavy and foggy. I don't want to be awake right now. I must be sick, or else why would I feel this way? Maybe I'm still asleep enough that I can get back to it before I wake up too much.

My stomach churns when I turn my head from one side to the other. God, I'm so nauseated. I think I'm going to throw up, and the sensation only gets worse when I move my head again. I should stay still. Ride it out. Whatever this is, I can sleep it off.

But something is wrong. I can't shake the feeling of something being very wrong. It won't let me rest. What I need more than anything is to sink back into oblivion, but my brain won't let me. Like now that the lights are starting to turn on, the rest are flipping on, too. They flood my head with light forcing me to remember whatever it is I should've been thinking about. But what is that?

My mouth is so dry, like cotton. I try to moisten it, but it's no use. My eyes are still closed, but I hear what sounds like the hum of an engine. I'm not bumping around, though, and I don't feel tires rolling along a road underneath me. I'm not in a car. But there's machinery around somewhere, something like that. The incessant whining is like an ice pick in my ear. No wonder I couldn't fall back to sleep with all this noise.

What is it I need to remember? Maybe Christian would tell me if I could only wet my mouth enough to ask.

It slams into me with all the force of a wrecking ball. All it took was remembering Christian. Pulling up his face in my mind's eye. It's been him all along. He's the stalker. He's the one who's tormented my life all this time.

And he's somewhere near. I can feel him. I don't dare open my eyes to show I'm awake, but I know he's somewhere close. And knowing him, he'll notice the slightest flutter from my eyelids. He's been watching me long enough. So even though my heart is racing and my body starts to tremble, I pull it together as best I can and stay very calm and very still.

All this time. I trusted him. I believed him. I let him into my life. He's a twisted, sadistic monster. He's known what he was doing all along. All this time, he's been taking pictures of me like the ones I found in the apartment. Of Kyla, too. I bite my tongue to keep from making a sound at the thought of her. I was so stupid not to believe her!

And now I don't know if she's alive or dead. I don't know if I'll ever see her again. Where is he taking me? Now that my thoughts are clearer, it's obvious I'm on my way somewhere. That's definitely an engine I'm hearing. Is it a plane? Dear Lord, I think it is. He's flying me somewhere. How will I ever get back?

And the other things I found. I take the deepest breath I dare in hopes of fighting off the rising wave of nausea. Bile rises in my throat and threatens to give me away. I can't let that happen. I've made every wrong decision possible up until now. This time, I have to be smart. I have to control myself.

So even though the image of Taj's cuff link sits directly at the forefront of my mind's eye, along with the photos of my family and everything else Christian's been collecting over time, I force my breathing to stay slow and even.

"Mr. Russo? I have this for you to sign." The soft voice comes from my left. So he is nearby. Not reclined directly beside me, though—the voice wasn't directed toward me, and I was sitting with the window to my right. I can feel the inside wall of the jet against my hand. So he's on the other side of the aisle? I don't want to open my eyes and look. Everything is so much heavier now, so dangerous.

"Thank you." I hear paper shuffling and the sound of someone walking away before Christian speaks again, raising his voice slightly. "I know you're awake. Don't play games, topolina."

Again, I have to fight off the impulse to throw up. His voice is still so gentle. Like he's admonishing a child, talking to me that way. There's still affection. Warmth. How is that possible?

"Come now, Siân. I imagine there's plenty you would like to discuss. Why hold back? We're alone. No one will hear us."

As much as it pains me to do it, I roll my head to the left and force my eyes open. It takes a second to adjust to the brightness in the cabin, especially since the window to Christian's back is unshaded. It's so bright behind his head, like a halo. Ironic. He's the furthest thing from an angel I've ever known. He might be the devil himself.

He's genuinely smiling, too. "There you are. You've been out for a few hours now. We'll be home soon."

My voice croaks when I speak. "Where is home?"

"You'll see soon enough." He frowns, though. "You sound hoarse. Here. Have some water." There's a table set up nearby, with bottles of water and juice lined up. He grabs one, cracking it open. Only because I hear the plastic seal break do I accept it. Otherwise, I might worry he already drugged it. I can't believe I have to think these things about him.

And he was always like this. I chose not to see it. I'm seeing it now, though.

"There." He sits down again, leaning forward, elbows on his knees. Like he's ready to negotiate. "Now we can talk."

Damn right, we can, even if my voice trembles with fear. "It was you. You killed Cynthia, didn't you? All this time, you tried to comfort me and act like you were my rock. You were the one who made this happen. You set everything in motion."

The more I talk, the more real it becomes. More solid. And the dumber I feel. I ignored every sign. Every warning. I was so sure I knew him, even denied the things Kyla and Taj said about him—and look where it got us. I'm captured like prey, and they—oh, God, I don't want to think of what he's done to them.

And I made it so easy. That's the worst part. Even now, I can feel him on me. I can smell him. I gave myself to him, body and soul. I even told him I loved him. I feel so filthy and used. I almost wish he had killed me to put me out of my misery.

His mouth pulls downward at the corners. "Why do we have to start off talking about her? I want to talk about us."

"There is no us, not after what you've done. There never was an us because you've lied to me from the beginning. You were never who you said you were."

"But you were oh, so willing to believe what you wanted to believe, weren't you? You behaved exactly how I wanted you to, like the good girl I know you can be."

"You're disgusting. You have no right to talk to me that way."

He's so fast, almost supernatural in the way he lunges for me, like a snake striking its prey. One second, he's seated across the aisle. The next, he's almost on top of me, one hand on either side of my head. I'm pinned to the seat with no hope of freeing myself.

And he's right here, in my face, sharing the same air. I recoil in disgust, but he only chuckles. "Are you afraid of me? Don't lie. I see it all over you."

"Then why are you asking?" I whisper.

"Because I want to hear you say it. I want you to admit how scared you are right now. There's nothing in the world that excites me as much as your fear. It brings out all my protective instincts. It makes you seem so much more precious."

His fingertips skim my jaw, and I bite back a whimper, but just barely. I'll be damned if I give him what he wants so easily.

"Sweet, Siân," he croons, his breath hot on my face. "I can't wait to make you mine forever."

"That will never happen." I force myself to look him in the eye even though it chills my blood. This murderer, this monster. "I hate you. And you're fucking deluded if you think there's ever going to be a future for us."

"I think you're the deluded one." He touches me again, this time letting his hand stray over my chest. I can't help but grimace in revulsion, which only makes him chuckle again. "Don't pretend. You can grimace all you want, but your body knows better." He proves this by flicking my now hard nipple.

"Don't you touch me." I swat his hand away, but he only laughs. "I'm not going to be a toy for you to play with for the rest of my life. I'd rather be dead than let that happen."

"You only think that."

Jesus, he actually believes himself. He is earnest, maybe more so than I've ever seen him. Why not? He's finally being honest. Finally showing me who he truly is.

I have to get away from him. Short of jumping off the plane, the only thing I can think of is the bathroom. "I have to pee." He backs away, letting me get out of my seat. I'm surprised he let me do that much. My legs are a little wobbly, but I manage to make it to the middle of the jet, holding on to the seats as I pass them.

The bathroom is tiny, as I expected, but it's private. I need my privacy. I have to think.

I don't have my jeans pulled down yet when the door opens. "Get out of here!" I try to yank my pants back up, but he only laughs. The sound brings to mind a crazy kid torturing a small animal.

"What, you think there's a single part of you that doesn't belong to me? If I want to watch you take a piss, I will." He leans back a little, looking up and down the length of the jet in both directions. With a quick jerk of his arms, he closes a pair of curtains on either side of the bathroom, blocking us from the view of whoever else is flying with us. What would they do if I started screaming? If they work for him, probably nothing. I don't want to waste my energy.

Nobody will stop him. My heart's hammering hard enough to hurt, and I might faint if I can't get my breathing under control. "Stop it, please," I whisper, and now I don't care if I sound weak. "This isn't a game. We can talk when I'm finished."

"No, we'll talk when I feel like it." He looks me up and down with a familiar hunger in his eyes, eyes I used to love gazing into. "Now piss if you have to go so badly. I'm not going anywhere, so you might as well do it unless you like wetting your pants. I don't care either way."

I've never hated anyone as much as I hate him right now. I move as little as possible, lowering my jeans just enough that I can sit on the metal toilet seat without getting them dirty. The sound of urine hitting the bowl threatens to bring tears of humiliation to my eyes, but I force them back.

"See? That wasn't so bad." Only he doesn't back away when I'm finished —instead, he pulls my hands away from the waistband so I can't button my jeans back up.

"Stop it," I whisper, trying to smack his hands away. He won't let me this time. Instead, he backs me up against the wall opposite the toilet and shoves a hand between my legs.

"You really think you could live without me fucking you for the rest of your life?" He rubs me, chuckling softly against my throat. His hand is anything but soft. He's so rough that it almost hurts.

I close my eyes, willing this to all be over. I'm not here. I'm somewhere else, anywhere else. This isn't happening.

"Stop pretending," he growls before brushing his lips against my throat. I shiver, but is it revulsion or something else? "We both know nobody can touch you like I can. Nobody can make you feel like I do. I own this body. I own all of you."

"No, you don't." But there's not as much fight in my voice now because, oh my God, it does feel good. My body betrays me, wetness seeping out of me as he works my clit. He's not even being gentle or skillful about it. He's rough, using me. And all it does is make me wetter.

"See? I told you." He laughs softly, lifting his head to look me in the eye. No. I can't look at him this way when it reminds me of when I thought things were good. I have to turn my face away from him while at the same time fighting back a moan. Why is he doing this? What's happening to me? I'm going to kill him for this. I'm going to kill him for so many things.

He presses his body against mine until my ribs ache, and all it does is make me gasp with pleasure. Damn him. Damn him more for laughing, taunting me. "Don't pretend I don't know you, Siân. I know everything there is to know. Your mind, your soul, your body. Especially your body. I've practically got you trained." He touches his forehead to my temple.

"I hate you. You don't know me." Yet when he slides a finger inside me, I shudder again. I have to fight the urge to rock my hips and ride his hand as he massages me inside and out.

"Yes, I do. And you're going to be mine forever."

"I'll get away from you."

"You don't stand a chance."

"You think so?" I pant as every part of me tightens in preparation for an orgasm. "No matter what you do, I'll get away from you. Or I'll die trying."

"Now, now." I don't know whether to be glad or regretful when he pulls his hand away before I have the chance to come. "It doesn't have to come to that, especially since you'll never be successful. Why would you try when we both know you belong to me?"

I have to force myself to look at him and deal with the amusement in his eyes. That's what that performance was all about? His way of proving he owns me or something? I wish I hadn't proven him right. "Because the alternative is allowing you to control me, and that's not going to happen." My fingers shake, but I manage to button my jeans.

"So you're going to waste time and effort trying to run away? No matter where I take you, no matter where we go?"

"That's right."

He leans in, and my head taps the wall when I try to back away. "You know what?" he growls close to my face. "I hope you do try. In fact, I can't wait."

He smiles, and somehow that's the scariest part of all this. How happy he looks. "I can't wait to drag you back kicking and screaming. The louder, the better."

MONSTER

2

CHRISTIAN

I stare at her for a moment, watching the rise and fall of her chest. Her breaths are hasty, her mouth ajar, and despite how badly she's fighting to keep them open, her eyes flutter shut. A smile tugs at the corner of my lips. Siân can pretend all she wants. She can claim to hate me, to be disgusted by me, but her body tells the truth.

Slipping my finger from her dripping cunt, I gaze down at her, enjoying the disappointment that washes over her. And when I lick her juices from my digit, she shudders. Realizing that I notice her disappointment, she stands upright, pulls her shoulders back, and pushes past me.

She hates herself for enjoying my touch, just like the day in the alley when she swallowed my cock. I rather like this game, this feistier side of her. It'll make taking what I want so much sweeter.

Siân returns to her seat, flopping down in the cream-colored chair and crossing her arms over her chest. When I settle in next to her, she attempts to scoot away from me, lodging herself as close to the window as possible. With tension in her shoulders, Siân points her attention out to the clouds, and almost instantly, she starts to relax. It's as if, just for a moment, everything in her world ceases to exist, and it's just her and the large pillows in the sky.

As I watch her, I admire her features. Even with her clothes and hair in disarray, she's fucking gorgeous. And the worse part of all is she doesn't even realize it. That's okay, though. I have every intention of bringing out the best and worst in her. Now that we're on our way to Italy, where we belong, she'll soon take her rightful place next to me.

Soon she'll appreciate the things I've done for her, and in the end, she'll see that we belong together. And no, I don't expect her to bend easily, but I sure as shit am going to enjoy forcing it out of her. Whether that be with my dick or through her fear is entirely up to her.

It isn't long before Siân succumbs to sleep again, and I can't stop myself from watching her. She is at peace in her dreams without a worry in the world. Too bad that isn't the reality she'll be waking to when we land. At the thought, my jaw ticks, and I adjust in my seat, my mind going back to the brief conversation with my father.

Yet again, he's ordered me home, interfering with my plans. It's because of him I'll need to reassess how to get Siân to trust me. We were close, everything I'd done had finally paid off, but then he had to ruin it all by forcing my hand and causing this new ripple in our relationship.

And throughout it all, the bastard still hasn't given me much detail as to what was so fucking urgent. Much like always, he's remained cryptic, sparing all the important details. I have been able to gather that shit must not be good. It's the only time he orders me to be anywhere. When shit hits the fan, and he needs me to handle it.

It's the only time we have any real discussions. If it doesn't involve business, we have nothing to say to one another. I try to think of a time when my father didn't treat me as just a member of his army, and it's pointless.

I learned ages ago that the only thing my father cares about is his money, his power, and asserting the dominance he thinks he holds over everyone. We've never been close, not in the traditional sense. Where other boys grew up playing catch and being raised to be gentlemen, my upbringing wasn't so touching. There were no bedtime stories, or positive affirmations, only wrath and ridicule. And the only praise I got was when I proved how valuable I was to his organization.

Boys my age played sports and chased girls around the courtyard, while I learned how to disable and reassemble an H&K G11 in under a minute by the time I was eleven. And by my fourteenth birthday, I'd made my father proud when I murdered a man for the first time. Not that he used his words to bid me a job well done. No, he rewarded me with pussy and a handgun of my own.

Shortly after that, the orders came. I took care of anyone my father wanted gone with no questions asked. He's never been a man who explained himself, and I'm convinced that's where I get it from. We do what we want, when we want it, and dare a soul to deny us that.

Siân thinks I'm a monster, but she hasn't met the man who raised me, the man who ordered her family be murdered—who ordered she be murdered. I stare at her again, sucking in a breath as I contemplate the reaction my father will have when he lays eyes on her. Or better yet, how Siân will behave when she meets the man responsible for every horrible thing that's happened to her.

Fifteen years ago, I told him she'd died in that fire with her family. That's something I would only know because it was my duty to end her life the same way I had Marco Giuliani. But I couldn't, she was meant to be mine, and my father's greed wasn't going to get in the way of that.

"Buonasera signor Russo, tra venti minuti arriveremo a Milano." *Good evening, Mr. Russo. We will be arriving in Milan in twenty minutes.* The pilot's voice blares over the intercom, pulling me from my thoughts.

With a heavy sigh, I sit up in my seat and lean over to fasten the seat belt around my topolina's tiny waist. Inhaling her scent, I brush the tattered strands of hair from her face before fastening my own belt into place.

Tony pokes his head into the aisle and glances back at me. "The car is already there. Your father wants to see you immediately once we get back to the estate," Tony rambles on, then darts his gaze to Siân. Heat builds in my chest, but I manage to keep from slapping him for daring to look at my woman. "What do you plan to do about her?"

I stare at him, my face void of all emotion. "She's none of your concern," I deadpan, boring my eyes into him, silently challenging him to combat me.

"Your father isn't—" Tony continues, but I cut him short.

"Mi occuperò di mio padre," I snip. *I'll handle my father.*

Tony raises his hand in surrender and faces forward again. I shouldn't have snapped. Tony may work for my father, but he's the closest thing to a brother I've ever had. We fight and debate, but in the end, he always has my back. So I know when he questions me about Siân, it's not done maliciously. But it doesn't mean I'll ever allow him or any man to question me where she is concerned.

She belongs to me. Her safety, her happiness and pleasure, and even her fear is mine and mine alone. Tony, my father, and whoever the fuck else will do good to remember that. I'm easily tempered and deadly when I'm angered. For months, I've hidden that side of myself from Siân, and now that she knows the truth, I no longer have to live in the shadows.

I'll still need to practice patience, though. The mission never changes, only the circumstances in how I will win her over—mind, body, and soul. It'll come in time. She thinks she hates it, but soon enough, she'll be begging to be a part of this world.

The plane jerks as the wheels underneath are released to prepare us for landing. We begin to slow, our descent from the air only moments away. When the tires hit the pavement of our private airstrip, the cabin rattles as the pilot floors the brakes, bringing us to a complete stop.

Once the overhead lighting comes on, I unfasten both my seat belt and Siân's. The action startles her from her sleep.

"What are you doing?" She cowers into the corner, attempting to put space between us.

"Come. We've landed," I say while stepping into the aisle.

Siân doesn't move. Instead, she throws her gaze around, then squints out of the window. "Where have you brought me?" she quizzes without budging.

"Home," is all I offer her before holding my hand out to her to take.

"You've kidnapped me," Siân accuses.

I breathe in through my nose, mentally telling myself to relax. This is new for her, and because she's still getting to know the real me, I'll give her a pass for testing me.

"Topolina." I keep my arm outstretched, tipping my head to signal once more for her to take my hand.

Siân slaps my palm. "I'm not going anywhere with you, you sick bastard. You've killed my friends and Cynthia. I'm going to make sure you rot in—"

She doesn't get a chance to finish her empty threat because I'm in her face in an instant, caging her between the seats with my hands on either side of her.

"Non vuoi mettermi alla prova, topolino," I seethe. *You don't want to test me, little mouse.*

She stills. The only indication she's listening is her heavy breaths. Siân's jaw clenches and her lashes flicker in rapid succession. She wants to be strong and not let me know she's afraid. A grin teeters on my lips, faltering almost instantly.

It's amazing, really. Siân isn't even aware of how tempting it is to snap and play this little game with her. The sadist in me desperately wants out. Hasn't she learned by now that I like the chase? All this false bravado she's displaying only makes me want to break her—show her who's really in charge here.

"It's cute you think you have a choice." With a finger under her chin, I tilt her head to make sure she can look me in the eye. "You don't. And the sooner you realize that, the better off you'll be. You're mine, Siân." I peer down at her pouty lips, my dick twitching against my zipper from thinking about having her mouth around me. "When I tell you to do something, you do it."

"Or what?" she challenges me.

I inch closer, and she stares at me over the bridge of her nose while craning her neck until her head hits the window. I huff. "Whatever it is—I'll be sure to make it hurt."

"I hate you," she vents.

"But you've already confessed your love as you rode my dick, topolina," I tease and stand upright.

"Fuck you," she spits.

"Soon enough. Now up," I bark.

Finally, she does as I instruct, but not without a fight. She pushes past me, jerking her body away from my touch while glancing back at me every so often. We reach the exit and take the steel staircase one at a time. The bright sun is damn near blinding, and the familiar smell of my country fills my senses.

Home sweet home.

"Welcome back to Italy, topolina," I announce behind her.

Her body stiffens at my words, the dread ripping its way through her body. I knew that bringing her back here wouldn't be easy, but she's just going to have to get used to it. Something in her posture tells me she's going to run, and just as I fix my mouth, she proves me right.

"And Siân, run, and I'll—"

She bolts before the words leave my lips, her arms flailing as she runs wildly. Tony chases after her, but she dodges him only to have him corner her at the hangar. She attempts to open the door, but her efforts are useless. It's locked, and she bangs on it while screaming for help.

Tony grips her by the bicep and drags her toward me. I meet them halfway, and Tony releases her. She attempts yet again to get away, but I'm much quicker than she is, snatching her by the back of her neck and tugging her to me. Her arms fly out as she tries to balance herself against my grip.

"Get your filthy hands off of me." She reaches back, clawing at my wrist. "I'm going to kill you for what you've done."

Bringing my mouth to her ear, I click my teeth, and she immediately tenses up. "Ooo. Who knew you had such a dirty little mouth, topolina? Keep it up, and I'll fuck it."

She shudders, her shoulders shaking with each forced breath from her lungs. That silences her, though, and all the fight she had a second ago disappears. What's left now is a woman torn between hating and undoubtedly wanting what I just promised.

I recognize the reactions running through her, the fake sense of self-deprecation. Something she's put on to trick herself and those around her that she's modest. Something she uses to convince herself that she doesn't like what's happening.

She certainly does. Why else has she moved the way she has the entire time I've followed her. This moment right here is the most effort she's put into saving herself, and even then, her exertion is weak.

"You'd like that, wouldn't you? Want me to fuck your throat like I did in that alley?" My dick stiffens at the memory of her on her knees in that piss-riddled alleyway with my cock in her mouth.

She inhales, and I notice the subtle tremor of her lips. "Why are you doing this? I thought you were different."

"I told you—you're mine. And you only have yourself to blame for not seeing me for who I am."

"I'll never stay with you," she deadpans and locks her legs to strengthen her stance.

Releasing my hold on her neck, I quickly scoop her up over my shoulder. Siân yelps and punches at my back. With a firm slap to her ass and a hard squeeze, I carry her just as I promised, kicking and screaming to the blacked-out SUV waiting for us.

I toss her into the back seat, and if she didn't try to escape from the other side, I'd be offended. The driver thinks fast and locks the doors just as she wraps her slender fingers around the handle.

"Let me go."

"And here I was thinking you wanted to see your precious Cynthia again," I add and slip in next to her.

That gets her attention, and her tussling stops. Siân stares at my profile, patiently waiting for me to direct the driver to take us home. With Tony in the seat next to him, he starts the engine and peels away from the runway.

MONSTER

3

SIÂN

I have to think of a new way to get out of here. I have to come up with something That's the thought that hammers at the inside of my skull with every beat of my heart as the sun sinks below the horizon. Every second that passes feels like a wasted second. I should be planning and coming up with ideas. There has to be something around here I can use to fight my way out, right?

Except there isn't. I've already checked. This room is a little better than a cell, with nothing but a narrow bed that looks even smaller than it really is, thanks to the size of the room around it. High ceilings, plenty of space, gleaming hardwood floors. I could do great things with a room like this and an unlimited budget.

Unfortunately, it's the opposite of what I need right now.

Once again, I try to turn the doorknob. What did I expect? For it to magically be unlocked this time? Like standing in front of an open refrigerator and waiting for something new to materialize. The tiny window in the attached bathroom is way too small for me to get through, even if I could break it open.

Besides, that would be a waste of time. All the windows in this room are sealed shut, but I can tell just by looking out that I'm far off the ground.

Three floors, at least. I would have no way to get to the ground without breaking something. Probably my neck.

Right now, that doesn't seem like such a bad idea. With my luck, though, I would break everything but. Then I'd have no choice but to let Christian use me however he wants while telling himself he's taking care of me. Because that's how his twisted mind works.

He didn't even bother telling me where he was going when he left. Only that he had things to take care of. I shudder to think about what that means now that I know what he's capable of. Is that his way of saying there's somebody to kill? Or kidnap? Maybe both. Like Cynthia. What did he do to Cynthia?

And how sick does a person need to be to pretend they're offering support and kindness when they're the one who caused the pain in the first place? No, he didn't admit his exact role in Cynthia's disappearance, but he didn't have to. I could see it on his face. He didn't bother correcting me, either, did he? No, instead, he used my desire to see her against me.

And he says he knows me. I know a thing about him, too. Maybe not as much as I wish I knew—otherwise, I would have stayed away from him—but enough to know that he's bluffing.

Even the sight of the pitiful little bed makes me yearn for rest. Much like my freedom, I don't feel like that's something I can enjoy right now. I'm too afraid to sleep since anything could happen. What if he sneaks in here and does something to me? I'd put nothing past him, especially now that I know about his twisted version of our relationship. He takes pride in embarrassing me, humiliating and scaring me.

What if I could strip the bed and tie the sheets together? Would that give me enough to escape? I look out the window, and once again, I try to open it. No luck. I could break it, sure, and there would be plenty of room to get through. I look down again, then look at the sheets. I don't know if they'd be long enough, even tied together. I don't even know if I have the upper body strength to lower myself, either. And I sure as hell can't scale the wall like Spider-Man. "Goddammit." I smack the glass with my open palm and shed a hot, frustrated tear that wants to turn into a deluge.

Maybe I do need to get some rest, after all. Take care of myself. I can't let my mind unravel. I have to stay sharp if I'm going to fight him.

Naturally, this line of thinking leads me to the bathroom attached to what's basically my cell. I flip on the lights this time and take a look around. Should I be surprised to find towels, soap, and shampoo on the counter? Along with them is a pair of soft pants and an equally soft shirt, both of which are in my size. How long has he been planning this?

My fingers curl around the fabric, my body trembling. All this time, he's been planning for this. And I was so oblivious.

I don't want to give him what he wants. I don't want to use these things he's left for me. On the other hand, I'm a mess. Filthy, sweaty, my own smell disgusts me. I could stay this way in hopes of keeping him off me, but I get the feeling he wouldn't care either way. Or he'd force me to bathe with him, which is an even more disgusting idea.

No matter what he thinks, I'm doing this because I want to. That's what I tell myself as I run a hot bath and strip off my dirty clothes. I gather the soap and other toiletries and leave them on the edge of the tub, then lower myself into the water. Instantly my muscles start to loosen. Everything but the tension in my chest, that is. That's not going anywhere.

I dunk my head a few times first, rubbing my fingers over my scalp to loosen any dirt or oil. It doesn't take long to shampoo, and I stick my head under the running faucet to rinse my hair. Settling back again, I pick up a washcloth and a bottle of fragrant soap. I'll be able to think better when I'm clean and dressed in fresh clothes. I'm already more relaxed, too, which can only be a good sign.

That relaxation lasts roughly as long as it takes me to blink an eye since the door leading from the bedroom opens before quickly closing again.

I cross my arms over my chest, drawing my knees up close to the rest of my body. Footfalls echo in the mostly empty space just as Christian appears in the doorway. The water suddenly feels much colder.

He doesn't say a word. His only communication is a glance at the counter before returning his attention to me. He's glad I took his suggestion and used what he left for me. It's probably confirmation in his sick mind that he knows best.

"Where did you go?" I ask. "Why can't you tell me anything? Why am I locked in here?"

The only sound coming from him is that of his breathing. It's not the cool air on my wet skin that makes me tremble. No matter what he says, even if it's something filthy and depraved, it's better than his silence. Not knowing what's coming next.

He crosses the room, his eyes raking over me. A part of his lower lip disappears beneath his teeth, and now I know exactly what he has on his mind. Yet instead of stripping and getting into the tub or demanding I stand and show myself to him, he lowers himself to one knee beside me. The washcloth floats on the surface of the water where I dropped it. He picks it up, soaps it, and begins rubbing it over my shoulder, moving it slowly down my arm.

What is this? I would ask, but something tells me I wouldn't get an answer. Nothing that makes sense, at least. He's not demanding or rough when he takes my wrist and lifts my arm to wash the underside, repeating the process with my other arm. I'm too surprised to react.

Until he moves down to my chest and the nipples peeking out over the water's surface. Reflex makes me try to fold my arms again, to cover myself, and this time, he's less gentle as he pulls them apart. Still, he doesn't say a word, not even when I clamp my legs together tight enough to make them shake while he soaps my calves, ankles, and feet.

I never realized how strong he is. No, that's not true. I can't forget how he overtook me in the alley and forced me. It's still hard to believe that was him, but not so hard when he's determined to part my legs and wash between them.

"You don't have to do that."

He ignores me, abandoning the cloth in favor of running his fingers between my lips. Unlike when we were in the jet's bathroom, he's gentler now, stroking my clit with a firm touch.

And it takes no time at all for my body to betray me like it did before. I can't help but arch my back, moving my hips in time with his strokes against my most sensitive places. He doesn't say a word, but his breathing deepens, quickening until he sounds like a rutting animal while I'm lost in sensation.

It's so wrong. I hate this. But God, I hope it never stops. That's the last conscious thought I have when an orgasm slams into me, knocking my head back and making my hips buck until water splashes out onto the floor.

And he doesn't stop, either, continuing to finger me even when I try to throw him off. He won't let me win. He won't stop until he's ready to stop. Another orgasm tears through me, and I can barely bite back a scream. I'm ready to beg him to stop since I don't think I can take anymore but thank the lord, he withdraws his finger then.

By the time my eyes are open, he's gone again. But he hasn't left me alone, not really. I still hear him walking around in the empty room next door.

I have no choice but to get out of the tub and get dressed. My pussy is still twitching in aftershocks, and my legs are shaky, but I need to get up. I don't want to leave myself vulnerable to him.

Why didn't I try harder to stop that? And why did I have to come so fast, so hard? All I'm doing is proving him right, and he can't be right. This is only encouraging him. How am I supposed to get out of this if I can't stop encouraging him? I'm even weaker than I thought.

At least the clothes are soft and comfortable, the only comfort I have right now. And they cover me up, which is another plus. The less exposed skin, the less chance of getting him hot.

I walk barefoot into the room and stop short in horror to find Christian pulling his T-shirt over his head. "What are you doing?"

For the first time since he rejoined me, he speaks. "What does it look like?"

"Why are you doing that here?"

"Why do you think?"

I wrap my arms around myself, shoulders up around my ears. "You're never going to touch me again the way you just did. I hope you know that."

He only snorts, then drops his pants. "Come on. It's getting late. You need to rest."

"I'm not getting into that bed if you are."

He turns slowly, facing me head-on. "Either you get in that bed on your own, or I put you in the bed." For a moment, I contemplate my next move, but it's like he can read my mind and instead says, "Tell me you don't think I'll do it." He grins, teeth flashing in the moonlight now shining through the window. "I want you to. I want you to challenge me. Do it. It'd be a pleasure to prove you wrong and put you in your place."

This heartless bastard. I make sure to glare at him as I cross the room and lower myself to the bed, pressing my back against the wall. "That's fine with me," he grunts and sits down. "Less chance of you trying to get past me. And by the way, don't even bother to do that."

He stretches out, taking up more than half the mattress since I'm lying with my back to the wall. "We're locked in. And we're not leaving this room until I say we are."

I know he's right. And I'm too tired to argue. Too tired, too sad, and too disappointed in myself. How can I ever trust myself again when I was so blind to who he truly is? And if knowing the truth isn't enough to keep him from manipulating my body, what is?

He's on his back, one arm under his head, the other across his midsection. A man without a care in the world. What would it take to kill him here and now?

Instead of wondering, I dare to ask the question heaviest on my heart. "Where is Cynthia? What did you do to her?"

The room is dark, but I can make out his eyes opening. "Can't you just go to sleep?"

"Not until I know. I won't let you go to sleep, either, so you might as well tell me. Did you kidnap her? Are you holding her somewhere? Did you…" I can't even bring myself to say it.

He spares me that, at least. "She's safe. Alive. I have her somewhere remote, but she's in one piece. You can believe that, trust me."

"Trust you? Do you hear yourself?"

He turns his head slowly until he's facing me. "Did you think I would kill her? Or even hurt her badly? I only hurt her as much as I needed to in order to take her. That's all. But I know how much she means to you. She did keep you safe and protected all these years. I can't forget that, either."

"Then why did you do it?"

"She recognized me. I couldn't let her move around freely when she knew who I was. But she's perfectly fine. You don't need to worry about her."

I damn near roll my eyes. Right. I'm sure that's the truth. Because he's been so honest in the past.

"I need to see her." He turns his face toward the ceiling, but I can't let it go. I won't. "I need to see for myself that she's okay, and I need her to see me, too. I'm sure it's not easy. She's probably worried sick, the way I am about her."

All he does is grunt, and my resentment grows. "You expect to keep me locked in this room? Do you want me to behave myself? Then I want to see Cynthia. You just said you know how much she means to me. You're right. I want to see her."

"And you'll behave yourself?"

Why do I feel like I'm making a deal with the devil? Right. Because I am. "I will. I'll do what you want. Anything, so long as I get to see her for myself."

Silence unfurls between us, and every passing moment ratchets up the tension that's found its way back into my muscles so soon after my bath. Is he going to toy with me some more? I can only imagine that's exactly what he's going to do. And there's nothing I can do to stop him.

"Fine. Behave yourself, and I'll take you to her. I promise." He closes his eyes again. "Now go to sleep before I change my mind."

I know better than to look a gift horse in the mouth. Besides, I'm exhausted. I have no choice but to close my eyes when they start to close by themselves. And soon, there's nothing but darkness.

4

CHRISTIAN

"Come on," she grunts. The sound of Siân's voice, followed by her panting and the wiggling of something, pulls me from my sleep. "Open, dammit."

Wiping the sleep from my eyes, I first check the space directly next to me. Not that I expected to see her tiny frame tucked in beside me. I already know she isn't. But it's my brain's way of confirming the obvious. When I finally direct my attention to the other side of the room, Siân is kneeling at the door, using something to try to wedge the door open.

She has her shoulders hiked around her ears, and her concentration is so deep she doesn't notice me watching her. It doesn't surprise me one bit that she's already trying to escape, and if I'm honest, I'm glad she did. It'll give me a reason to punish her.

I slip out of bed, my toes nestling in the rug beneath it, and when my bare feet hit the cold wooden floors, a shiver runs the length of my spine. Siân remains focused on her attempt to free herself, but she's no longer kneeling. Instead, she gives the knob one more shake before succumbing to defeat. Sad shoulders and an exasperated breath are the only reactions she has.

At least until she catches a glimpse of me from the corner of her eye. She sucks in a shaky breath, her bottom lip quivering at the sight of me. I stalk toward her only to peer down at her, torn between whether to kiss her or spank her for defying me.

"Are you done?" I ask while reaching out to stroke her cheek.

She turns her head to keep me from touching her, and when I inch closer, she presses her back as far as she possibly can into the door. Undoubtedly she wishes she could disappear or somehow magically slip through the hard surface just so that she could be anywhere but here. Sorry to disappoint, topolina. This is the only place she'll ever step foot in again.

"Yes," she huffs out, her body trembling in fear.

Running the back of my hand along her collarbone, I move her hair out of her face. I need to look at her, to see the fear etched into her features. Still, she tries to get away, but I hook my palm at her nape and force her to me.

Siân struggles to keep from meeting my gaze while pushing at my chest to create even the smallest amount of distance between us. I yank her forward, dragging her back over to the bed despite how difficult she's making this. Siân falls only for me to snatch her up, then claws at my wrist until she breaks the skin. There's a sting when the air hits the newly opened wound, but I push it to the back of my mind.

"No, Christian. No. Please, I won't try to run again."

I tilt my head, a soft chuckle bubbling in my throat. "Now see, I don't believe you. You promised me you'd behave, and already you're lying to me."

"All you've done is lie," she points out.

I halt and snap my gaze to her while aggressively pulling her to me. "Wrong. You just didn't pay attention."

Siân continues to hold on to my wrist, but it does nothing to alleviate the hold I have on her neck. Tears brim her eyes, and her chest falls in sharp waves as she tries to keep it together. I survey her face, letting my eyes roam her features, just hoping for a glimpse of fear. My silence makes her uncomfortable, and I can feel the tension building in her body. And then I see it, the consternation she's fighting so desperately to keep at bay.

Her efforts are useless—pointless because, in the end, I will always get what I want. Until she accepts me for what this is—accepts herself for who she is, I will always hold this level of power or control. I get that she sees me as a monster, and so fucking be it. It's a hat I wear proudly. But until she opens those beautiful eyes of hers and sees that we aren't that different. She was born to live at my side through the blood, the pain, and carnage.

"What do you want from me?" she asks as warm tears trail her cheeks.

"Just what you're giving me, topolina. You. Your tears—"

"And my fear, right? That's what you said."

"Right now, I want your cries," I admit and return to coaxing her over to the mattress.

Her flight or fight instincts kick in, and she swings at me, landing a blow to the side of my head. I stop, my jaw clenched, but she ceases hitting me. From my peripheral, I can see the panic seeping from her. The painful anticipation as to how I will react is almost crippling for her. Her knees give out, but I keep her upright.

"What are you going to do?" she screeches.

"Teach you a fucking lesson." I toss her over to the bed, and she catches herself with her hands bunched into the comforter. Quickly I'm behind her, and in an instant, I slip my fingers into the waistband of her sleeping pants and yank them down until her tight ass is staring back at me. Blemish-free olive skin is just waiting for me to mark. My cock twitches at the sight of her naked flesh, and it takes everything in me not to take her cunt right now.

"Christian, no, please." She squirms to get free.

Gripping her hair, I tilt her head back and hover over her, my already hard dick nestling against her ass through my pants.

"Run again, and I'll break you. I've told you not to test me and to behave, yet not even twenty-four hours into this new life together, you're disobeying me. That's a problem, so now I'm going to punish you."

"I'm sorry. I won't act up agai—"

Her words fall short when I land a slap on her ass, the sound of my palm against her skin echoing through the otherwise empty room. The hit stings me just as much as it does her. Siân flinches, her cry muffling out as she buries her face into the blanket.

Smack.

I slap her ass again, this time rubbing away the handprint I've left behind. She fists the sheets, and her breathing grows erratic. I spank her some more, and with each hit, she whimpers. From this angle, I see her biting down on the comforter.

"Mm," she moans, although it is barely audible thanks to the mouthful of fabric.

Fuck, I think to myself. Seeing her like this, her ass exposed for me, my mark on her skin, and the moans she's fighting to hold back are enough to drive me wild. But I contain myself, ignoring my raging erection. I have one goal today, and that's to show her what happens when she tries to run, to teach her that her actions have consequences.

Continuing her punishment, I raise my hand to strike her bottom one more time but stop when I notice the arousal seeping from between her thighs. I stare at her for a moment, her sweet little pussy lips pressed tightly together from how hard she's holding her legs together.

"Topolino, non smetti mai di stupirmi," I groan. *Little mouse, you never cease to amaze me.*

I run the pad of my thumb over her lips, scooping her honey up in one go. Suddenly, she jumps, completely caught off guard by the change in pace. Using my tongue to clean her juices from my finger, I peer down at her, gripping my cock through my boxers.

"You like being spanked, don't you?"

She doesn't answer me, so I slap her ass so hard she has no choice but to react. Maybe not with words, but her body says it all.

"Yeah, you like it. Is that why you've done a piss poor job of hiding? You were hoping I'd find you."

"Fuck you," she seethes, her words muffled through the blanket.

Smack.

I expect her to squirm some more, to run, to cry out, but she doesn't. Instead, she squeezes her thighs together and attempts to hide the moan that escapes her. Tracing her lips again, I part her slowly, watching her expression closely. When I press against her entrance, she shudders, and I get to see just how turned on she is.

I don't give her what she wants, though. Instead of slipping my finger into her cunt, I trail her moisture up to her ass and rub it around her puckered hole. Siân tenses up, and a laugh builds in my chest.

"The next time I tell you not to do something, you listen, or it'll be this tight little ass I punish next."

She tightens up at my threat, but her disappointed sigh gets my attention. So fucking greedy for pleasure even when she should hate me. I back away and find my shirt at the foot of the bed and slip it on. Siân lies still for a beat, not budging until her breath normalizes. She's embarrassed, and I can bet she's hoping I leave so she doesn't have to face me.

Think again, sweetheart. I want to see every ounce of dread and be present the moment she realizes that the rest of her life belongs to me.

"It's time for breakfast."

"I'm not hungry." She sits up and redresses herself, but she doesn't look at me. She can't. Her cheeks are flushed, a deep shade of red painting her skin.

"Do I need to spank your ass again?" I ask without looking at her as I straighten out the hem of my shirt.

Siân remains still, her features twisted in a mixture of things—hate, fear, and even disgust. She wants to challenge this, but somewhere in her mind, she knows that would be a bad idea. And I have to admit, this feistiness is a side of her I'm not used to. After what I've witnessed with Kyla and Taj, she's always been somewhat of a pushover.

With them, she allowed them to walk all over her, something I will never understand because she is the daughter of a mafia king. His reign may have ended fifteen years ago, but his name still carries weight in Milan. Marco was just as ruthless as my father and made lessons out of anyone who crossed him. I may have been only a boy at the time, but I've heard the tales, witnessed the war that brewed between our families, and saw the bloodshed. A legacy like that doesn't just go away. It's ingrained in the blood of the daughters and the sons, generations after generations. How she could allow those people to get away with the disloyalty and betrayal disturbs me.

One way or another, she's going to become the queen she was always meant to be. Even if it means she'll hate me for the rest of our lives together. People can call it what they want, but the truth is, there is a paper-thin line between love and hate, and the sex is amazing either way.

When Siân doesn't move, I stalk forward, pull her to her feet, and aggressively fix her clothes on her body. She's a disheveled mess but gorgeous nonetheless. She's stubborn, or at least attempting to be.

I drag her by her arm to the locked door and knock three times before finally, we hear the latch release. On the other side is Helga, our maid. She steps aside for Siân and me to exit the room, and from my peripheral, I notice the pleading glance Siân gives to her. It's pointless. In this house, no one questions me or dares to interfere. So any hope Siân has for escaping me will get her nowhere.

Siân continues to tussle with me, working overtime to get free, but my grip is tight. We reach the kitchen and are immediately met with the aroma of breakfast. This is something I'm excited about, considering how much I've missed Italian cuisine. The kitchen is empty except for the chef, who's wiping down the counters and clearing dirty dishes.

"Signor Cristiano." *Mr. Christian.* He tips his head in my direction, and just like Helga, he doesn't even bother glancing at Siân. "La colazione è nel patio questa mattina." *Breakfast is on the patio this morning.*

"Grazie, Aldo. E mio padre?" *Thank you, Aldo. And my father?*

"Scenderà più tardi, c'era una riunione a cui doveva partecipare." *He'll be down later, there is a meeting he needs to attend.*

I nod and head for the sliding door that leads out into the patio area that sits just off the kitchen. Siân huffs and puffs, silently cursing me for forcing her to be here, for all the things I've done—yada yada yada.

When we make it to the table, I yank out a chair and push her into it. Her body shakes from the sudden movement, and a frown forms on her face.

"Ouch." She jerks her arm away and rubs at her wrist. "You're hurting me."

Bringing my face to hers, I grip her chin and make her look me in the eye. "Topolina, what happened this morning was nothing to the pain I can truly cause."

She swallows, the bob of her throat rolling against my hand. I squeeze a little harder, but not enough to actually cause her pain this time. Just enough to let her know that hurting would be easy. I survey her features while roughly sliding my hold from her chin to the piece of flesh right before her throat. I crane my neck, the memory of how good it felt to fuck her throat replaying in my mind.

Unease washes over her, and she manages to be brave enough to snap her head back until I am no longer touching her. I smile at her, loving to see how easy she is to rouse. This is going to be fun—our very own game of cat and mouse.

"If I want your tears, I'll have them. And if you continue misbehaving, your punishment will be a lot worse than me spanking your ass."

"Where is Cynthia?" she says.

I laugh out loud. "You can forget that." I step around her and take the seat next to her.

"No," she whines. "You told me you would take me to her."

"And you promised you'd behave. So I'm going to tell you how this will work. This is your home. You belong to me, and if you continue to disobey—"

"I'm not your fucking property. You don't get to steal me away from my life—"

"Steal you away. I can't steal what's rightfully mine."

She shakes her head. "Why are you doing this? Why have you been stalking me all these years? Tormenting me? Killing the people closest to me?"

I suck in a breath, reach for the pitcher of water, and pour it into the glasses in front of us.

"Answer me, dammit," she demands.

Siân jumps when I slap the glass table, and the dishes atop it rattle from the impact.

"*Maledizione, Siân. Tutto quello che ho fatto è stato per te. E prima o poi lo capirai. Ora mangia.*" *Goddammit, Siân. Everything I've done has been for you. And sooner or later, you'll get that. Now eat.*

"*Io non ho fame.*" *I'm not hungry.*

I smile, proud to hear her using our native tongue. She's erased that part of her identity, denied her roots, all to live this deluded life she and Cynthia have drummed up.

"And all of this sick and demented shit wasn't for me, you fucking psycho. You don't get to harm people and say it's because of me. I didn't even know you before you weaseled your way into my life. You manipulated me, lied to me, abused me, and I'm supposed to believe it's because you care. You're sick, Christian. And I will get away from you. I will find Cynthia, and somehow, I will make you pay for this."

She continues to defy me, and while I hate being challenged or questioned, I'm also proud. Finally, in all the time I've watched her, she's putting up a fight. When it comes to me, she'll lose every time, but at least she's not going out so easily. Not to mention, it makes it that much more fun. Siân doesn't really know the lengths I'm willing to go to get what I want, but she's sure as shit about to find out.

"You and what army? Hm? You think you can take me on, *topolina*?"

She doesn't respond.

"You've known me longer than you think, little one."

She frowns. "What is that supposed to mean?"

Reaching for the frittata, I pick up a serving with my hands and drop it on the plate in front of her. "Think. When was the first time we ever met? And I'll give you a hint, it wasn't at that fucking bar."

Her chest rises and falls in sharp bursts as she stares at me, conflicted. I can hear her mind racing while she racks her brain to figure out what I'm talking about.

"This has all been about my father, hasn't it?"

"Enough questions. Your food is getting cold." I adjust in my seat and begin to load a helping of food on my plate. I need to change the subject. Now is not the time to go down that road because if I do, the truth will come out, and I can't have that. Not yet. Not until after she is completely mine.

Siân forcefully pushes the plate from in front of her, causing the other dishes to shift to the opposite end.

I drop my fork and inhale deeply. "This little tantrum of yours is starting to piss me off, and you don't want to see me angry. So this is how things are going to work. My father is going to visit. You're going to eat your fucking breakfast and be a good girl. And maybe I'll take you to see Cynthia."

"You promise." Her entire mood changes, the fight turning into desperation.

I don't like it, but I can't tell her that. Instead, I give her the only truth I feel should matter. "I'll never break a promise to you, topolina. Never."

We stare at each other for a brief second, the moment fleeting because we're finally joined by my father, Samuele Russo. Dressed in a pair of slacks and a crisp white button-down shirt, he confidently settles into the seat next to me.

He doesn't speak, but then again, he never does. He makes no introductions but simply commands the attention of everyone around him.

My father watches Siân, his expression blank and almost lifeless. I know this look all too well and notice the familiar veins in his forehead before they start to protrude. It's his one and only tell. All my life, he's been hard to read, his anger just as temperamental as mine. But I learned early on that when he's gotten to be so perplexed by something, the veins make an appearance. And normally, that means he'll be ordering me to kill someone.

There is a shift in the air as the two stare at each other. Siân's posture goes rigid, and her breathing hastens. As if she recognizes him but can't quite put her finger on it, she inadvertently scoots closer to me. She keeps her gaze trained on him, and she curls into herself like a baby gazelle about to be pounded by a lion.

The need to protect Siân nags at me, and before I realize what I'm doing, I find myself leaning toward her. Samuele then directs his attention to me, and a barely-there smirk forms at the corners of his mouth.

"Quindi non solo sei un rompicoglioni, ma sei anche un bugiardo," he intones. *So not only are you a pain in my ass, but you're a liar as well.*

My jaw clenches, but not because of his choice of words—no—this is a typical conversation for us. My father isn't gentle, not when I was a child, and certainly not now. So it's not what he says to me that gets a rise out of me but the meaning behind the words.

Siân breaks my concentration with a soft touch on my forearm. "I don't want to be here," she whispers to me.

I place my hand on top of hers but don't get the chance to provide her even the slightest comfort.

"Speak up, girl. Ain't no need to be shy," he interjects, his accent heavy.

Siân swallows while shifting awkwardly in her seat. She's afraid but quickly pulls it together. Heat builds in my chest at the thought of her being scared of him or anyone else. And I have to calm myself so that I don't lash out. I still my desire to smack that smirk off his face. Usually, seeing Siân's fear fuels me, but right now, it only pisses me off.

"You know…" Samuele takes the pitcher of water and pours some for himself. "You must be a lucky girl to have survived the fire that murdered your family."

Her spine snaps straight. "You knew my family?"

He takes a sip and releases a sarcastic chuckle. "Christian non te l'ha detto?" *Christian hasn't told you?*

Siân darts her gaze between us, confusion written all over her face. "Told me what?"

I stare at him, seething. This bastard and his mind games. He wants to ruffle her feathers, wants to get under my skin. It's his game—we all have one, really. I like to watch, and dear ole Dad loves the seed of doubt. It's the only thing that's gotten him where he is today. It's the only reason Marco failed that night.

"Nothing," I deadpan. "Eat something so that we can go."

"È questo che hai fatto? Spendere soldi e risorse in America per un po' di figa?" *Is this what you've been doing? Spending my money and resources in America for some pussy?*

"Guarda la tua bocca," I bark. *Watch your mouth.*

Samuele lifts his hands in mock surrender. "Sì, così arrabbiato." *Aye, so angry.*

Siân watches our interaction, and it is obvious she is growing even more confused. If I had to guess, while she remembers some Italian, she isn't as fluent as she once was. She steals my attention, forcing me to finally peer away from my asshole of a father.

"It's fine," I say to reassure her. "You don't need to worry about him." I stare him dead in the eye.

"Non fare promesse che non puoi mantenere, figliolo. Potrei ucciderla in questo momento solo per sport." *Don't make promises you can't keep, son. I might kill her right now just for sport.*

"Kill? What?" Siân starts to stutter as she deciphers bits and pieces of the conversation.

"Devi essere uno sciocco a portare questa puttana a casa mia quando dovrebbe essere morta. Mettimi alla prova, figliolo, e potrei semplicemente accusarla del debito di suo padre." *You must be a fool bringing this bitch to my house when she's supposed to be dead. Test me, son, and I just might charge her with her father's debt.*

"She's going to be my wife and the mother of your grandchildren. So you might want to think twice about what comes out of your mouth next."

He laughs. "That's what this is about? You've chased her all these years for that?"

I frown.

"Yeah, I know all about your little trips to the United States. You can keep nothing from me. I only allowed you to think so because you're doing my bidding. But get out of line, Christian, and I'll make sure it happens this time."

His words—his threat burns through me. My father stares at me, a smile on his demented face. If it weren't for Siân sitting next to me, I'd dig into him. I'd allow my temper to get the best of me. I can't, though. It's evident to me that Siân knows my true colors, and despite what anyone thinks, I need her to trust me—to love me.

Choosing to take the higher road and not show my father just how deep my affection for Siân goes, I take a sip from my water. But I know my father well, and this brief back and forth is more than enough to fuel whatever twisted plan he's formulating in his mind.

MONSTER

5

SIÂN

I can't be hearing this. Did I ever wake up this morning, or is this all a weird, uncomfortable dream? Do family members actually talk to each other this way?

Not only to each other but about other people who happen to be sitting at the same table? I might as well not be here except for the filthy looks from Christian's father.

That's not even the worst of it. His son's wife? The mother of his grandchildren? I know better than to think Christian doesn't mean it when he says things like that, but he's also out of his freaking mind. Married? To him? I'd kill myself before the ceremony.

That's what this is all about for him. He said something on the jet about how he can't wait until I'm his. Something insane like that. He meant marrying him. Where does he get that idea from? Where does he get any idea from, I guess. I get the feeling it would be a waste of time trying to understand.

Once Samuele stands and stalks away, it's easier to breathe. Christian notices the way my body slumps a little now that it's just the two of us. "You did well."

"Excuse me?"

"With him. You did well. You didn't cower in front of him." His lips twist in a bitter smile, and he raises a glass of water to his mouth. "Trust me. He hates weakness more than anything."

"Trust you? What, did he bully you into not being weak?"

His brows draw together, and for a second, I think he's going to open up. I might get him to talk about himself, the real Christian. Not the fake persona he's presented to me from the beginning. I might be able to use this to my advantage.

"Did he?" I prompt as carefully as possible. I can't be too obvious about this.

"Do you believe he did?" he counters. It's like we're dancing without music. Or playing chess. I make a move. He makes one.

"It would make sense. You two obviously don't get along."

He lets out a long breath through flared nostrils. This is it. He's going to share something real. He might start trusting me a little more. I practically have to bite the inside of my cheek to keep myself calm.

Suddenly he stands, wiping his mouth and tossing his napkin to the table. "Come on. We're going out."

I can't keep up with these sudden shifts of his. "Where are we going?" I ask, wiping my own mouth. I'm not fighting, no way. I'll go wherever he wants. Maybe there's a chance I could catch somebody's attention and beg for help.

"I'm taking you to see Cynthia."

Amazing. Just like that, trying to run away is the furthest thing from my mind. "Seriously? Right now?"

"Or a few minutes from now, if you insist on asking questions." Again, he's treating me like a child. I don't care right now. I only want to see Cynthia again. To think, this is where he took her. So far from me.

He leads me out to a Town Car and opens the passenger door rather than allowing the driver to do it for me. Such a gentleman. If he's waiting for a thanks, he can keep waiting. I slide into the back seat without a word. He pauses for just a moment before closing the door harder than needed. I wonder how many times he's been denied what he wants. I'm sure this is new for him.

At least he doesn't seem interested in having a conversation about our happy future and how glad I'll be once I give him what he wants: my hand in marriage. Even now, away from his father and the rest of the household, the thought makes me want to gag. Instead of bugging me, he makes a phone call, angling his body slightly away from me as if to close me out while he conducts business.

"*Ciao. Che cosa hai sentito? Sì, sono tornato in campagna.*" He barely speaks loud enough to be heard, though thanks to the fact that he's speaking in Italian, I can only make out bits and pieces anyway. He's telling somebody he's back in the country and asking what they've heard. Heard about what, I wonder.

After that, most of it comes too fast for me to make sense. I wish I wasn't so rusty, but then Cynthia and I stuck to strict English once we made it to the States. We couldn't give away our origins. It wasn't easy at first, but I lost my Italian over time while my English got stronger.

Now I wish I knew more so there'd be less chance of him hiding things from me. Maybe it'll get better with time. Oh, no, am I already thinking about this in the long term? Have I already given up hope of getting away?

Maybe Cynthia can give me some ideas on how to escape. Wait, who am I kidding? I doubt we'll be able to spend any time alone. I can hope. I have to hope.

We're on the road for maybe ten minutes, and the driver turns into a thickly wooded area. Of course, he'd keep her somewhere remote. Cynthia's too much of a badass not to get away if there was any chance of escaping without getting herself killed somehow. I'm sure she's weighed the pros and cons of trekking through unknown woods on foot.

I need to think of her this way. I don't want to believe Christian hurt her permanently. He said she's fine, but I suspect our definitions of that word are different.

"*Sì, facciamo in modo che ciò accada. Come ora. Nessuna scusa. Fammi sapere quando è finito.*" Something about making things happen. No excuses. Let him know when it's finished. What's he talking about? Do I even want to know? What if it has to do with me? My anxiety rises with each thought.

He ends the call, sliding the phone into his jacket pocket. He's gritting his teeth. Clearly, something made him angry. "What was that all about?" I venture. "You seem upset."

"Nothing you need to worry about." He stares out the window, looking away from me.

"No offense, but you've sort of pulled me into your life. What bothers you worries me, especially if I might get caught in the crossfire."

He snorts, looking my way from the corner of his eye. "It was business. It has nothing to do with you."

"What kind of business?"

"The kind of business that gets people's brains blown out when they fuck up." He turns my way, his face blank. Daring me to react. *Message received.*

I stare at him for a long moment. It's stupid how gorgeous he is and how attracted to his face and kindness I am. I was a lamb being led straight to the slaughterhouse, and I don't know why it took me so long to see. I turn away from him in favor of looking at the scenery without really seeing any of it. How did I ever think he was sweet and kind? I could never have imagined this version of him back then. Either that or I didn't want to see it.

Turning my attention back to him, I murmur. "You know who you sound like when you talk like that?" I don't wait for him to respond. "Your father. You sound mean. You weren't like that in Florida."

"That was then. This is now." He even sighs like he's bored.

"But you expect me to be happy with you now when you act like him? If you hate him so much, why do you want to be like him?"

"Hate is a strong word," he observes in a low voice.

"It's the only word that came to mind earlier. Why is it like that with you two?"

"You don't need to know why." Another sigh. "As for happiness, that's entirely up to you. If you behave yourself, there's no reason I won't afford you privileges. Shopping, dining out, trips. Whatever you want in time, once you've earned my trust. Until now, you've done nothing but defy me, yet you blame your unhappiness on me."

I itch to slap him, but instead, I use my words. "I didn't ask for this."

"We rarely ask for what we end up getting." He lets out a soft, bitter laugh, looking away from me. "We can only do our best with what we're given."

It's obvious I'm not getting anywhere with him right now. He's not in the mood to converse. Not that it matters once the car pulls to a stop in front of a quaint little cabin in one of the thickest parts of the woods we've passed through so far. So thick it seems to go from day to twilight, thanks to the crisscrossing branches above us once we step out. Christian guides me inside, opening the door to the cabin like he owns the place—which I suspect he does.

Immediately my eyes fall on a pair of burly men sitting on either side of a small card table. It's obvious from the glass beer bottles and wrappers that they've been playing cards, eating, and drinking.

Until we entered, anyway, and they set sights on Christian. He holds up a hand like it doesn't matter, giving neither of them a chance to speak.

His other hand wraps around my arm so he can lead me through the small front room. My eyes dart back and forth as I take in the rest of the cabin. It's clean and warm. There's a kitchen with food lined up on shelves.

We stop in front of a heavy wooden door. She's behind a locked door. So it might as well be a prison.

"I'll be in the room with you the entire time, so don't bother with any ideas." He unlocks the door and swings it open so slowly that it hurts. My heartbeat thunders in my ears, and I swear if anything happened to her...

The words cut off when I see her on the other side. She's here, sitting on the bed, facing me from the other side of a modest bedroom. *It's really her.*

"Thank God!" I run to her, falling on my knees, throwing myself into her open arms. "I thought you were dead!"

"I thought I was too, for a minute there." She's gotten thinner since the last time I saw her, with dark circles under her eyes and extra lines bracketing her mouth, but she's still Cynthia. The strength hasn't left her voice. It gives me strength, too, even with Christian standing behind me.

"How are they treating you?" I touch her face, her hair, her arms, and hands. Anything I can reach. I need to prove to myself she's real.

"I'm fed and given clean clothes, the whole nine yards. I wouldn't recommend it on TripAdvisor, but I know it could be worse."

I frown. "You don't need to make jokes."

"Who's joking? Truly, I'll be fine. You don't have to worry about me here." It's her turn to take my face in her hands. "How are you?"

"As good as I can be." I try to offer a brave smile, but I know it's nothing near what I need it to be. Tears fill my eyes, and I can't blink them back before they spill over onto my cheeks.

"My poor girl." She kisses my forehead.

"I wish I knew why this was happening," I confess in a whisper that I hope he can't hear. His eyes burn holes in the back of my head. How could I have ever thought I loved him? Look what he did to her. And he probably thinks he's a good guy because he didn't kill her. He thinks he's sparing me the pain when all he's doing is causing it.

With her lips against my skin, she whispers, "I tried to warn you, but it wasn't enough."

"I don't understand." I breathe as softly as possible.

"Don't trust him. Don't trust anyone in his family. They're the ones who killed your family."

I don't have time to react, to even speak before a steel band clamps around my waist. *No!* I want to scream as Christian hauls me to my feet, pulling me away from her, but my throat seems to tighten. No, it's not long enough.

"No! Not yet!" My voice finally escapes my lips, and I reach for her, our fingers almost touch, but he turns me away from her. She screams, cursing him, but he ignores her just the way he ignores the kicks I land against his shins and knees.

I'm screaming, too, shrieking and wailing, and for one split second, I know I'm losing my mind. This is where I break. I'll never be whole again. I'm going to cross the line and fall over onto the other side, never to return.

But I don't. And no matter how hard I fight and scream and claw at his arm, Christian's hold on me remains. He clutches me tight to his chest, his possession.

"A pleasure as always, Cynthia," he taunts.

She spits on the floor and mutters an Italian curse. He only snorts in amusement and drags me out of the room. The last thing I see is her stricken face before the door swings shut.

Then her words start to playback in my mind. *His family killed my family.* All I needed was to hear it from her lips. I hope he doesn't punish her for this.

I bounce off the back seat when Christian throws me back into the car. "Goddamn it," he snarls after climbing in and slamming the door. "That little display was beneath you. How am I supposed to trust you to behave yourself when you act like a child?"

"It's true, isn't it?" I'm not letting him get away with blaming this on me. "Did your family really kill my family?"

"Yes." He leans across the seat, bringing his face close to mine. "My father ordered a hit on your family. Are you satisfied?"

I stare up into his eyes and know he's telling the truth. "Why? What did he want?"

His nostrils flare, the muscles twitching in his jaw. "Everything your father had."

My mouth falls open, making him snort before he backs off.

"And for the record, he also wanted you dead. I refused to let that happen, and I still do."

"Why does he want any of that?"

"Does it matter? The result is the same. You are under my protection from him, but the only hope of solidifying that protection is by marrying me. Which is what you're going to do, as soon as possible."

His words trickle through the horror movie rolling in my head. "That's not going to happen. I'm never marrying you." He wanted me dead. That's why my parents died. Because of me. The shitstorm just keeps growing, like a hurricane.

"That's what you think."

"It's what I know." I want so much to curl up in a ball and cry until the pressure in my head eases. I can't take this. It's too much. But I won't humiliate myself like that. "You tell me your family killed mine, then tell me we're going to get married? Why would I want to marry you after everything you've done? After what you just told me?"

He cocks his head to the side. "Knowing I'm protecting your life isn't enough?"

"If living means being married to you, my life isn't worth all that much."

His eyes light up, and I understand I've stepped into a trap. I don't need to hear it to know what the trap is, either. It's obvious.

"What about Cynthia's life?" he murmurs before a slow smile spreads across his lips. A genuine smile that's so much scarier than the cold, harsh kind. "Is her life worth much? Because if you don't marry me, she'll be the one who suffers the consequences, and after that little show, I'll bet, even if you don't think your life is worth something, you're not willing to let Cynthia die because of your poor choices."

I clench my teeth. "I hate you, and I mean it. With every fiber in my soul."

Christian merely smiles. "You can hate me all you want, but no matter what happens, you'll become my wife."

MONSTER

6

CHRISTIAN

Siân sits across the table from me with her arms folded over her chest and her lips pouted. She hates me, or at least she likes to pretend she does. I laugh internally because we both know the truth.

She may not necessarily enjoy the circumstances, but she's already admitted to loving me once. Something tells me that to save her precious Cynthia, she'll do everything that I ask. After our visit, after she'd learned that my family was responsible for her loss, I knew that this would be hard.

But she's mine in every sense of the word. My ways may not be that of Prince Charming, but she means everything, and a part of me came to know that a long time ago. Which is probably why I decided to watch her instead of taking her early on. I knew that if my father found out that I did not kill her like he ordered me to, he would do it himself. Or better yet, it'd be some sick, tormented thing where he takes her and adds her to the list of girls that he sells.

At the time, I thought nothing of it. It would be just like always, another young girl sold to the highest bidder in the name of keeping the wrath of my father at bay.

Plenty of girls have come in and out of our possession, and Siân was no different. My father was to take her as a trade, only things didn't work out the way they planned. There was more to the story, and before I ever laid eyes on her, I knew that. Maybe it was the urgency of the deal or something else entirely.

I had remembered seeing her a time or two in passing. She's four years younger than me, so I never saw anything but someone innocent with the kind of pureness that could save even the damnedest of souls. But it's as if the moment I heard the words slip past their lips, something shifted. It was written in ink, she would be ours—his for the taking, and this war between Samuele and Marco would finally end.

My father was loveless, only sharing the occasional fuck with women who didn't always leave our home intact. So the fact that he agreed to the offer surprised me. What was he supposed to do with a child? I needed to see for myself why he would accept but, more importantly, how a mother could betray her child. Or why Marco wasn't there himself making the deal.

It's no secret the things my father is involved in. He's proud of the role he played in the corruption and disruption of Milan. And for the most part, so am I. Being his son, hated or not, comes with perks. Our name carries weight throughout this world. Marco was no different. He was cold, calculated, and ruthless, and had shed more blood than a mortuary. But knowing that Marco would agree to give his only child to a notorious trafficker didn't make sense. But more so, why wasn't he man enough to do it himself.

Instead, his beloved stood in my father's office, signing her child over to the devil. Whatever beef he had with her father, Marco, runs deeper than what meets the eye. And when I learned the truth behind that deal, it was me who put a stop to it all. I watched them sign on the dotted line, a conspiracy in the making. The truth is, it wasn't Marco's doing at all, but that of the woman who was supposed to protect her.

I wasn't about to have it, and that's why I hid her from him.

Sooner or later, he would figure out what I did. I thought maybe if I took my time and let her get to know me, she'd come to terms with the fact that we are meant to be together on her own. No, I'm not the romance hero. I'm the fucking villain. And I own that. But the only thing that really matters to me is her. Her safety, her pleasure. And yes, her tears, but only when they come from me.

It took everything in me not to blow my father's brains out right in front of her for threatening her. But then that wouldn't have been good either. There are things that we have to handle. Killing my father isn't gonna make any of it easier. It'd be a hell of a mess that I'd have to try to figure out while still trying to get ahold of Siân. But also, he's my father. He is the man who raised me. And despite how fucked up our connection is, I'm his child, and I'm going to play the doting role of the honorary son because that's what we do in this family.

Siân clears her throat, breaking my concentration. When I glance up, instead of looking at me, she throws her gaze out at the large expanse of lawn as we sit on the patio waiting for breakfast to be served. Just like yesterday, she swears up and down she isn't hungry. But after going nearly two days without food, she hasn't eaten since my father's visit to the table yesterday, ruining her opportunity.

The last thing I need is for her to wither away, at least not before I'm done fucking her until my heart's content. I make a mental note that while making nice with people and trying to win people over isn't necessarily my thing, I want to try to be a little different with Siân.

At the end of the day, she will be my wife, and there is that old tale about a happy wife, happy life, right? So I need to find a way to show her that there is at least a little part of the Christian she thought she fell for inside me. I need to show her that while yes, I have done some things in the name to make her mine, I would never really hurt her. Most of all, I need her to trust me enough that even when she finds out I was the one who pulled the trigger, she won't try to go.

Not that she could ever escape me. She'll have the rest of forever to get used to our new reality. Aldo exits the house, the sound of the sliding doors alerting us to his presence. Siân sits up, trying desperately to hide the fact that she is indeed hungry. The closer he gets to our table, the louder her stomach growls, and she hugs herself as if it'll muffle the sounds.

"Buongiorno, signor Russo," he says without greeting Siân. *Good morning, Mr. Russo.*

She looks at him weirdly for a moment. But he knows the rules. Servants, housemaids, and everyone else who works for us have been warned against speaking to her. Their only responsibility when it comes to her is to provide her anything she needs. If they cross that line, there will be consequences.

Aldo removes the silver lid. As always, he outdoes himself with an array of different choices; waffles, meats, and other traditional breakfast items. I expect Siân to continue pretending she isn't going to eat. But to my surprise, she immediately reaches for the bread, tearing it in two and popping a piece in her mouth.

She loads her plate with other items, so focused that she doesn't notice the tiny box sitting in the middle of the tray right away. When she moves the waffle from the top of the stack, and her eyes take in the black velvet box, her mouth falls open, the uneaten piece of bread falling to the ground.

Siân swallows a breath, but it doesn't do anything in settling the wheels that are so obviously turning in her mind. "What's that?" She darts her gaze to mine, her shoulders hiked to her ears.

"Your engagement ring," I deadpan.

She stares between me and the box, dumbfounded. "Why are you doing this, Christian? Why are you trying to force me to marry you? It'll never work. I'll never love you. You think bringing me to some fancy house after all the horrible things you've done and then putting a ring in front of me will make me love you? Well, that'll never happen."

"It's cute that you think you have a choice in the matter. We've already talked about this. And I've made myself pretty clear. You belong to me. And you always have."

"You keep saying that. *I always have*—what the fuck does that mean? Does this have something to do with whatever you and your father were going back and forth about in Italian yesterday?"

For a moment, I allow her to go on as I watch her with my elbows propped on the arm of the chair and my fingers locked under my chin.

"Lower your voice, topolina."

She's seething, and I must say, it's sexy as hell.

"No, I won't lower my voice. Why don't you tell me what is really going on, Christian? Why did your father kill my family? Why did you take me? Why are you forcing me to be your wife? There's more to this story, and for whatever reason, you're trying to hide it from me."

She pauses for a beat, only to start right back up again.

"And on top of all that, you've done nothing but mistreat me."

"The only thing that you need to know, Siân, the only thing that matters is that we are getting married. I've already told you the only way to keep you safe from my father is for you to marry me. Unless you want to end up like your family. You want to see something happen to Cynthia? I suggest you put on the fucking ring and eat your food."

As soon as the words leave my mouth, she jumps up, sending her chair falling over with a loud thud. I can see her mood shift, and part of me likes it. There haven't been many times when she's been this angry and stood up for herself. Yes, she has been feisty on and off with me. But that was more because she was flirting.

This pushback. This is who she is. This is who she's supposed to be. Not that it's gonna matter with me. At the end of the day, she will do what I say every single fucking time, but she shouldn't take it lightly. She shouldn't just sit back and allow me or anyone else to force her to roll over. But don't tell her that. Not yet. I need more time with her. I need to break her down a little more before she realizes that while she may have the power to stand at my side and be the reigning queen of Italy, she'll have to learn her place. She'll have to learn who's really in charge.

I'm on my feet, and in seconds I'm around the table, hovering over her tiny frame. "Where do you think you're going?" I snatch the ring off the table.

"Anywhere that you aren't," she spits and attempts to stomp off.

I'm quick at grabbing her wrist, keeping her in place. She twists in my grasp, fighting to get free, but it's no use. Someone clapping in the distance steals our attention, and we look to see Samuele walking toward us.

"Well, look at this," he taunts. "Trouble in paradise?"

With a snarl, I ignore him, choosing to focus on Siân and her defiance. She's immediately uncomfortable at the sight of him. She doesn't cower away, though, and tries not to allow him to see that he rattles her.

Good girl. It seems she does listen when it's convenient.

"Siân. I'm getting angry. Put on the fucking ring," I demand, keeping it so that only she and I can hear.

With shaky breaths, Siân snatches the box. "You know what you can do with this fucking ring," she yells and tosses it with the ring in it across the field.

From the corner of my eye, I notice my father watching along with me as it falls in the distance, landing next to the flower bed. Flowers I don't give two shits about, but they are there. Curb appeal is important, I guess.

I size her up, staring down at her, but she doesn't budge. In fact, she stands her ground while never dropping her gaze. Fuck. She's so goddamn tempting. I love this version of her, fierce and unapologetic. Something about the determination to stand up for herself does something to me. It makes me want to take that from her, to break her down and show her that she can have as much fucking fight as you want, but in the end, I will win.

"Siân, I'm not going to tell you again not to fucking test me."

Samuele lets out a whistle while clapping his hands together loudly. "Feisty one, isn't she."

I snap my gaze back at him. "Stay out of it."

"I'd never let a bitch talk back to me like that. It's about time she is taught the meaning of respect," he interjects.

"Watch your fucking mouth," I seethe and throw back at him, mentally telling myself not to react any more than I already have.

The last thing I need is for him to see that Siân is a weak point for me. He'll exploit it, use it to get his way. I won't have that. I won't let him see that he's getting to me. And until she's my wife, she isn't completely safe from him either.

But he's not wrong. She does need to be taught a lesson.

Grabbing her by the elbow, I force her over to where I think the ring landed. After a brief second, I spot it nestled between the bushes. Siân struggles to free herself from my grasp, but it's no use. She's not strong enough, and she knows it. But still, she fights, probably some eternal thing she does to keep from feeling defeated.

"Pick it up," I order.

Siân stands her ground, rolling her shoulders back to hide the discomfort she feels from my touch. "Fuck you," she seethes through her teeth.

"Pick up the fucking ring, or there will be serious consequences."

She inhales deeply. "There's nothing that could be worse than what you've already done to me. Keep me prisoner. But you'll never be able to force me to marry you. I won't make it that easy."

Speechless, I bend down and snatch the box from the ground, thankful that the ring is still inside it. Calmly, I remove it, then toss the box back to where it previously rested in the shrubs. Siân stands still, her chest rising and falling in sharp bursts. She knows she fucked up, but she's smart enough to continue to stand up for herself.

I'm proud of her, actually. She's putting her foot down and not backing down. Great. Finally, while a part of me loves seeing this from her, the other half needs to punish her.

Siân slaps my hand away when I try to grab hers. We tussle for a bit before I eventually get a hold of her, twisting her wrist to force her to stop.

She winces. "Ouch. Christian. You're hurting me."

I forcibly slide the ring on her finger, watching the red bruising that forms from how hard it scraps against her flesh. Then I scoop her up, throwing her over my shoulder and stalking away, past my father, up the stairs, and through the patio door. And I don't stop. Siân kicks and screams, but I continue until we reach the room she's dubbed her prison.

Removing the key from my pocket, I unlock the door and kick it open. It slaps against the wall, startling Siân, who continues to squirm. Once we're inside the room, I return her to her feet. She attempts to flee, racing toward the door, only she isn't fast enough.

I grip her by the hair, pulling her back while using my free hand to slam the door shut. Siân claws at my hands for me to free her hair, and I do. We stare at each other, both equally out of breath. I have to admit, I like the fight, the fear in her eyes right now as she tries to figure out how to get away.

With nowhere to go, she rushes to the left. I catch her with a hand around her throat and force her to the wall. My body brushes up against hers, and I watch her eyes grow wide when she realizes she's trapped, completely at my mercy.

Her throat bobs against my palm, taking me back to the night in the alley and how sexy it was to feel my dick against my hand through her throat. Fuck, I should make her swallow me whole right now.

"This is what you want?" she asks, her voice strained. "You want to hurt me? Spank me? What else can you do to break me, Christian? You can force your ring on my finger, but I'll never love you."

Running my gaze over her features, I admire her beauty while tracing the curve of her face with the index finger of my other hand. "I think you forget you've already told me you love me as you rode my cock."

"That was a lie. I didn't tell *you* that I love you. I told the man I *thought* you were."

"It's semantics, really. The fact remains that you belong to me. To lick, fuck, and suck. To break until nothing is left. I'll take what I want when I want, and I'll make you fucking hate yourself for enjoying it."

She tries to push me away. "You're insane. I'll never enjoy being with you. Not again."

I smirk. "You really believe that, don't you?"

She doesn't respond. Instead, she stares at me with her brows pulled tight and her nostrils flared. "I hate you."

"I don't think that's true. You love when I touch you. I bet your pussy is wet right now." I reach between her legs, pressing my fingers against her sex through her jeans.

She tries to keep me at bay, closing her thighs as tight as she can, but with a tight squeeze of her throat, she stops fighting. Using my knees, I manage to push her legs apart, a groan building in my chest from the heat radiating from between her legs.

"You want to know what I'm going to do to punish you? Hm?"

She turns her head to the side to avoid my gaze, but I make her look at me. Fumbling with the buckle of her jeans, I undo them at the same time she closes her eyes.

"I'm going to make you come and enjoy every second of you wishing like hell you never met me," I threaten as I slip my hand past her zipper and into her panties. "I'm going to finger your tight little pussy, until you can't see straight."

Her breath is hot on my skin, and her exhales grow short and labored. And just like I knew she would be, her pussy is drenched for me, and I haven't even touched her yet. Not fully. I know because my knuckles feel the damp spot of her underwear.

"And as you come, hating yourself for loving it so much, I'll have won. You can hate me all you want, topolina. Just be prepared to do it for the rest of your goddamn life."

Finally, I slide two fingers between her slit, not bothering to tease her clit as I aim straight for her tight channel. I slip in with ease, and Siân's legs start to give out.

She gasps. "Mm," she bites back a moan.

I smile, knowing I was right. Just look at her trepidation rolling over every inch of her flawless skin. She knows I'm right, and I've barely even started to wring an orgasm out of her.

"I hate you," she groans.

"And you look pretty damn good while you do."

That's the last thing I say before finding her G-spot and pounding my fingers into her sweet pussy until she's clawing at my forearms for me to release her. Until sweat beads across her skin and her head falls back against the wall. Until her legs give way, and the only thing keeping her standing is my hand on her throat and my fingers in her cunt.

I finger her like it's the last thing I'll do, ignoring my hard-on because right now, all that matters is following through on my promise. She can hate me all she wants as long as she comes hard as hell while doing it.

Her walls tighten around me, and I inadvertently inch closer.

"There it is."

"No." Siân shakes her head, trying once more to close her legs to keep her body from betraying her. "No."

I lean forward, bringing my lips to her ear. "Yes, topolina."

She continues to shake her head, her moans coming out like gargled cries.

But then I kiss her ear and pull her lobe into my mouth.

"Fuuuuck." The word is hard, throaty, but oh-so fucking sweet.

Her back buckles, and she has no choice but to rest against me as I pull every last drop of cum from her.

"That's a good girl. Let me have it." I encourage her while removing my hand from her throat and guiding her to rest her head on my shoulder. I cup the nape of her neck, gently petting her hair until her body and pussy relax.

When she's completely done, I give her G-spot one last stroke for good measure. Siân jerks from the sensitivity, and I have to fight back a laugh. After a beat, I carry her over to the mattress and place her on the center of it. She crawls into the fetal position with her back to me.

I stand upright and run my hand down my erection to hopefully make it go down. There's no time to tend to my needs right now. But sure enough, when I finish meeting with my father, I'll be ready to chase my own release.

"If I have to tell you to keep that ring on your finger again, you won't like what I do next. But if you behave yourself, I'll give you some time with your beloved caretaker." And with that, I leave her to stew in her thoughts, satisfied that I know her better than she thought I did.

Once on the other side of the room, I lock her inside and head to my father's office with her scent still on my fingers. I push into the room to find him sitting behind his oversized desk, a cigar in hand, and a stack of papers in front of him. The farther into the space I get, the more I can see that there are pictures. Of what I don't know yet. But whatever has him flustered, his face is expressionless as he pulls a drag from a cigar.

"Can we get some work done now that you've had a quick fuck?" he asks while staring at me nonchalantly.

"What do you want?" I say instead of what I really want, and I hate it. I hate him talking about everything. For the way he is, for the things said out of his mouth about Siân.

But I don't react. I don't give in to his tactics and instead take the seat in front of him. He pushes the envelope across the desk, and I catch them before they fall.

"I need you to handle this." He takes another drag of his cigar.

I pick up the images, completely unfazed as I flip through one after another. Bodies. Dead and mutilated. Some of them I recognize, and others I don't. Bullet wounds, severed limbs, guts sliced open. The normal type of shit we see in this life.

"What is this?"

"That's what you're going to find out. While you've been away, chasing your little bitch—"

"Fucking watch it. Keep her name out of your mouth."

"Or what?"

I stare for a moment, and when I don't offer him a retort, he continues.

"While you were out chasing your new wife-to-be, shit's been going crazy here. Someone has been going around Milan and the surrounding cities taking out families. Who, I don't know. But I need you to figure it out."

I drop the photos on the surface. "I'm interested. It seems the people in these photos are people we've been trying to get rid of for a while. Seems to me like whoever this is, is doing us a favor. Sloppy but good work."

"Christian. His work isn't the fucking point. He's taking out families, which means if he's going after our enemies, who's to say he's not on his way here now."

"Then let them come."

He shakes his head. "How was your little fight?"

When I glare at him, he holds his hands up in surrender.

"What goes on between Siân and me isn't your business. The only thing you need to worry about is the family. What do you want to do?"

"We need to figure out who this is and stop them. They haven't made their way over here to us yet. But who's to say that they're not.

"And when they come, we'll handle them. We have the biggest fucking organization throughout all of Italy." I don't have to tell him what I'm referring to. He knows every detail of the events that started all of this mess. He wanted what Marco had, his territory, and as a result, we own half of Milan. Everybody in the Giuliani organization either joined our family or met their leader in death.

"I'll see what I can find out. But I have to admit, he does nice work."

"Dammit, Christian. Stop admiring the sick bastard."

I laugh. "Sure. But who do you think it is?"

"Besitos."

I shrug. "It's not their style. I don't see the Espositos, but then again, it's not like them either. Every major crime family is in these photos. Tesla hasn't been a part of shit in forever, so I highly doubt he has the balls to go after everyone on this list.

"I really don't care, Christian. What I need you to do is get this shit under control. Whoever this is obviously has connections. They're getting too close, taking out soldiers and making their way up."

"That won't be us." I stand and tap my knuckles on the desk. "I'll get with Tony. We'll deal with it."

"Good. Don't disappoint me," Samuele says to my back.

When I reach the entryway, I rest a hand on the door. "And, Samuele?" I throw over my shoulder.

He stares up at me, cigar in hand and the other filled with the images.

"I know you're the boss and my father, but don't you ever disrespect my woman again." And with that, I exit the room, not bothering to wait for a response.

MONSTER

7

SIÂN

*T*his has got to end somehow.

My incessant pacing has gotten me nowhere. I've chewed my nails down to the quick but am no closer to a solution. The longer I stay around here, the more opportunity I give Christian and that sick father of his to tear me down. They want to break me for some twisted reason. I see where Christian gets it from because his old man is no better than he is. He might actually be worse. How lost does a person have to be to get to that point? Is there any humanity left in him?

What does it matter? I can ask myself these questions as many times as I want, and it doesn't solve anything. What would solve something would be getting out of here. Far away. I don't know where that would be or how I'd get there, but I'll be damned if I hang around here to be used and hurt for their amusement. I did nothing to deserve this.

Locked in this bedroom, though, I have limited options. Christian went somewhere again and, of course, didn't see any reason to tell me where he went. There's no way to know how long it will be before I'm allowed out again. I could have hours of this in front of me. Would it be too much for him to leave something to help me pass the time? I'll have to ask him about that when he returns.

When the door opens out of nowhere, I think the time is now. Only it isn't Christian who steps through the door. It's a dark-haired young woman in a stiff gray dress that's a little too big for her tiny frame. A uniform. She's carrying fresh linens for the bed and towels to replace the ones in the bathroom.

I've never been so happy to see anybody except maybe when I saw Cynthia at the cabin. "Hi," I say with a smile and a little wave. "How are you?"

Instead of answering, she offers a weak smile, then makes a beeline for the bed. She works quickly and efficiently, stripping the sheets and blankets, and pulling the pillowcases from the pillows. I might as well not be here.

"My name is Siân. What's yours?" When all she does is aggressively shove the pillows into new cases, I clear my throat. "Can you not hear me? I asked what your name is."

She turns her head barely enough to look at me from the corner of her eye. "We aren't allowed to speak to guests." Her voice is hushed, tight, with a thick Italian accent. The pillow has begun to shake.

She's terrified. Samuele's cruelty doesn't stop with me, I guess.

What matters more right now is the fact that she left the door cracked open. Does she even know she did it? She never got the memo I'm supposed to be locked up.

This is it. The chance I've been waiting for. I back away slowly, my feet barely making a sound. She's already turned her full attention back to the bed, so I make my move by ducking out through the partly open door and into the hall.

I can't believe it. It worked. But my plan never went any further than getting through the locked door. What good does that do me if I don't know where to go?

This house is a maze. I've tried hard to remember how to get around, but now my heart is pounding so hard, and my thoughts are flying so fast that I can barely remember how to get down to the front door. I run blindly down the hall, passing one closed door after another before coming to a dead end. Dammit. I missed a turn somewhere. I double back, turning down another hall jutting off from the wing my room sits in. This time, I think I'm going the right way.

A man dressed in all black steps out from one of the rooms up ahead. I duck inside a deep doorway, my heart hammering, pressing myself to the door and hoping he can't see the tips of my shoes sticking out. His footsteps fade away. He went in the other direction. For once, something is going my way.

I poke my head out, and finally, the coast is clear again. I dart back and forth across the hall, from one doorway to the next, coming to a familiar set of stairs that leads down to the first-floor foyer. I'm almost out.

My head's on a swivel as I run down the stairs. I don't hear voices or footsteps, so I dash for the front door and open it just enough to slip outside, then close it quietly.

I'm out. I'm out! It's exhilarating, just having the fresh air and sunlight on my skin. Only now, I have to figure out where to go. I'd rather die out here alone and starving than live another minute as a captive.

Yet I'm not ten feet from the house when the door opens, and someone shouts at me in Italian. Rather than freeze, I run, tearing across the front courtyard. Where am I trying to go? I have no idea. Away. That's all that matters. Away from here.

No such luck. A hand closes around my arm and yanks me hard enough that I nearly hit the ground. The guard catches me before I do and hauls me to my feet. He's still growling something in Italian as he starts to drag me back to the house.

"No!" I swing at him with my free arm, hitting his shoulder and his chest. He takes hold of that, too, and tears spring to my eyes when his fingers press into my flesh. I settle for kicking, yanking my arms until my shoulders scream in protest.

And through it all, I scream at the top of my lungs. "Stop it! Let me go! Take your hands off me!"

It's no use. He pulls me back to the house a little at a time, cursing me. "Get off, get off me, you son of a bitch!" He only gives me a hard tug, making me trip. I hit the ground on one knee and cry out in pain, but he's unsympathetic as he continues to drag me along.

"Hey!"

We both stop dead at the sound of the shout, as sharp as the crack of a whip. Christian is charging at us, fists clenched, his teeth bared in a snarl. "What the fuck do you think you're doing?"

"She tried to escape." The guard is out of breath. "I caught her. I was only trying to get her back inside."

Rather than thanking him, Christian pulls me out of his grip. "You think you can hurt her like that? Didn't you fucking hear her? Anyone could tell she was in pain, thanks to you."

In a flash, he reaches into his waistband and withdraws a gun. I don't have time to gasp before he aims at the guard's head and pulls the trigger.

My scream fills the air, loud enough to drown out the sound of his body hitting the ground. Blood immediately pools beneath what's left of his head. He was alive just a second ago, and now he's nothing but a mass of flesh lying on the ground, staring blankly up at the sky. All because he was doing his job.

"Do you see what you made me do?" Christian tucks the gun back into his pants, then takes my wrist in his hand. I'm frozen in shock and unable to pull away. "Remember this, Siân. Your life is safe with me. I won't kill you, but that doesn't mean your actions have no consequences. Insistence on having your way got this man killed. A good man, too. Think about that the next time you want to defy me."

"Don't blame me for this!" His eyes widen, and it's good to know I can get through to him. "You decided to do that. You didn't have to!"

And now it's me he's baring his teeth at, but I'm not going to back down. He did say he wouldn't kill me, right? I believe him.

On the other hand, it's clear his emotions are all over the place now. Between the tension with his father and that tense phone call I overheard, he was clearly already under some kind of stress. Now he's walked up to a guard and killed him without blinking. Not the act of a man with his shit under control.

Maybe this isn't the man I need to challenge right now. Yet I still have to. I can't let him win.

"Get inside the house." Danger runs through his voice like a current. "Now."

"No. I won't. Why would I go anywhere with you? I don't want to be here. You don't own me."

He lifts an eyebrow. "Oh, no?" He picks me up like he did at the cabin, lifting my feet off the ground and carrying me into the house. It doesn't matter how I scream. Nobody pays any attention.

It's when he doesn't head up the stairs that true, icy fear touches my heart. He's taking me somewhere else. Knowing that drains a lot of the fight out of me. "What are you doing? Where are you taking me?" He doesn't answer. Instead, he marches past the foyer and opens a small door I hadn't noticed before now. He flips on the lights, revealing a stone staircase leading down to a dark basement where any number of things could be waiting. "Why are you doing this?" I might as well be talking to myself.

The sight of bars makes me whimper. There are several cells down here. What could they be used for? Do I want to know? Christian drops me in front of them, and I land in a heap, trembling. "What are you doing?" I croak when he begins unbuckling his belt. "Are you going to beat me?"

"No, you'll enjoy this a lot more than that." He pulls me to my feet once his belt is free, standing me up with my back to the bars. With his body pinning me in place, he raises my arms above my head and cinches my wrists with the belt. I hiss in pain when he pulls the belt tight enough to bite into my skin.

I'm trapped. He's tied me to the bars. And now, his growing erection stirs against me. It's almost too dark to see, but I can make out the gleam in his eyes. "You're laboring under the misconception of being the one who calls the shots. Perhaps I need to remind you who's truly in charge. Don't pretend you won't like it."

He yanks my pants down along with my underwear, exposing my skin to the cold, damp air down here. "I own you," he growls, his hands running up my thighs, over my hips, and now beneath my shirt. He lifts that above my head, twisting it around in such a way that it's knotted around my arms. "I own this body. These tits." He slaps one, then the other, striking me hard enough to bring tears to my eyes.

"This ass." He digs his fingers into it, his short nails scraping my skin. I bite down on my lip, struggling not to show how much it hurts.

"And this pussy. I think we both know this pussy is mine." He wedges a hand between my thighs, cupping my mound and rubbing it frantically, laughing when I groan and squirm.

It only makes him rub harder. "What? I thought you liked it this way."

"I don't."

"Then why do you keep forcing me to behave this way? I wouldn't be rough with you if you wouldn't be such an impulsive little cunt." He shoves his fingers inside me, pumping them in and out without mercy. With the other hand, he slaps my boobs again, and now I can't help but cry out in pain and humiliation.

"Look at you. Just as weak and helpless as I always knew you were." He closes his hand around my throat, still fucking me with his fingers. Three of them from the feel of it. His hand tightens, constricting my airway. "Completely under my control. And already oozing cream from that sweet pussy."

Yes, I am. Because no matter how sick this is, part of me likes it. I must, or else why would the sounds coming from between my legs be so wet and sloppy? Why would my muscles clench around his fingers like they are, even as I struggle to breathe?

Yet before I go over the edge, he releases me, taking a step back. I pant for air, coughing, and wheezing. "Look at you. You're pathetic. Thinking you have any control over the situation. Or your body. You belong to me."

He closes a hand around my throat again, squeezing. "Isn't that right? Tell me. Tell me your fucking life belongs to me." I shake my head, glaring at him. His hand tightens. "Say it. I might not kill you, but I can hurt you. And the more I do, the more I like it."

"I... belong to you," I gasp, and the pressure lessens. I suck in as much air as I can, the fog that starts to close around me clearing up—only for me to realize he's unzipped his pants.

"We both know what you want." He drags the tip through my wetness. "Deny it all you want, but your pussy needs this cock. You need me to fuck you hard until you don't know anything else but the feeling of me pounding you. Isn't that right?"

Before I can answer, he enters me with enough force to make me cry out. The metal bars are cold against my back, pressing into it hard enough that I know I'll have bruises. He pushes me up against them with every thrust. He either doesn't notice my pained gasps or doesn't care.

No, that's not true. He likes it. He gets off on my pain. But it's too much for me to hide.

"That's right." He pulls my thighs wide open and wraps them around his waist, then takes hold of the bars on either side of me and uses them as leverage. I'm nothing to him right now. Just a hole to fill. And he does, punishing me, pulling tears from my eyes every time he slams home. I feel him inside me, feel him pushing against my cervix.

"Does it hurt?" he asks through gritted teeth, panting in my face. "This is how you like it. This is what gets you wettest. I could swim through your slit right now if your tight little cunt wasn't squeezing like it is."

He's right. And it's squeezing tighter all the time because this is doing exactly what he says. Pushing me higher, bringing me to the edge. I want to fight against it almost as much as I want it to happen. I crave that release that only comes when I'm with him.

"Filthy slut," he grunts between thrusts. "You love being used. I'm going to fill all your holes again and again until you're covered in my cum."

I want so much to turn away from what he's saying, but I can't. Not when the mental image he's conjuring has me clenching around him. There's no stopping this. I'm teetering on the edge when he pulls out, leaving me hanging when I was moments away.

He takes himself in his hand, pumping furiously and coming on my stomach. I don't know if I'm glad he's finished with me or disappointed I didn't get to finish, too.

"What are you doing?" I whisper between gasps for air, watching him scoop cum off my skin. My sharp gasp cuts through the air when he shoves his fingers inside me, depositing it deep inside my quivering tunnel.

"Now, once you're pregnant with my child, maybe that will shut your fucking mouth." He pulls his fingers free. "Maybe that will settle you down." I can only watch, aching and humiliated, as he tucks his dick back into his pants.

Then he turns and walks away, leaving me helpless with his cum dripping from me.

MONSTER

8

CHRISTIAN

Stepping out into the hall, I rake my hands through my hair, dread and remorse flicking across my skin. Tentatively I turn and hold my hand out, hovering it over the knob. Then I pace the floor, alternating between wanting to leave her there to stew in her thoughts and wanting to comfort her.

This, the torture, the way I fucked her—that is who I am. Through and through. I fuck and suck until I am done, and I sure as shit don't feel sorry for how I leave things. Yet here I am, feeling remorse for something I've done.

I'm torn, trapped in a headspace I don't like one fucking bit. She deserved it. Every vile thing I've done, she's earned. I told her not to test me, but she did it anyway. And while I fucked her, tied and bound, I reveled in it. This is me—hard, demented, and chaotic. So why in the hell is there a pit in my stomach? Why do I want to go back into that room and hold her to my chest?

With Siân, this is different. I want to be different. Over the past few days, I've battled with trying to be softer with her while keeping to my truest self. But who am I kidding? No matter how well I pretend, my darkest desires always present themselves. It never fails. I am who

I am, and Siân is just going to have to figure out a way to deal with that.

She talks about hating the way I am, yet at every turn, she challenges my authority. A part of me is starting to believe she purposely pushes my buttons because she wants me to react, to punish her. There's something inside her that wants to be with me. Even the sick, sadistic version she claims disgusts her so much. But she can't admit it, not to me and not to herself.

So the only way she can have her cake and eat it too is by force. Siân presses my buttons because she wants me to react, to take from her what I want. That way, she gets her fill and never has to face her own dark desires. She never has to say to herself that she is as screwed up somehow as I am. The one true difference here is that I own who I am.

A criminal.

A tyrant.

A sick motherfucker.

But she, on the other hand, has a lot of self-reflection to do. She's mine now for eternity, and it'll go a lot smoother if she accepts that. But at the same time, I recognize that I need to make some concessions of my own. Yes, I love her fear, her tears, but what I've learned is that I love it more when she wants it too. The rush I got in the alley was largely in part because her body showed me that she enjoyed it. Her words and her tears were all a show, but the skill, the effort she put in getting me off, and the subtle shift in her body weren't the actions of a person who hated it.

Hell, every time I've touched her, she was wet for me. Now all I need is for her to be open about that. I shouldn't want to hurt her, not when I need her to trust me. That fact never changed. Out of all the things in this world, trust is important to me, right next to loyalty.

I stare at her through the peephole, her body slumped and arms bound. She's just there, the weight of her body straining against the bounds around her wrists. It doesn't skip past me that she hasn't called out. Not to me, not for help.

My chest tightens, and regret seeps into my bones. I try to push it away, telling myself that she tested me and paid the consequence. Maybe now she'll think twice before disobeying me. But I can't help feeling that just maybe this was too far. With my thoughts clouded, my nerves on edge, I snapped. There's too much at stake, too much going on in this world that she isn't privy to. So dealing with her bratty behavior triggered me.

"Shit, topolina," I mutter to myself and push the door open.

Immediately, the air feels different, and I know it's from the painful silence that fills the room. Siân doesn't budge, almost as if she knows it's me. Her head to her chest, her breathing out of control, and my cum dripping from her body. She's broken and has me to thank for that. I attempt to force a smile, but it falters. As much as I enjoy the pain of others, of hers, I don't this time, and it's truly fucking with me.

Her eyes stay pointed at the ground, and she doesn't even pretend to acknowledge me. So fragile and perfect, and she doesn't even know. She doesn't get me and thinks this is all some sick game for me, but she's wrong.

Everything I've done has been for her. She's spent too long on the run, and now is the time for her to accept who she was meant to be. Who she should have been had things not gone south with her father.

The memory of the ordeal flashes in my mind, and I realize just how much she doesn't know. But I need to break her so I can build her back up. If she were to learn the truth of it all now, she wouldn't be able to handle it. There are too many lies and secrets. She thinks I was a wolf in sheep's clothing, but the reality of it all is that nothing that's happened to her is what it seems.

I recognize the part I played in that, but she's alive today because of me —because of this moment right here. As twisted as it may be, everything that happened was for this, for me to finally have her as she was promised to me. Only I'm not sure how she would be able to deal with the circumstances of the deal.

And before it all comes to light, I need to cement what we have by building her trust to ensure nothing will get between us. I was different for her once. Maybe I can give her that again. Maybe the mask I wore in Florida, the Christian she loved, is still around, and if I can give her that, it'll make the transition smoother.

When she learns that I was the person who killed her father, everything will change, but I'm hoping she won't want to leave by then. I won't be able to protect her this time if she does.

Sucking in a breath, I step closer to her and lift her head so that she can see me. Siân doesn't, though. Instead, she points her eyes to the left while turning her neck to free herself from me. My gaze skated over her body, taking in the bruises I left behind on her inner thighs.

I rub her softly, tracing my thumb over the marks, and like the sadistic person I am, my dick twitches. But quickly, I pull myself together and, at the same time, take in the trail of my cum dripping down her leg. No longer wanting to see her this way, I reach for the belt and unbind her wrists.

She falls, and I catch her, holding her to my chest for comfort. I expect her to speak, to tell me to get my filthy hands off her, but she doesn't. When I scoop her into my arms, she wraps her arms around my neck, allowing me to carry her past the threshold of the cell, up the stairs, and to the room I've been keeping her in.

Once we make it inside, I head for the bathroom and gently set her on the toilet. Siân remains silent as I turn on the water in the tub, and she doesn't fight me when I guide her over to the bath. She steps inside, immersing herself under the water.

Rolling up my sleeves, I grab a washcloth and lather it with soap. She flinches when I touch her legs, and I hold my hands out to silently let her know I'm not going to hurt her. She's hesitant but eventually allows me to work. I did this to her, so the least I can do is try to make it better.

Neither of us speaks for several minutes. It's only the sound of the water as the tub continues to fill. Once she's nearly submerged and the soap has dissipated into the bath, I shut off the faucet and re-lather the cloth.

I move on to her back, and she helps me by sitting up. Siân holds on to the edge of the tub for balance, and something tells me it's so that she doesn't have to hold on to me. Can I blame her? No, but that doesn't mean I like it. Before she knew who I was, she flocked to me for safety and comfort despite me being the person who made her feel threatened in the first place. I miss that.

Not the façade, no, I hated being someone I wasn't, but being the person she came to became my favorite part of this charade. Though it was all an act, it was a side of me I was sure I wasn't capable of. I softened—for her. Feelings that I had as we lay together in my loft return, and I realize I feel the same. With her, I feel everything, not just anger and darkness but maybe even a little kindness. Remorse is high up on that list right now, whereas, in the past, I would revel in the discomfort I've caused.

Finally, she makes eye contact with me as she settles back into the tub. "Why are you being nice to me?"

I stare at her while lifting her leg and washing her feet, then her ankles, and finally her legs. We simultaneously stare at the bruises on the inside of her thigh, and for a moment, a lump forms in my throat. I take care in washing her there, massaging the soreness away.

"Because I care for you," I admit.

She huffs and tilts her head. "Funny way of showing it."

"I never said being with me would be easy."

"You never said anything about kidnapping me either. Nothing about stalking and tormenting and certainly nothing about violating me."

"You're right." What's the point in deflecting? I've done all those things and more, and I want to feel bad about them, but that's hard for me. I don't like the aftermath but feel the way others do.

"Then why are you doing this? Why won't you let me go?" Her voice cracks, and a numbness works its way through my body.

"I want your love."

Her eyes widen at my confession. "Love? This isn't what you do to a person you love or want to love."

I don't speak. All I can do is look at her as she rages out.

"What is wrong with you?"

I peer down into the tub while softly lowering her leg and reaching for the other. She jerks away, pulling her legs to her chest.

"Stop it. Stop trying to take care of me when you're the reason I'm hurting in the first place."

Settling back on the heels of my boots, I pinch my lips tight, allowing her to have this moment. She needs it, and it's the least I can do. It's what I've been trying to get out of her since I ran into her at the coffee shop. For far too long, she's hidden and not spoken up for herself, and the darkest parts of me knew I would be the one to bring this out of her.

"Do you think this makes it all better? You've killed people, Christian. You've taken Cynthia and are forcing me to marry you. Washing away your betrayal changes nothing."

"I know."

"Then fix it." She pauses for a beat with her hands on either side of the tub. "Let me go home."

That causes me to snap—that word—home. Springing to my feet, I toss the washcloth into the water, and she flinches from the droplets that splash her face.

"This is your home," I bark.

"It's not," she combats.

I lunge forward, balancing myself on the edge of the tub so that my mouth is only inches from hers. "It is. This is where you belong, and you will be my wife."

"And are you ready for me to hate you forever, then?" She shrugs. "Because that is what's going to happen. Love isn't this, Christian. It's gentle, it's patient, it's—safe."

Without putting any space between us, I peer into her eyes and her into mine. "Then teach me."

Siân frowns and cranes her neck to get a better look at me. "What?"

I drop my gaze, my breathing hasty. "Teach me how to be gentle. How to love you?"

Siân is speechless, her brows knitted tightly together as if everything I've just said to her was in another language. I push off the tub and pace the bathroom.

"I'm not letting you go. This is your life now, but that doesn't mean I don't want to make it pleasurable for you."

"Pleasurable?" She laughs sarcastically. "You can't be serious." She stands, completely unbothered by the fact she's naked and soaking wet in front of me.

Not that I mean to, but my eyes trail the droplets of water that runs from her neck down over her breast before beading on her nipple. I swallow and force my attention back to her face. I may not feel the way others do, but getting hard right now wouldn't bode well in my favor.

"After everything you've done, you're now asking me to teach you how to be nice to me. That should be pretty fucking simple, Christian," she raves and throws her hands around. "But you know what, after meeting your father, I'm not surprised. What happened to you?"

Licking my lips, I allow a sigh to roll through me. "Look, Siân. I don't feel emotions like you or anyone else. I've had a hard life because I was born into a world that would fucking demolish me if I didn't toughen up. I don't feel sorry, and I like to hurt people. By the time I was fourteen, I'd killed a man, and I felt nothing but contentment. I don't know how to be gentle or patient."

"But you do. Well, maybe not so much on the patient part, but you were gentle with me once."

"And I still had to hurt you to feel something," I announce, and she freezes, the weight of my words seeming to finally sink in for her. "But if you can teach me what you need, show me how to be softer with you, then I can do that. I'm not letting you go. You will be my wife, and you will do what I say and if you can prove that I can trust—"

"Pot-fucking-kettle, Christian," she interrupts.

"*Trust* you, I will let you be with Cynthia whenever you want. But you don't have to hate it here," I propose.

She shakes her head. "You're a psychopath."

All I can do is stare at her for what feels like an eternity. "I am. You're going to need to get used to it."

MONSTER

9

SIÂN

It's been days since the basement, and I've barely spent five waking minutes with Christian since then. He always sleeps with me but usually doesn't fall into bed until well past midnight, when I've already been asleep for a while. By the time I wake up, he's gone.

Whenever I ask about it, he gives me the same explanation. *Business.*

It isn't that I care about him or that I'm worried. I only wish I knew what he was doing. If he's going to keep me here, force me to love him, the least he can do is answer my questions. With each passing day, the sense of having no control over my existence looms larger, threatening to smother me. I'm not even allowed to know what goes on elsewhere in the house. A bird in a gilded cage.

In truth, I should thank him for this sudden removal of himself from my presence. Otherwise, I might fall into the trap of latching onto his kindness and tenderness after he used me so brutally. I might want to look at the way he cared for me afterward and tell myself that he was the real Christian. The one I fell in love with. This cruel, dismissive, hurtful version of him is only an act. I might twist myself into knots out of desperation to believe he didn't really fool me.

At least I'm allowed to have some books in my room now. I think it's more a way of distracting me, so I don't plot my next escape attempt, but it's something to do. I've just cracked open a book about the history of medieval Italy from the library downstairs when the bedroom door opens.

Immediately, I sit up on the bed, clutching the book to my chest like it's a shield.

Then I drop it, too surprised to worry about myself when I see the blood on Christian's clothes. "What happened? Are you hurt?" My heart's in my throat, and I can't believe I care, but who wouldn't be surprised?

He only brushes off my concern with a bitter laugh. "You're worried? Over what? I thought you hated me. Shouldn't you wish I was dead?" He's still scoffing on his way into the bathroom. Within seconds, I hear the water running. I guess that's all I'm going to find out.

I shouldn't take him seriously, but I can't help mulling over what he said. I should want him dead. And I do. I wasn't kidding all the times I've said it. I meant it with all my heart, and I still do.

There's another truth on the heels of that one. He's lied to me about a lot of things, but there's one point on which I believe him: he's the only thing keeping me alive. Somehow, I survived the hit on my parents. Only thanks to Cynthia's bravery am I still breathing. If Samuele Russo still wants me dead—and I have no doubt of that considering what I've seen from him so far—Christian is the only thing keeping me alive. And if something happens to him, that's it for me. I don't stand a chance.

Son of a bitch. I hate him, but I also need him. The thought of it turns my stomach almost as much as the memory of thinking I was happy with him does. I wonder how many people he killed before I ever met him.

I'm still thinking this over when he returns, dressed in clean clothes, his hair still wet. The sight of him like this used to make my heart flutter. Now I don't know what to think.

"What have you been up to today?" he asks, rubbing the towel over his hair.

The question is so ridiculous that it makes me laugh. "What does it look like? I've been here. I was about to start reading." I hold up the book.

He stops drying his hair, now frowning at me. Great. What did I do wrong this time? "Would you like to go out?"

Once again, I blurt out a laugh before I know what's happening. "Really?" I venture. His expression doesn't change. He's not smirking or laughing. Could he be sincere?

"You could use a little sun, I imagine." He looks me up and down. "And new clothes. You deserve to choose something you want to wear. I had to choose your clothes for you, but I never expected them to be all you ever wore."

"You want to take me shopping?" Can I believe him? I want to.

"I told you, Siân, you don't have to be a prisoner here. That's not how I want it to be." He sits on the edge of the bed. "You aren't here to be my slave. I know we can be happy together. Let me show you how it could be, how I want it to be."

It will mean playing along. Not searching for any chance to escape. Can I do that? If it means getting out of here for an afternoon and having a look around, it's worth it. "Okay. I'm ready whenever you are."

I'm so happy for the chance to get out and act like a normal person that it doesn't hit me until we're in the car. This is the first time in fifteen years I've explored my home country. I don't remember much of anything—up until this point in my life, only brief flashes of half-remembered moments have reminded me of my former life.

It's a brilliant, sunny afternoon without a cloud in the sapphire sky. I admire it along with the hills and mountains all around us. The car weaves along a road cut straight from the mountainside. Beyond it is a sharp drop-off and a sparkling body of water. I don't know which body it is, and I'm too afraid of a sarcastic answer to ask.

It doesn't matter. Right now, my heart is lighter than it's been in days. I don't want to ruin it.

All the while, I feel him watching me. The energy in the car is easy, though. There's still something weighing on him, but it's not bothering him right now. Maybe he's already forgotten whatever it was he did earlier to get those bloody clothes. I wish I could forget seeing them.

We end up in a plaza where dozens of people wander cobblestone streets, ducking in and out of shops, and eat at tables on the sidewalk. It's almost too perfect. And it brings back a memory I've had buried deep in my subconscious all these years. I used to come to places like this with Cynthia—and my father. The three of us walked around, window shopped. I had a gelato, didn't I? Chocolate. It was so good, and I had to eat it quickly to keep it from running over my fingers. I can almost hear Dad's indulgent laughter along with Cynthia's soft giggles while she searched in her purse for a tissue to clean me up. How could I have forgotten that?

"Is everything all right?" When Christian places a hand on my arm, the memory pops like a bubble. But I still feel its warmth.

"Memories," I explain with a shrug. "It's crazy."

"I hadn't thought about that. What's it like, being home?"

"Is it really home if I spent more of my life in the States than I did here?"

"Home is always home. No matter how far you go or for how long." Something in his voice tells me he's not talking about me now. I wish I understood him. If he would only open up a little, I might be able to.

Then he smiles. "Are you ready to spend some money?"

"How much are we talking about?"

"How much are you willing to spend?" I can only imagine how skeptical I must look to make him laugh like he does. "I'm serious. Whatever you want, go right on ahead."

It's almost too much to believe. I guess there's nothing to do but test him by entering the first shop we come to. I'm glad to hear people speaking English. At least I'll be able to communicate.

"Mm, I would like to see you in something like this." He jerks his chin in the direction of a mannequin wearing what I guess could pass for a dress. It's barely a scrap of fabric and looks like it might be sheer in the right lighting.

"I bet you would." I roll my eyes before I realize what I'm doing, and my stomach sinks.

He only laughs it off with a shrug. "Hey, I'm a man. You can't expect much from me." His smile is contagious.

"Let's deal with the basics first, shall we?" I can't believe I'm actually smiling. What choice do I have? I can be miserable and make things more difficult, or I can try to get along. I can't pretend it isn't nice seeing him like this. Like the Christian I thought I knew before. As he follows me around the store and even offers to help hold things as I pull them off the racks, I can almost remember why I fell for him.

"Oh, forget it." I stop admiring a light, pretty sundress on seeing the price tag.

"Why?" He reaches out, touching the fabric. "That would look nice on you. Add a sunhat, and you could be any one of the girls strolling around outside."

"But it's, like, a lot of money."

"And last I checked, I told you not to worry about that. I meant it." He makes a big deal of removing the dress from the rack and draping it over what he's already carrying in his other arm. "I want you to have everything you want."

"Price checking. Force of habit," I confess with a shrug.

"A habit to drop." He follows me to a curtained-off dressing room where I try a few pieces on. By the time I'm ready to settle on what I want, I'm almost giddy. All of this, for me? This is only the first store we've gone to. I need shoes, underwear, and pajamas. Maybe a new purse?

After an hour, I have much more than that. We're both carrying bags by the time we leave the fourth store we've visited. Christian is having just as much fun as I am, if not more. "What the hell? Why not," he replied when I couldn't decide between a pair of designer sunglasses. "Get both." So I did, along with shoes, boots, jeans, T-shirts, and lace panties that are so pretty I'm almost afraid to wear them.

I could be a princess in a fairy tale if I hadn't been kidnapped and brought here on a jet while drugged. Why did I have to remember that now? It's such a beautiful day, and I'm having fun for the first time in so long.

We leave the bags in the trunk with the driver, who's waiting patiently for us. "Are you hungry?" Christian asks once the driver's closed the trunk. "I imagine all that shopping would work up an appetite. And we haven't yet found you any evening clothes."

"You plan on taking me out in the evening?"

"I would love to show you off. No matter where we go, I will have the most beautiful woman in the room on my arm."

My heart hurts. I want so much for this to be us. The real us, the way it used to be. When he would spoil me and pamper me and shower me with compliments and praise. When there wasn't any pain or murder. No blood.

"Food. Please." He takes my hand, and I let him lead me to a small restaurant with a few tables scattered out front. There's only a counter inside, nothing fancy. Not that I care. And something tells me anything that comes out of there would be better than I'd get at a fabulous restaurant back home, anyway.

Before we step inside, his phone rings. "*Merda*," he mutters, reaching for it and sliding me an apologetic look. "I have to take this. Why don't you wait inside where it's cooler?" Yes, the sun is really beating down now. It would be nice to step inside.

Before I can, something catches my eye from around the side of the building. Peeking out from the shadows of an alley between this building and the one beside it is a shabbily dressed man. His gnarled face is covered in gray whiskers, and his clothes could use a wash. He's also painfully thin, with veins visible beneath his papery skin.

"*Scusi.*" I inch my way toward him, so he doesn't feel threatened. "Hungry?" I pat my stomach, then point at him while smiling.

His head bobs up and down, and he rubs his stomach, his face scrunched up in pain.

"I'll buy you something." I point at myself, then inside the café. If Christian can afford thousands of euros worth of clothes, he can afford an extra sandwich. I'm glad he gave me his card so I could do the purchasing while he looked on. It's sort of nice that he trusts me, too.

I don't know what the gentleman outside wants to eat, so I settle on a simple ham and cheese on crustless white bread. It's ready in less than a minute and quickly wrapped up. As an afterthought, I ask for something cold to drink, as well, and settle on a bottle of Coke. Some brands are universal.

"Here you go." I can't believe how good it makes me feel to hand the man the sandwich and soda once I'm outside. He looks so happy, so grateful, repeating the word *gratzie* again and again. I wish I had enough Italian to ask if he needs anything else. It seems a shame to spend all this money on myself when I don't need very much.

When he reaches out and hugs me, I hug him back—gingerly, but I don't want to be rude by refusing, either. "*Prego*," I murmur with a smile as he lets me go.

"What the fuck?" A blur flashes past me an instant before Christian slams the man against the wall. He drops the Coke, and it shatters on the ground. "What the fuck do you think you're doing?"

"Wait—" That's all I have time to say before Christian takes him by the shoulders and slams him against the wall again, this time hard enough that I hear a sickening crack when his head strikes the stuccoed brick. The man's eyes roll back, his body twitching once, twice, before sliding down the wall and landing in a heap.

"Oh, my God!" I back away, bumping up against the wall behind me. "Why did you do that? He was thanking me for buying him food. Why did you kill him?"

He turns to me, breathing heavy, his eyes flashing. There he is. The real Christian, the one he hid from me all along. A simple shopping trip isn't enough to erase the truth or take me back in time to when I only thought things were good for us.

They'll never be good for us. He's crazy and dangerous and violent.

And I have no idea what else he's capable of.

MONSTER

10

CHRISTIAN

"Why are you constantly testing me, topolina?" I stalk toward her, my teeth clenched.

She peers up at me, wide-eyed, her features soaked in fear. Siân is screaming at me, but her words fall on deaf ears. All that matters is the jealous rage coursing through me. She pounds on my chest, yelling over and over, sweat and tears running down her face.

"You're fucking insane," she huffs out, her words finally registering. She attempts to step around me, but I keep her in place. "Stop it, Christian. Let me go."

There she is with those words again.

Let her go.

It angers me, her constant need to get away from me. Her insistent desire not to heed my words. Her actions come with consequences.

"Where do you think you're going?" I ask when she tries once more to yank herself from my hold.

"Away from you. You're sick. Why did you kill him?" Her voice cracks as she glances down at his lifeless body slumped awkwardly against the yellow brick of the café.

"No one fucking touches you."

"He was being nice."

I tug her toward me, spinning her so that she has no choice but to look me in the eye. "Do you think I give a fuck about how nice he is? No one touches what's mine."

She blinks in disbelief. "I'm not a property for you to claim."

"Too fucking late for that," I seethe.

She pushes against my chest, working overtime to pry herself from my grip. "You're hurting me," she whines while twisting and turning to free her wrist.

My grip is tight, so much so I feel my nails digging into her skin, and I should care that I'm hurting her, but I don't. Once my buttons have been pushed, there is no turning back. And with everything that is going on right now, she can't be this fucking reckless.

Being nice. I huff at her words ringing out in my mind again.

All it would take is for whoever is out here killing the crime families to take her naïvety for weakness. Nothing is as it seems in this world, and I won't apologize for protecting her at all costs.

"And you're being foolish."

She gasps, resentment for me written in the frown lines forming above her brow.

"You don't know who that man was. He could have hurt you, taken you!"

"Oh, what? Only you're allowed to hurt me?" she asks, and I know her question is rhetorical.

She's testing me, pushing me to prove her point. It's useless, though. Hasn't she learned by now that I don't care about the typical social conventions of the world?

"Exactly, and I will kill anyone who dares to challenge that. You can't go around being nice to every Tom, Dick, and Harry. People are after us, men who will do whatever it takes to get to me—to get to my father—and that includes posing as lowly street scum to seek your pity."

"He wasn't going to hurt me."

"And I wasn't going to find out if he would. You're not going to find any sympathy in me, Siân, so you might as well give up hope."

She shakes her head. "So today was all an act? Another fucking lie to manipulate me?"

"Let's go." I pull her toward the alley entrance, but she plants her feet.

Rooted into place, Siân tugs with all her might until she is finally free. I go to snatch her wrist, but she moves away, sidestepping me and nearly falling over the man's corpse. A yelp escapes her, and she shifts to back away, bumping into my chest.

With her back against my front, my need to prove to her she is mine only grows. I snake my hands down her sides quickly and grip her hips, pulling her into me even more. "You're mine, Siân, and whether you want to see it or not, I was fucking protecting you." I move again and lock my arms around her waist.

She shakes her head and claws at my hands. "No, I'm not!"

I've tried to be patient—or at least as patient as I can be—but this back and forth nonsense is starting to piss me off. Without another word, I grab one wrist and turn her to face me. Stalking forward, I don't stop until she's pressed between the brick of the building and my body.

When she opens her mouth to speak again, I promptly cover it. "Shhh. We're done talking, topolina." I can feel her teeth sink into my flesh as the last word leaves my mouth. It makes my dick swell and strain against my slacks.

I force her head back using the hand I have over her mouth, then slide the other one between us and unbutton my slacks. Her shoulders tense as her arms try to wiggle between us, but I just force my body against her even harder.

"You can say you're not mine all you want," I use my knee to spread her legs, "but the moment my fingers grace your pussy, I know you'll be dripping. You always are."

Dropping the hold I have on my pants, I slide my knuckles past her dress and up the inside of her thigh. Her skin is already hot, and when I brush the front of her panties, she's wet, just like I knew she'd be. I hook my fingers into the delicate fabric and pull, ripping her panties, then let them fall down her legs between us.

Gripping my dick through the hole of my zipper, I rub the head against her slit. Her eyes are still full of anger and contempt, but her body relaxes the slightest bit. "See, little mouse. You're mine," I hiss.

She shakes her head as tears well in her eyes but doesn't dare try to fight me anymore.

Slowly, I push into her and relish in the soft, muffled moan that slips from her lips. With every thrust, I keep my eyes locked on hers, waiting for the last bit of fight she has in her to leave, but it doesn't. The sooner she realizes this is how shit is, the sooner shit can get better. She just needs to give in to me.

I let go of her mouth and move both hands back to her hips. Turning her around, I force her onto the ground next to the man I murdered. The sound of broken glass crunching under my shoes only adds to my senses. The sea of voices from people passing by, a slew of individuals who are oblivious to what's happening only a few feet away.

Siân holds out a hand as if she is begging for someone to see her, to save her, but it's pointless. Her words are trapped in her throat. Only low grunts leave her, though soon, even those are mixed with soft cries of pleasure.

She loses her balance, falling forward on her elbows, bringing her face closer to the dead man. Without even trying, she tilts her ass up for me, calling me to drive deeper into her. She tries to lift herself, but I shove my hands into her hair and keep her in place.

"You care so much, look at him," I grunt around my thrusts. "I told you actions come with consequences, topolina."

"Ah," she bites back, and I can tell she's attempting not to moan.

That's okay. She doesn't have to. I know the truth. As it always does, her pussy squeezes me tight, milking my cock for all I've got.

"Ah. Ouch," she whines when I dig my nails into her ass and tighten my grip on her hair.

Siân tries to move her face from directly in front of the man, twisting and turning, all while her body rocks as I pump into her. Her balance slips, and she falls forward, her right hand sliding into his blood. The thick, dark liquid paints her pale skin and adds to my arousal.

"Fuck, you're so fucking perfect. That's right, feel his blood on your hands."

"N-No." She shakes her head. "I won't."

I pummel into her, our skin slapping loudly against echoes between the two buildings. Yet still with the liveliness of patrons, the music coming from nearby establishments, and the roar of engines as cars roll over the cobblestone streets, no one notices what's happening.

And even if they did, no one would bother to interfere. The people of Milan know my name and what I'm capable of. To protect themselves and to save their families the heartache of burying them, they'll steer clear. They could be standing inches in front of us, watching as I fuck while the man she caused me to kill isn't even cold yet.

Bringing my large palm down on her ass, she yelps from the sting. "Please, Christian." Her tone is shaky.

"Every time you disobey me, I'll make your punishment ten times worse."

"I'm sorry," she struggles to get out.

"Too late for that now. Smear his blood on your face. Maybe then you'll think before you hug another man."

She shakes her head in jerkish movements. I slap her ass again, and her sex pulses around me. Shit, I think. The body never lies. You can fight, kick, scream, and swear to the heavens, but your body will always tell the truth.

"Do it, or I'll take your tight virgin ass right now."

She outstretches her arm, her fingers jittery as she hesitantly coats her hand in his blood. Siân slowly brings her hand to her cheek, but she doesn't do as I say. Instead, a wave of silent cries hits her in a burst, and I love it, every fucking minute of it.

I tried to be gentle, but this is more me. The hurt, the pain, the murder. This is who I am, and unless she learns to comply, she's going to have to start getting really acquainted with me.

I watch her closely, losing myself in her sweetness. My lust, unchecked and disturbed, I piston into her over and over, digging my nails deeper into her flesh until I draw blood. From my place behind her, I notice her wince, the infliction giving her the courage she needs to heed my demands.

Finally, she touches her cheek, rubbing her trembling hand into her skin hard and painfully slow. The sight alone is enough to send me over the edge, and no sooner than I see her skin painted in our victim's blood, my balls draw tight, and I plunge into her one more time, emptying my seed and not pulling out until her pretty little pussy drinks it all up.

MONSTER

11

SIÂN

This can't be my life.

I don't know how long I've been staring at the ceiling, watching as the light from the windows moves across it while the hours pass. None of this feels real. Maybe I just don't want it to be. Because the pain in my body is most definitely real. Evidence of what he did to me today.

That pain, combined with the searing pain of remembering that poor, innocent man lying in a heap in that alley, makes sleep impossible.

Somehow worse is the way Christian can sleep soundly by my side. I know the way he breathes when he's asleep, and he's out cold. How? How could he do all those terrible things—committing murder, using me, being so callous about both—and sleep like a baby? How broken does he have to be to make that possible?

And his ring is on my finger. I'm trapped here with him. A soulless monster only pretends to be human when it fits his plans. That's what this is, too. He only wanted to throw me off guard today. Make me behave myself. A whole carrot and stick thing. Now, all those pretty clothes mean nothing. I'll never be able to wear any of it without remembering today. That poor, clueless man. All he wanted was something to eat.

And now he's dead because of me.

I don't realize I'm crying until the tears begin to pool in my ears and run down the sides of my face. I sniffle as quietly as possible and try like hell to fight them back. I don't want him to wake up. I don't even want to hear his voice.

I turn on my side, away from him, staring out the window. Not that I can see much this high up. Only the dark outlines of the mountains in the distance. I may as well be on the moon. I'm so far from normal reality.

What am I going to do? How do I spend the rest of my life like this? Eventually, I'm going to break. It's inevitable. After watching Christian kill not one but two men without flinching, something tells me my breaking point can't be far away. No matter what he says, no matter what happens, there's nothing true between us. How could there be? He doesn't even have a soul.

I pull the pillow up to my face when the crying over everything I've lost gets to be too much. It's soaked by the time Christian touches my shoulder. "What's wrong? Did you have a nightmare?"

"I don't need to have a nightmare." I shake his hand away. "My life is a fucking nightmare."

"You've been through a shock." He touches my hip this time, his body closer to me. I squeeze my eyes shut against my natural reaction. Even now, having seen what he's capable of, I want to melt against him. How sick is it that I want him to make me feel good so I can forget, even if for a little while? He's twisting me up with him. Turning me into a sick, depraved animal like he is.

"You put me through it." I try to roll away, but he holds me in place. "Please. Don't do that. Listen to me for once."

"Why are you so afraid of me? Can't you understand I did that for you? I believed he was attacking you."

"Why would a random person attack me? I'm just me. It's a ridiculous excuse."

His fingers dig in to the point of discomfort. Any more, and I'll be flirting with pain. "You don't know what you're talking about."

"And I'm sure you wouldn't want to tell me." I glare at him over my shoulder. "Why don't you tell me why somebody would try to kill me in a random alleyway? If you were so concerned, why did you even take me out shopping, then?"

"It's complicated."

"It's very simple. You're a possessed maniac. You can't stand to see anyone touch me, not even a random stranger thanking me for kindness. That's all he was doing."

I can't see him well in the darkness, but there's no missing his low growl. "I didn't know that."

"No, and you wouldn't want to wait three seconds to find out, either. You would rather act first and apologize later."

"I didn't apologize." He sounds proud of himself for it. "I only explained why I did it. You're taking this way too hard."

"You can't believe that. I'm only taking it the way a normal person would. You know, after seeing an innocent person killed in cold blood over something so harmless."

"He was nothing but a lowlife with no family or friends. No one will miss him."

"Is that supposed to make me feel better?" He makes a shushing noise and tries to pull me in close. I'm sure he only wants to press his erection against my ass since that's all he wants me for. I'm not going to let that happen. Not tonight.

I get out of bed before he can stop me, backing away until I'm almost pressed against the window. What am I thinking of doing next? Jumping? Right now, the idea doesn't seem half bad, but I know I don't have it in me.

Christian sighs as he sits up. The sheet falls away from his bare torso. I even hate him for taking away the thrill of seeing him like this. "Get back into bed."

"No. I don't want to be in bed with you. I don't want you to touch me."

His mouth twitches. "We both know that's not true."

"Don't do that. Don't act like anything about this is normal. You have no right to touch me."

"The ring on your hand says I do."

"What, this?" I hold up my left hand, snorting in disgust. "Is this a ring or a handcuff?"

"Which would you rather it be?" He rests his arms on his bent knees, the picture of ease and calm. His hair is tousled, and his eyes are still slightly blurry with sleep. I can't even pretend he's not hot like this. If the situation were different, I would be too happy to crawl into bed and pull him on top of me.

"I would rather it not mean I have to be ready for you whenever you want me, however you want me, no matter how I feel."

"It's only how you think you feel. Your body knows the truth."

"A physiological reaction isn't the same as wanting something here." I put a hand over my chest, where my heart is thumping like mad. I almost can't believe I have the courage to stand up to him, especially after what I've witnessed. But if I don't do it now, I never will. "You have no right to do the things you do to me. And even if I do want you to touch me, even if I like it, it's still wrong."

"Why?"

"Because of what you've done, obviously." He only stares at me like I've grown a second head. Could he be this obtuse? "Remember? You killed my ex-boyfriend. You stalked me for years. You terrorized me, and then you had the nerve to pretend to comfort me when you were the one who set everything in motion. Everything was calculated."

"You're right." He's sneering openly now. "It was almost too easy, making you do what I wanted. I only needed to set the pieces in place."

"You're proud? You hurt me. You hurt everybody I cared about. Taj and Kyla and Cynthia. And I'm supposed to lie there in bed with you and let you touch me? I'm supposed to like it?"

"I never said I was a good man," he mutters. "I never lied to you about that."

"A good man? You don't even have a soul."

"I do have a soul. Everybody has a soul. The difference is, mine is black. That's the way I've always been."

He's so matter-of-fact, it chills me to the bone. "So you don't care? You really don't care about the lives you've destroyed?"

"No. I've never lost a moment's sleep over killing. But I don't kill indiscriminately. That much you need to know. When I do, there's a reason for it."

"What about the guard you killed? There was a reason for that?"

"He was hurting you."

"Not that much."

"No one puts their hands on you but me."

He actually believes himself. I guess crazy people have to believe the insanity that comes out of them.

"And the man in the plaza? You couldn't have thought he was any sort of threat. A stiff breeze would've knocked him over."

He lowers his gaze to the bedspread. "I had reasons for that, too."

"Like what? What could possibly have been bad enough for you to do that?"

"Here's something you need to understand." His eyes are hard, glittering in the moonlight flooding in from behind me. "I consider your protection and welfare the most important thing in life. If it even appeared anyone was thinking of hurting you, I'd kill them. I believed that man was trying to hurt you. So I killed him. End of discussion."

"That is not the end of the discussion."

"Yes, it is. Right now, what you need to do is get back into bed and go to sleep. I'm tired of you questioning me."

I wrap my arms around my trembling body. I will not cry. I can't cry. "How can I not? I have no control over anything. And you never tell me anything, either."

"You'll be my wife soon enough," he murmurs. "That will make us equals. Then maybe you'll learn more of what you need to know."

"Equals?" I would swear the top of my head is about to blow off. I clasp my hands on top of it as if to keep that from happening. "How could we ever be equals after what you've done? You raped me, Christian."

He averts his gaze.

"What?" I challenge. "You don't like that word? We can talk about the other things you've done, instead. You stalked me for years. You made me run from you. I had to look over my shoulder everywhere I went. You pretended to want to protect me when you were the one I needed protection from. How is that us being equals? How does the exchange of vows erase everything that's already come before? It can't. I'll never forget it. Every time I look at you, I remember what you've taken from me. And who you've taken."

Did I say all that? My brain and my mouth weren't connected. That must be it. I don't know where the courage came from, but I'm glad it showed up. He deserved to hear all that and more.

Seconds pass, and now I wonder if I'm glad or not. He's hardly moving, his body still as marble. What's he thinking? Convincing himself not to kill me the way he's so indiscriminately murdered others?

He takes a breath, and I brace myself for what's coming. "Are you finished?" I can't find my voice to answer. He must take my silence as an answer instead because all of a sudden, he gets out of bed and crosses the floor. His dick swings with every step. I wish he'd wear something when he sleeps. Somehow I'd feel safer.

I creep closer to the bed in hopes of seeing what he's pulling from his dresser, but his body blocks my view. I have to wait for him to turn back to me. He's holding a thin stack of paper.

Not just paper. Photo paper. Pictures which he strews across the bed before stepping back and turning on the bedside lamp so I can get a decent look.

I still don't understand what I'm looking at. First, I recognize Taj. My heart feels like it's going to burst out of my chest. No, things didn't end well for us. He was worthless as a boyfriend. But he didn't deserve to die.

There's a photo of him on the sofa at his place, taken through the window. His pants are around his knees. Who's that under him?

"Remind me of everything I took from you." Christian's voice somehow makes its way through the sirens blaring in my head. "Because from what I saw, Siân, you can't possibly be missing much now. I did you a favor."

I want to look at him, but I can't pry my gaze away from the photos. Some of them are at Taj's, some are from my old house. His partner is always the same.

Kyla. Taj and Kyla. How did I never see it? They're all over each other. Some of the pictures were shot in full daylight, some at night. He's behind her in this one. She's riding him in that one. She let him take her ass while she leaned over the kitchen counter. They sixty-nined on my sofa without even a blanket or towel under them.

So many examples. How long was it going on? She pretended to be my friend. He pretended to give a shit about me. My chest is so tight I can barely breathe. When I try to do it, a sob bursts loose.

"You don't want to share the bed with me tonight?" he asks, still standing on the other side of this sea of horror. "That's fine with me. Share the bed with them, instead." My head snaps up at the sound of the door opening. He strides out, still naked, leaving me alone.

Alone with all this. The evidence of my blindness. It wasn't just Christian I was oblivious to. Everything was a lie. My relationship with Taj, my best friendship. Was anything real?

I sink to my knees beside the bed and immediately regret it when my torn skin screams a reminder of its existence. Right. Because it's not enough to have this thrown at me. I have to remember what I went through earlier today, too. With that poor, dead man lying feet away. It was as obscene as what I can't stop looking at now. No matter how much it hurts, no matter how many of my tears drip onto the images, I can't stop looking at them.

Maybe I deserve this. The pain of having my blind trust thrown in my face. The pain throughout my body reminds me of how stupid I was to ever believe in Christian. Kyla was a shitty friend, but at least she tried to warn me about him. She was smarter than me. And now she's gone, too.

Exhaustion sets in before long, and I sink into the bed with the photos still spread out next to me. Tears are still rolling down my cheeks by the time I drift off to sleep.

12

CHRISTIAN

For the past week, I've been away tracking down any and everything I can on who has been killing off the crime families. There hasn't been much development in that department, and now I have to walk into this house and tell my father that we are no closer to figuring this all out than we were days ago.

Every lead I chased led to a dead end. The only solid piece of evidence I've been able to find is that it's a man. Whoever this is doesn't want to be found. And if I'm honest, I kind of admire his tactics. The level of demented thinking that goes into each of his kills, the precision, the skill, it's my aphrodisiac. If I weren't looking for him to put an end to all of this, I'd be more interested in picking his brain.

I exit my car and take the stairs two at a time until I reach the top. It's a long way up, and I'm slightly out of breath by the time I reach the door. When I push it open and step past the foyer to the kitchen off to the left, I notice Helga walking toward me, carrying a tray of untouched food.

She doesn't have to tell me it's from Siân for me to know, but I ask her anyway. "Perché stai riportando un piatto pieno di cibo in cucina?" *Why* are you taking a full plate of food back into the kitchen? I adjust my slacks up on my hips, and we stop halfway at the center of the hall.

Helga shrugs, a remorseful expression on her face. "Mi scusi, signor Russo. Ho provato. Semplicemente non mangerà nulla." *I'm sorry, Mr. Russo. I've tried. She just won't eat anything.*

My blood starts to boil. I've been away for nearly six days. Is she telling me Siân hasn't eaten anything the entire time?

"Per quanto?" *For how long?* I follow her, waiting patiently for her answer.

Helga sets the tray on the counter and nervously turns toward me while holding out a water bottle for me to take. Servers dash throughout the kitchen, tending to their duties to keep this place running. It's massive, and while Aldo and Helga have been with us the longest, they can't do it alone.

I break the seal and take in a large gulp of water, finishing it in seconds. She clasps her hands together in front of her, a shaky breath rolling off her shoulders. Helga doesn't look at me, but then again, she never does.

"Da quando te ne sei andato." *Since you left.*

I'm fuming, disappointment and anger making an appearance. "Non mangia da sei giorni?" *She hasn't eaten in six days?* I bark, but not at Helga.

She clutches her blouse, slightly slipping out of my reach. "No. Ho provato di tutto. Ha detto che puoi tenerla qui, ma non puoi costringerla a mangiare." *No. I've tried everything. She said you can keep her here, but you can't force her to eat.*

Tossing the empty water bottle to the floor, I storm off in the direction of Siân's room before Helga can get the last word out of her mouth. I race up the stairs and take one large step after the other.

Siân's insistent. Hell-bent on getting under my skin. For a person who hates being punished by me, she sure as shit seems to enjoy pushing me. When I reach the door, the key already in hand, I insert it and swing the door open in one fell swoop. The heavy wood slaps against the wall, startling a sleeping Siân.

She jumps up, inadvertently rolling to the floor. A second later, she pokes her head up, but I'm already at her side, pulling her up by her bicep. She's fragile, and her already thin body is almost nonexistent now. She's wasting away, and I don't like it one bit.

Is this supposed to be her version of a strike? Starving herself on purpose. Not smart if you ask me. For someone so determined to get away the first chance she gets, you would think she'd want her strength.

"Ouch. Christian, let me go." She jerks from my hold.

"Why haven't you eaten, topolina?" I demand to know while inching closer.

"Siân. My name is Siân. I'm not your goddamn topolina or whatever the hell that even means."

"You're whatever I tell you, you are."

"Just leave me alone, Christian. Haven't you already done enough?"

"Not until you eat something."

She walks to the other side of the mattress and climbs under the covers. I take her in, noticing for the first time that she is not only skin and bones, but she also stinks, and her hair is a mess atop her head.

"Get up." I meet her on that side and yank the covers back.

"No." She scoots across the bed, getting out of it on the other end.

I wide-step until I'm directly in her path, blocking her. Grabbing her arms, I pull her to me and tug her toward the exit. Siân fights me every inch of the way, using her body weight to slow me down, but it's pointless. And that's why she should eat. Maybe if she hadn't malnourished herself, she'd have enough willpower to really put up a fight.

We make it to the kitchen, and immediately, the staff disburses, leaving us alone. Siân swats at my hand, her nails cracking against my knuckle. Gripping her tight, I force her to look at me, shaking her hard.

"Stop it. You're being a child right now," I yell.

She stares at me, seething. "Fuck you."

I grab her by the throat but don't apply enough pressure to hurt her, only to get her attention. "You keep offering, and I'll bend you over this fucking counter. Let everyone watch me take your ass."

"You're an asshole."

"And you need to eat. Now sit."

"I'm not hungry," she exaggerates and tries to leave.

Spinning her around, I say, "Eat it anyway."

Siân continues to challenge me. I force her ass onto the barstool, and she springs back up, so I take the seat myself and pull her onto my lap, wrapping my legs around her to keep her in place. I bring the tray of food Helga left closer to us. Siân pushes it away, but I bring it back and then wrap my large arms around her small frame. She's pinned to me now, unable to move except to squirm against my lap.

It's harmless, an attempt to get free, but she doesn't realize that if she keeps grinding on me, she will get a lot more than just this food. Picking up one of the pancakes, I use my hands to break it, not bothering to cover it in syrup as I hold it to her mouth.

She tilts her head, causing me to drop the pancake.

"Dammit, Siân. I'm not in the mood for your bratty behavior." Picking up a handful of eggs, I hold them to her mouth, squeezing her tightly until she finally gives in.

Her mouth opens, and as I go to put the eggs on her tongue, I watch the way she bares her teeth.

"Bite me, and I'll spank your ass."

She glares at me, pissed that I read right through her. Siân gives a little, finally taking the food without any more fighting. I continue to feed her until soon the plate is empty. Taking a napkin, I wipe her mouth and then clean up the food that spilled all over her clothes.

"There. Now, don't you feel better? You were wasting away, and I don't like that. You need to eat."

"Why do you care?"

With my finger under her chin, I force her to meet my eyes. "I've told you. Your safety, even your health, is important to me. Don't ever starve yourself again."

Siân is about to speak but is cut short when Helga enters the room.

"Signor Russo. Il dottore è qui." *Mr. Russo. The doctor is here.*

MONSTER

13

SIÂN

"A doctor?" I look at Christian for an explanation. His face is strangely blank. Did he know about this? "I don't feel sick."

"She isn't that sort of doctor."

"What sort is she?" I don't like this. I don't like the sense of needing to be on my toes all the time, either, waiting for the next surprise. It's exhausting in body and spirit.

"You're going to be checked over by a doctor specializing in fertility."

At first, it doesn't register. "Why do I need that?"

"To ensure you'll be able to carry my children."

I know better now than to think this is a joke. He rarely jokes, anyway. "And what if I can't?"

"You're young and healthy. There's no reason you won't be able to, I'm sure."

"But what if I can't? It happens. Sometimes women go around without knowing they're infertile for years until they try to get pregnant."

He nods slowly. "Which is why we're going to the trouble now of ensuring that isn't the case."

"What difference does it make?"

"Don't be a child." His brows draw together, his mouth set in a scowl. "You know it's important."

"I know you think it is."

"In our world, it is. End of story. You don't have to like it. But the rules must be abided."

"I never agreed to any of these rules." And now, I have to submit to yet another violation. "Will you abandon me if the doctor says I can't have children?"

He blows out a huge sigh. "It's not worth getting into this since that's not going to happen. Now come on. It's rude to keep her waiting."

"I wouldn't want to be rude," I say sarcastically while twisting my neck mockingly.

"Keep up that bratty attitude and see where it gets you." He snickers almost cruelly. "Never mind. You like that too much. I wouldn't want you to think of it as a reward rather than punishment."

"Go to hell."

"I have no doubt that's precisely where I'm going." As always, there's no fighting his grip on my hand. I think I'm beginning to understand the mentality behind breaking a captive's spirits. I know that in the end, any effort I make will be useless. He's always going to catch me, then find some new way to degrade or humiliate me once I'm caught. It's easier to avoid it, which means behaving myself, which is exactly what he wants.

We reach a bedroom I've never seen before, but I'm not particularly interested in looking around once I catch sight of what's clamped to the footboard: a pair of stirrups. "Oh, no," I whisper, shuddering.

Of course, a man wouldn't get it. "What?"

"Let's just say there's not a woman in the world who looks forward to a gynecological exam." I shiver and turn away from them.

A middle-aged woman emerges from the attached bathroom, chuckling softly. "Not to worry," she murmurs, smiling. "I'll be as gentle as possible." In her arms is a towel that she spreads across one side of the bed. We watch as she opens a leather bag and lines shiny metal tools along the towel's length.

Before she's finished, she glances up at Christian and smiles. "You can go now. It's best if the patient can enjoy privacy during these examinations," she insists, her Italian accent thick.

I'm glad for that, anyway, even if being left alone with a stranger who's about to look inside me is the alternative.

"I don't think so."

Her smile falters slightly. She seems kind, patient, and thoroughly thrown off balance. "Mr. Russo, I can appreciate your desire to guard this lovely young lady, but I can assure you your concern is unwarranted. I've performed this routine examination more times than I can possibly count. Things will move faster and come more easily if you aren't present."

"That's not going to happen. I'm not leaving her alone."

It's a game of verbal tug of war, and I'm in the middle. My gaze ping-pongs between them. Has Christian finally met his match? It might be worth going through this exam alone if it means watching him sulk away in defeat.

She lifts her chin. "I didn't need to come out here on short notice. I'm performing this examination as a favor to the family. I can just as easily leave if I'm going to be disrespected."

It looks like this battle will rage on indefinitely until footsteps ring out in the hall beyond the open door.

"I heard your voices down the hall. Is there a problem?" Samuele strides into the room, casting a sharp look my way before turning to the doctor.

"I merely tried to explain to your son that the examination must be conducted in private. For the sake of the patient."

"I'm not leaving her alone," Christian grumbles at his father.

Samuele barely stops short of rolling his eyes. "Christian, allow the doctor to perform the service she came here to perform. The sooner we confirm your fiancee's worthiness, the better."

The word *worthiness* sets my teeth on edge. The way he looks straight at me as he says it tells me he knows how it'll make me feel. This is not a man who speaks without thinking. He knew what he was saying.

Christian's jaw works, sharp breaths making his nostrils flare. I wish I believed he was this angry because of how his father insulted me, but I know him too well by now to make that kind of mistake.

"Please, by all means, do your work." Samuele nearly pulls Christian out of the room, leaving me alone with the doctor once the door is closed.

She turns to me, wearing an exasperated look. "Men. Always thinking they know everything."

"You have no idea." If I didn't know anything I said would get back to Samuele, I would give her an earful. I might even ask for help.

"Undress, please. I will be performing a full examination." She hands me a folded paper gown. I turn my back, undressing as quickly as possible before inserting my arms through the gown's sleeves. After leaving my clothes folded on a chair, I turn around.

"On the bed. Move forward as far as possible and put your feet in the stirrups." She pulls on a pair of surgical gloves, her voice gentle but professional. "At what age did you begin menstruating?"

"Uh, ten? No, eleven." She drapes a towel over my knees.

"Were you sexually active from a young age?"

That's a strange question. Usually, a doctor will ask at what age sexual activity started, but then again, English probably isn't her first language. Her phrasing is probably off. The fact that there are still male voices coming from the other side of the door makes my face warm with added embarrassment. "No. I mean, I wasn't young."

"Have you had many partners?"

Now this is getting uncomfortable, and she hasn't yet begun the exam. "Excuse me, but is there a reason you're asking? What does that have to do with anything?"

"I assume the answer is yes, then?"

"No, it isn't, but I'd still like to know."

She settles herself between my open knees. "You are American, yes?"

"Yes." It's easier than going through the whole story.

"I see. There is, how do you say it, a cultural barrier. I suppose doctors in the States go about this differently."

That makes sense. "Sorry. This is very sudden, so I'm still trying to catch up."

"Not to worry." She turns her head slightly like she's listening for something beyond the door. I wait, holding my breath. How much weirder is this going to get?

"You are very tense." She lifts an eyebrow. "Would you like me to give you something to help you relax? If your muscles are too tight, I'm afraid the examination will be quite uncomfortable, and it will take me longer."

"No, I don't think so. I'll try to relax." I look up at the ceiling, breathing slowly. It's not easy to tell my muscles to loosen, but I'm sure the doctor is right. The more nervous I am, the more uncomfortable this will be, which I'm sure will only make things worse when the exam takes longer than it needs to.

"Normally, I have a little time to mentally prepare for an examination like this."

"Yes, I'm sure that would help." She hasn't put a hand on me yet, and I can't see her now because of the towel. "Perhaps if I performed a breast exam first, it would give you time to relax."

"Sure, I guess so."

"Remove your left arm from the gown to expose your breast. I promise this won't take long." She offers a warm, almost maternal smile as she joins me beside the bed. "Raise your arm over your head."

I do as she asks, then try not to flinch when her gloved fingers press against my breast. It's easier to look away from her while she's doing it, so I turn my head in the opposite direction. "I have to tell you, I don't know if there's any history of cancer in my family."

When she doesn't answer right away, I look at her again and find her looking at the closed door. Considering she's supposed to be examining me, I don't think confusion's out of the question. "Excuse me, but is everything all right?"

She answers by removing her hands from my breast and clamping them around my throat.

I grab her wrists out of reflex, but she's so strong, and she has leverage over me. I pound on her arms with my fists and try to claw at her face, but she pulls her head back so it's out of reach. Christian's words and his concern for me starving myself make sense now. Not that he knew this would be happening, but precaution—always take the necessary precautions.

My eyes are bulging, and my lungs are screaming for air, but I can't breathe. She's going to kill me. Why is she going to kill me?

I try to shout or make any noise to bring Christian back, but I can't make a sound. She grunts when I land a punch against her chest but doesn't lessen the pressure. If anything, her hands tighten. The world is going gray, and suddenly, everything seems far away.

The tools. I remember them, and my hand shoots out to grab anything within reach. I close my fingers around the first thing I find, a thin metal rod, and jab at her hands with it.

"You little bitch," she hisses, removing one hand and holding my throat with the other while trying to fight me off. It's enough to give me a little bit of room to breathe, and I gulp in as much air as I can manage before she tightens her hold again. She knocks the probe from my hand, and it skitters across the floor.

She's leaning closer now. I claw at her cheeks, her eyes, anything I can reach. If I could only scream, but all that comes out of me is a gurgling noise. This is how I'm going to die. After everything I've been through, I'm going to die here.

I clench my fist and swing it as hard as I can, hitting her nose. She groans, using both hands to clutch it, now spurting blood. That's all I need.

I let out a broken, choked, "Christian!" before she's on me again, more vicious than before now that I've hurt her.

She shakes me, putting all her weight against my windpipe as my head flops like a rag doll.

Then she stops. Reality comes back into focus, and I pull in a painful breath as a furious Christian drags the doctor off me. "What are you doing?" he snarls.

I hold a hand to my throat. It feels like it's on fire. "Tried... to kill me..."

She's quick, delivering a sharp elbow to his ribs. But he's stronger than she knows, maybe even more so thanks to the rage that makes him bare his teeth as he takes her by the throat and shoves her up against the wall beside the bed. She's like an insect impaled on a pin, flailing around helplessly with no chance of escape.

He looks back at me. "Are you all right?" I nod since that's all I can do without it feeling like bolts of fire are shooting through my throat.

He leans in close to her until their noses are almost touching. She claws at his arm the way I clawed at hers. Now she knows how it feels. "What is this about?" he snarls. I hardly recognize his voice. "Who are you? Who sent you?"

At first, she only glares at him, blood running down over her lips and chin, thanks to the single punch I managed to land. I don't have to see his hand tighten further to know he does it. The way her eyes bulge is proof enough, not to mention the way her clawing becomes more frantic.

"Answer me. Who sent you? Why did you do this?"

"Paid. I was paid."

"I figured as much. I want to know why. Who was it?"

Her eyes bulge, her lips working with no sound coming out. He must let up a little because she sucks in a ragged breath. "Don't know. No names."

"How do I know that's true? Maybe your nose isn't all I can break. Eventually, I'll break enough that you'll beg to tell me the truth."

"It's true!" she gasps.

I would feel sorry for her if she hadn't tried to kill me a minute ago. If she hadn't looked so cold and vicious while she was doing it.

"This is your last chance. I'm going to start breaking things. Maybe I'll start with a finger. Maybe I'll shoot a kneecap." He glances my way, wearing a sick smile. "Maybe I'll have Siân decide. I'm sure she has a few ideas."

I nod slowly, looking straight at her.

"I swear." The fight has gone out of her, her body almost limp. "No names. Don't know. Kill her. That's all."

"Very well."

I'm shocked when he releases her. So is she, her face going slack with surprise when he lets go of her throat.

He gives her a moment to process her freedom before taking her face in one hand and smashing her head against the wall. She doesn't drop like the man in the alley but instead stumbles forward, falling to her knees.

Christian stares down at her, his expression unlike anything I've ever seen from him or anyone. Seething, murderous rage. If she was anybody else, I might try to get through to him and beg him to back off. At the very least, I would close my eyes this time, so I wouldn't have to see.

She's not anybody else. She's the woman who tried to strangle me. This, I want to see.

But instead of murdering her, he steps back. "Tony." A moment later, the man in question appears.

If I could speak without it hurting, I'd ask where he was all this time.

"Finish this bitch, then get rid of her."

She must be too dazed to react since Tony has no problem hauling her to her feet and dragging her away.

That leaves us alone. Christian stands in front of me, shoulders heaving, breathing like a bull ready to charge. "Like I said," he grunts, "I'm worried about your life."

I'm beginning to see why.

14

CHRISTIAN

"Let's go," I order through clenched teeth.

She allows me to take her by the hand and lead her out of the room. We take the stairs with her struggling to keep up. Her breathing is ragged. I can hear it even though I'm not looking at her. Focused and on a mission, I have only one thing left in mind, and that's to protect Siân.

A part of me knew she would be in danger, but there was no way to know for sure. We haven't exactly told anyone the last living heir to the Guliani family was alive and well. Not that it should matter to anyone who isn't my father, but clearly, I was wrong.

Marco's legacy burned right along with his and his wife's corpse in that fire all those years ago. And his territory, his connections all came to be my father's possessions. Or should I say, he made sure it was his? Naturally, considering we're the people who killed them—I was the person who killed him. First on the scene, first to claim the prize. A part of me wondered back then if Samuele was ever really going to go through with the deal had Marco not found out the truth. Had he and Siân not been betrayed by the woman who vowed to love them both, would Marco have ever agreed to give me his daughter?

I doubt it, considering when he found out what Samuele and Siân's mother had done, he put an end to it that ultimately cost him his life.

"Slow down, Christian," she huffs through shaky breaths. "I need air." Her hold on my fingers falters.

Quickly, I face her, my chest tightening with a mixture of emotions at the screaming red bruises around her neck. Without a word and the need to get her as far away from here as possible, I scoop her into my arms and carry her the rest of the way.

One large, hasty step at a time, I rush to the room I'd been keeping her and place her gently on the bed. She releases my neck and uses her hands to balance herself against the mattress. I feel her watching me as I thrash around the room, pulling clothes from the closet and dresser.

Tossing the items next to her, I disregard the pieces that fall to the floor and exit the room. Hell-bent on taking her away, I don't even bother to lock her in the room. Three steps at a time, I climb to the next level and hit the corner, bumping my shoulder hard against the wall. Pain shoots through my body, but I push it to the back of my mind.

I make it to my room and retrieve my travel cases, then throw clothing for myself inside. It doesn't matter what the items are. I just need some things to tide us over for a few days. Anything else we need I can get while we're away. Halfway zipping up the suitcase, I race back to Siân's side. Even though we're inside and the threat has been neutralized, I fear leaving her alone.

"Fuck." I stop for a moment with my hand over my chest.

What is this? Fear? I'm not afraid of anything, have never been. So why the fuck does it feel like there is a band around my heart, tugging and pulling? I shake away the nerves and continue, damn near jumping down the stairs.

Siân sits up when I burst into the room. It isn't lost on me that for the first time since she's been here, she didn't try to run. The door was wide open, so she could have fled if she wanted to.

"We're leaving," I deadpan and make quick work of stuffing her things next to mine.

Siân frowns but doesn't fight me too much. She helps me by handing me the items that fell on the floor. "Where are we going?"

A deep breath escapes my lungs, but I can't look at her. I can't help but feel as if this is my fault. I knew I shouldn't have left her alone. There was a weird energy coming from that woman, and yes, I called her to examine Siân before I arrived home. But when you've been at this shit as long as I have, you get a sixth sense about these things. I know that, and still, I left her alone.

She could be dead right now.

"Topolina, I don't need your resistance. We need to leave now."

Siân stares at me for a moment, and it's as if she can read the unspoken concern in my voice. She moves slowly at first before sprinting into the bathroom for her toiletries. Then she makes her way to her closet for something else, but I cut her short.

"Leave it. Whatever else we need, we can get once we get to where we're going."

Siân nods and slips on a pair of sneakers. Smart girl, I think as I close the overstuffed bag and wait for her by the door. Once she's ready, she reaches for my hand, and we exit the room, head down to the first level, and out the side entrance to where we keep all of our cars.

I hear Tony behind us, rambling off something I can't make out. My thoughts are crowded, and while I normally count on him, taking him everywhere with me, I can't this time. Not if I'm going to keep her safe while I figure out who sent that woman.

"Cristiano. Dove stai andando?" he yells. *Christian. Where are you going?*

"Sto portando Siân fuori di qui," I answer without glancing back at him. *I'm getting Siân out of here.*

We cross the bricked lot with Tony hot on our ass. Opting to be a little more inconspicuous, I snatch the fob to the Mustang from the hook in the garage we never close. It's nothing fancy and will allow us to get through town without drawing any attention, but it's also fast enough if we need to get away in a hurry.

I hit the button and wait for the headlights to flash. Siân runs for it, and I hit the unlock button for her. Once she's inside, I finally turn toward Tony.

"I'm coming with you."

"No," I blurt. "I need you to stay here, find out everything you can about who she was working for." I point, then turn away and run to the driver's side of the Mustang.

"I'll keep you posted."

I nod, snatch the door open, and sink in next to my woman. Siân fumbles with her seat belt, hissing when she doesn't get it the first few times. I place my hand over hers to still her trembling hands.

"Breathe, topolina."

She makes eye contact with me, mimicking my display of even breaths. She nods rapidly, then successfully fastens herself in, falling back into the seat when I shift the gears and floor the gas.

*

THE RIDE IS quiet except for the sound of cars passing and people out enjoying themselves as we make it through town. Once we get on the autostrada—*highway*— I pick up speed, flying through the countryside.

The entire way, Siân remains silent, staring out the window. For a moment, she looks peaceful, almost as if she's reminiscing about a time when everything wasn't this hectic. I like seeing her like this, despite the fact that it will be short-lived.

Until I can make sense of everything that is going on, she won't be at peace—I won't be at peace. None of it makes sense, Siân hasn't done anything to anyone, and I can't help wondering if maybe the person who is killing off members of the crime family is behind this.

Did they come for her, in my house, directly under my nose to get at my father and me? To show us that we are indeed on their list and to demonstrate just how resourceful they are. Or is it something else entirely?

Now, I'm starting to think that bringing her back may not have been a good idea. But my greed, my sick need to own her, blinded me. But my need to have her overshadowed my logic. I knew my father would be something we'd have to worry about, considering he ordered her dead and doesn't like unfinished business, but now with all the bodies piling up and us being no closer to figuring it out, I regret taking her.

After a while, Siân dozes off. Where we're headed is hours outside of Milan, a quaint villa that is more touristy than anything else. No one would think to look for us there, out in the open. We'll still be staffed, staying under the radar, but I want her to be comfortable. I made her a prisoner, but I won't allow her to be a sitting duck.

I turn down an uneven road, stirring Siân from her brief sleep.

"Mm." She stretches. "Where are we?"

I glance at her, then back to the road. "We're just about there. The hotel is just up ahead."

She nods and adjusts in her seat while craning her neck to peek out the front window." This is beautiful. I think I remember coming here before."

I dart my gaze to her and back.

"Yeah. I was with Cynthia and my dad. I couldn't have been no more than five or six. But I remember it vividly because I fell and scraped my knee right over there." Siân points across me to a section of seating just feet away from a statue. "I was climbing on the statue and fell. How do I remember that? I don't remember much after I was ten."

"Repressed memories. You went through a traumatic experience. Your little brain must have hidden thoughts of anything before you got away. You were protecting yourself."

She's quiet, and I have to look at her to be sure she's okay. Her face is grim, and her shoulders rigid.

"I didn't mean to make you uncomfortable."

She shakes her head while picking at her nails. "No, it's fine. I knew that. It's just still surreal. Growing up here and never knowing about this world is overwhelming."

"It can be. But, you're strong, and like I told you in Florida, risk makes you stronger."

"What is that supposed to mean?"

"Everything that has happened, it's a risk—trauma. It'll make you tougher."

"Are you seriously trying to negate me almost being murdered into a pep talk?"

"No. Not at all. But it's a fact."

"Yeah, well, Christian, we all can't be heartless."

I don't respond to that because she's right. I don't expect her to be like me, but she needs to be stronger, especially now that people are out to get us. But like I've told her, her safety is important to me, so whoever this is just fucked with the wrong motherfucker.

MONSTER

15

SIÂN

"Here you are." The clerk on the other side of the counter slides a key card across the marbled surface. "Have you any bags to be carried to the room? One of our employees—"

"No need. We'll manage it." With a firm grip on my hand, Christian leads me away from the front desk of the sprawling hotel we've checked into. This whole experience is such a whirlwind that I can't keep track of the surprises. The biggest surprise of all being how sweet and attentive Christian is now.

All it took was me being moments away from death.

"Are you hungry?" he asks on the way to the elevator. "Would you like something to eat before we go to the room?"

"What I want more than anything now is sleep." Then as an afterthought, "Though maybe we can order a pot of tea. Something hot." I touch a tentative hand to my throat, which still hurts.

"Of course. I should have thought of that." He looks disappointed with himself. "Whatever you need. Perhaps something for pain?"

"We'll see." When he doesn't look any less concerned, I try to give him a smile. "Thank you. I'll be fine." It's overwhelming how he's swung all the way back to how he was before. I wish he would stay this way. I hate always wondering in the back of my mind what's going to cause him to swing back to that cold, degrading version of himself. When he's like that, I would swear he hates me. It's hard to imagine why he wouldn't want me dead when he treats me like garbage.

Right now, I'm a treasure. He even strokes my hair on the way up to our penthouse, then keeps me close to him when we step off the elevator and into the spacious, luxurious suite. It's enough to take my breath away, and the views beyond the windows are even more stunning. I could sit here all day and gaze out at the expanse of mountains, the lake, and gorgeous villas spread out in front of me. I could be God sitting up here, looking down on creation.

Instead, I'm a very confused, very tired girl who can't remember a time when life was normal. It must have been at some point, right? At a moment like this, it's tough to remember. So much has happened so fast.

Christian checks everything out while I gaze out the window. I watch his return in the reflection on the glass. "There's an electric tea kettle in the kitchen. I've turned it on for you. Why don't you freshen up, and I'll bring you a cup?"

"You don't have to go to the trouble."

"It's no trouble."

And it isn't worth it to argue. I go to the bathroom and take a quick shower, then wrap myself in a thick, warm bathrobe provided by the hotel. All the while, I hear Christian talking on the phone. His voice is muffled by the walls, but it's obvious he's tense. I wouldn't want to be the person on the other end of the line.

By the time I'm finished, the water is boiling away in the kettle. Christian is distracted, typing furiously on his phone, so I go to the kitchen and fix a cup of tea using the complimentary bags offered. There's honey, too, and a small bowl of lemons. I cut a few slices and add them to the brew. A few sips are enough to take the edge off the soreness.

How much longer is this going to go on? I have no doubt Christian has the resources to hide me away wherever he wants to, for as long as he wants, but we can't live this way forever. And I don't want to. Always on the run. I've had enough of that—ironically, thanks to him.

"I'm sorry. I was supposed to do that."

I didn't realize he was watching. "It's okay," I insist. "You're busy." As if to prove my point, his phone rings, and he turns away to take the call.

I should go back to the bedroom. It's late, and I'm beyond the point of exhaustion. But while my body is wrung out, my brain won't slow down. I know any attempts at falling asleep would be useless, and I would only be hopelessly frustrated after lying in bed for ages with nothing to show for it. It's not like Christian would join me, either, since I'm sure he'll be on the phone for a while. So I would be alone. Nothing but me and my thoughts and the memory of nearly dying at the hands of a woman who pretended to be a doctor. Or maybe she was a doctor with a side hustle.

Rather than go to bed, I curl up in an armchair near the window and admire the lights twinkling on the lake below. It's so peaceful. I wonder what it's like for people down there right now, people whose lives don't involve running from hired assassins. Why would anybody want to kill me? It wasn't long ago that I doubted Christian when he claimed my life was in danger. I still don't understand why, even if it's clear he was right.

He finishes yet another call made in rapid-fire Italian before leaving his phone on the coffee table. "Aren't you going to try to rest?"

"How can I? I can't stop thinking."

"That's understandable." He comes to me, stroking my hair like he did before. It's a comforting gesture, one I wouldn't mind him continuing, but it's still so out of line with the way he's been lately. I wish I knew what to expect. I can't enjoy this or even relax very much if I never know what to expect.

"Why are we here?" I look at him in the reflection. "Why did you bring me to this place?"

"To keep you safe, of course."

"Safe from what?"

"To start, from assassins. I would think you'd understand that by now."

"But why? Why did she do that? I've never hurt anybody. I've never done anything."

"I know that."

"Then why?" All he does is snort, derisive, before turning away. The teacup shakes so hard it splashes liquid on the bathrobe. I set it aside and stand. It's time to get some answers. I doubt he'd want to leave me alone right now, so he has no choice. There's no escaping me.

"Remember when you talked about us being equals? You said it would happen once we're married." It's still hard, not choking on that word. "Why wait? Why not start treating me that way now? How am I supposed to ever trust you or believe you if you won't be honest with me? This is my life. Don't I at least deserve to know why it's in danger?"

"Why is it not enough to know I'm doing everything in my power to keep you safe?"

"Because I would like to know what to look for, too. I was completely unprepared for that woman."

"Because you didn't believe me when I warned you."

"You didn't suspect her any more than I did."

"That isn't true. I suspect everyone. Why else do you think I'd been hesitant to leave you alone?"

Right, because he's never been possessive for no reason. Rather than throw that in his face, I reply, "If we're ever going to be equals, you need to start now. Unless you meant nothing you said. Answer my questions. That's all I want."

When he hesitates, I cross the room to where a well-appointed bar sits in one corner. Maybe if I loosen up his tongue a little, it will be easier for him to fess up.

When I turn around with a glass of whiskey in hand, he sighs and drops to the sofa. Interesting. When he knows he's cornered, he doesn't waste time keeping up the fight. I wouldn't be surprised if he got all forceful and demanding, but instead, he submits. Sort of the way I've learned to do with him.

I return to the chair and pick up my cup as he takes a few sips of alcohol. He sighs, sinking further against the plush cushions at his back. "It turns out you are not an easy woman to protect."

"Thank you?"

The beginnings of a smile stir his lips, but it never solidifies. "What do you want to know?"

"Only what I asked already," I remind him. My heart's beating like crazy. Am I really going to get answers, finally?

"Obviously, I brought you here to keep you away from my father's property for a while. Obviously, someone knows you were there, and they could easily send another assassin after you once it becomes clear their first mission failed." He sips the whiskey again. "I'm sure once it's clear they're not going to hear anything else from that bitch, they'll try again."

"Why would they send anyone after me at all? What have I done?"

"That's unclear. I'm sure you've done nothing but exist."

That isn't exactly comforting. I draw my feet up on the chair, covering them with the ends of the robe. Suddenly, I feel cold.

"We'll spend a little time here, out of sight. Hotel security is tight. I've already instructed them not to let anyone up to the room without my permission first."

If I have to be locked away somewhere new, I could think of much worse places. At least I have that going for me.

He stares into the glass, then begins swirling what's left of the whiskey. It's almost hypnotic, watching the funnel that forms. "We have a much more complicated history than I've ever shared with you, Siân."

"More complicated than the way your father called for my family's destruction?"

"My father." There's a growl in his voice that doesn't bode well. "The figure that's loomed largest in my life from the day I was born. There's never been any pleasing him. Never any understanding him. I've watched him make promises to countless people, and I've watched him break just as many of those promises. I've watched him smile and clap men on the back and thank them for their friendship, then cross them. Sometimes not even hours later. He's a master manipulator. The ultimate sociopath."

Having spent even a limited amount of time in the man's presence, I have no problem believing this.

"He taught me from a young age to say one thing when I mean another. How to be convincing. How to disconnect my true feelings and beliefs when it comes to handling friend and foe alike. Nothing matters more than getting what we want and protecting what's already ours. No friendship is greater than that. No other human life means more." There's an emptiness in his words, flat and cold. He might as well be reading from a book. That's how much emotion he's putting into this.

His gaze darts up from the glass, eyes meeting mine. "We were promised to each other a long time ago."

"We were what?"

"Our fathers agreed to the match." He smirks at my reaction. "A match made in heaven, it was not."

"So we were supposed to be married all this time? You mean, if he hadn't murdered them, you and I would be married by now?" No matter how I say it, my brain doesn't want to accept it.

"There wouldn't have been a choice in the matter. That's how these things are determined among the families."

"But I thought my father loved me."

"It has nothing to do with love. Even if you were the most precious thing in his life, he would still have used you to secure an alliance with my father. And he would have known you were well taken care of because otherwise, the alliance would suffer. I'm certain from his point of view, it was the only way to go."

"Without asking me about it?"

"You're thinking as an American and a civilian at that. For families like ours, emotion isn't brought into it." He savors another sip, leaving me hanging before he reminds me, "You were a child, too. Don't forget that. It's only business."

I'm sick of that word. I'm also sick of knowing he's not giving me the full story. He only thinks I can't see he's being evasive. He won't look me in the eye, and the fingers of the hand not holding the glass tap rhythmically against his knee.

"When I think back on Dad, though, all I remember is happy times. He was loving and sweet. He paid attention to me. He made me feel special and important."

"I'm sure he did. You'll have to tell me sometime how that feels since I certainly never experienced it for myself."

"I'm just saying. What you're describing feels so far from what I knew."

"Again, there's a personal life, and there's business. I'm sure he knew how to separate the two for your sake."

"While your father couldn't, I guess?"

"For my father, they're one and the same. Family is business. Business is family. He never makes a choice without weighing what it means for the Russos. For himself, in particular."

"How old were you when he brought you in?"

His smile is bitter. "There's never a time I wasn't in, as you put it. From the beginning, I was the heir apparent, and he believed in on-the-job training. Other kids were allowed to go out and play, to make friends." He snarls before draining what's left in his glass. "Me? I lived with the daily reminder that there's no such thing as friendship. In the end, everyone behaves in their own best interest. Might as well get what you can from them while you can."

"I'm really sorry."

"Why? You didn't do it."

"No, but I'm sorry that happened. Being brought up that way must have been miserable. You never knew if you could trust anybody."

"Simple. I don't. That leaves me with a lot less to wonder about."

"But that can't be easy, either. You're always looking over your shoulder or judging everybody through the most cynical lens possible."

"It's kept me alive." I know he's trying to sound tough and unaffected, but there's pain in his voice. So much that it touches me deeply and reminds me that he's just a wounded, broken person who never had a chance. He talks about his black soul, his lack of conscience? No wonder. Anybody would have a conscience beaten out of them over time with a father like the one he's describing.

"But what kind of life is that? I'm so sorry."

He looks at me from beneath lowered brows. "Sorry for me? I'm not the person you should feel sorry for." He leans forward, plopping the glass on the coffee table before picking up his phone again. He's pulling away from me. We were so close to sharing something real, too.

"Please come and talk to me," I beg.

"We've done enough talking," he barks before storming off to the bedroom, where he closes the door and separates us once again. Within moments, he's back on the phone, rattling off instructions in Italian so I can't understand.

Why not? It isn't like I can understand anything else about him, anyway.

MONSTER

16

CHRISTIAN

I slept on the couch last night. Partly because I wanted to be near the door in case anything happened. But mainly because of how I reacted last night. After everything she's been through, she didn't deserve for me to flip out on her. And while apologizing isn't a thing I've done, I feel I owe her that.

She nearly lost her life, and I had a hand in every horrible thing that happened before that. Now, after nearly losing her, I don't like the way that feels. Almost as if the emotional dam has broken, and all of a sudden, I'm in tune with my feelings—remorse, regret, shame. Sensitivity is probably a better word for it, but that has no place in our world.

Shaking away my thoughts, I swing my legs over the side of the insanely comfortable sofa. I push my fist into the cushion, grunting as I lift myself. It's quiet, and when I glance to my right out the large window, it's barely sunrise. The sun slowly peeks over the horizon, painting the sky in various shades of orange and purple.

I walk across the large living space toward the bedroom. The suite is huge and should be for the amount of money it cost me. Not that money matters, because it doesn't, but there is no way I'm paying for anything less than what we deserve. The door is cracked, but I can't see anything through the slit. When I push it open, my heart jumps from my chest, and my ears start to flood with nervous pressure.

I storm in, shoving the door open farther as if that would make a difference. Then I pat the empty bed, a subconscious action to help my brain accept the reality in front of me. The bathroom adjacent to the room is vacant, and she's nowhere in the front of the suite.

She's gone—Siân is gone.

Panic rises, my palms sweat, and suddenly, I can't fucking breathe. When I race to the bar area where we set the keys and notice one is missing, I relax a little, but that doesn't exactly mean anything.

My nails scrape across the cold granite as I snatch up the remaining key card and my phone and storm out of the room without shoes. The hallway is clear, only the sound of a child crying in the distance, and as I stalk past doors, I can make out bits and pieces of conversations.

None of that matters, though. But, I keep my ears open just to be sure I can hear her, a laugh, a cough—a scream. Is this it? Has she finally found her out and decided to take it? To run from me despite me saving her, despite being wanted by an unknown assassin?

That hits me harder than anything I've ever experienced before. Not when I was shot, not when I was stabbed, and not when Samuele beat me to teach me a lesson. I've endured a hellish amount of things, but with the tightness in my chest and the way my lungs rub together like sandpaper, it seems losing Siân affects me the most. There's a name for feelings like that, a name I've never cared to say to anyone before.

Instead of taking the elevator, I opt for the stairs, running down them so fast my bare feet slap against the concrete surface. I grab onto the railing because I miss a couple and come extremely close to face planting.

I continue, one floor at a time. Twenty-three. Twenty-two. Twenty-one. I call them out in my head, hoping to help keep me from going batshit crazy. There was no telling when she left or if she was taken.

None of her stuff seems to be missing, but then again, if I were running away from my captor, I wouldn't take anything with me either.

I'd leave it all behind so that nothing holds me down. But where would she go? She doesn't have any money, nor does she know anyone here but me. I also doubt she'd leave without her precious Cynthia.

Finally, I make it to the bottom level and burst through the door like a madman. It leads into the lobby area next to the elevators. The sudden reaction draws scorned glances from those around me. But fuck them, my concern is Siân, not a bunch of people I know nothing about.

Dismissing their glances, I continue, looking in every direction, craning my neck to see around the other guests. It doesn't surprise me the number of people who are here, it is a popular tourist location, and we're in the dead of summer. The sun beams in through the large floor-to-ceiling window, blinding me. Squinting, I head past the lobby area, cutting in front of the line of people. Grunts and groans sound out behind me, but I ignore them.

"La ragazza con cui sono venuto, l'hai vista?" I say to the clerk who checked us in. *The girl I came with, have you seen her?*

"Sig. Russo. Credo che stia facendo colazione." She points to the left. *Mr. Russo. I believe she's getting breakfast.*

I can't breathe. Just like that, the restriction around my lungs releases, and I draw in the biggest breath. But as quick as the relief hits, anger sets in. Why would she leave the room without me? Doesn't she know how stupid that was?

Someone literally tried to strangle her, and she's getting breakfast. I swear she loves getting under my skin, doing things that she has to know will upset me. And now, the need to punish her has replaced the fear I had over losing her.

Heading to where the breakfast area is set up, I fish my way through the sea of bodies. Short, tall, skinny, and plump, I survey the crowd in search of her. Then I spot her, all the way at the back of the room, pulling a bagel out of the toaster.

I storm up to her, presenting myself at her back, my front against her soft ass. She startles and yelps when I grab her by the arm and bring my mouth to her ear.

"What the fuck were you thinking?" I seethe.

"About what?" she questions nervously, holding her plate to her chest with the bagel still in her hand.

"Let's go." I pull her away, but she stands her ground, though not as effectively as I'm sure she'd like.

She stumbles against me. "Christian, wait," she lets out. "My bagel."

Snatching the bagel and throwing it against the wall, I yell, "Fuck the bagel."

She gasps. "Why would you do that?" She follows the bread as it lands with the floral wallpaper before shattering into pieces.

Getting up in her face, I force her to look at me. "Back upstairs now." I point toward the exit, and when she doesn't move, I grip her bicep and force her to move.

"You're hurting me," she cries while fighting to free herself.

"Hey amico. Lasciala andare." A stranger interferes with his hand on my forearm. *Hey, man. Let her go.*

Wrong move.

Before he can even attempt to protect himself, I draw back and smash my fist against his nose. "Fatti gli affari tuoi, cazzo." *Mind your fucking business.*

I cock my arm back again, ready to clock him once more, but Siân grabs me, wrapping her tiny arms around my large one.

"Stop. Stop. Let's go."

I peer back at her with a fistful of the man's shirt. Blood gushes from his nose, and I'm sure it's broken. Serves him right for getting between me and what's mine. And if it weren't for Siân pleading for him or the room full of people, I would do a lot more than busting his fucking shit. He'd be a statistic, and I wouldn't think twice about it.

Actually, it would be the perfect relief to let go on him. I need to hit something, hurt someone. To bash a motherfucker's brains in to give me the fix I desperately need. But soon enough, I'll find whoever the fuck sent that bitch after her, and when I do, I'll skin them alive.

Siân doesn't let me go, and this time it is her who coaxes me away. We don't stop, ignoring the whispers of onlookers and the gargled cry from the guy. Maybe that will teach him not to interfere where he doesn't belong. Trying to be the hero never ends well. In my world, the villain always wins.

We make it to the elevator, boarding it the moment it opens. She steps in, puts her back against the wall, and crosses her arms over her chest.

"What is wrong with you?" She berates once it's only she and I without the ears of others around us. "Are you incapable of being a decent human being?"

"The question is, what's wrong with you? It's not safe. Why would you go anywhere without me?"

"I just wanted a fucking bagel. In case you forgot, Christian, we didn't eat. I haven't eaten in days."

"And I should spank your ass for that."

She flinches, her cheeks growing visibly flushed. She's pissed, yet my threat to spank her still does something to her.

"Stop. For once, just have a conversation with me. No threats, no trying to dominate me. Please. It's the least you can do."

"You don't get to make demands when I'm trying to keep you alive. You were almost murdered. Do you fucking get that? Someone somewhere managed to find a way into our home and tried to kill you. I don't give a shit about that asshole downstairs, the bum in the alley, or anybody else. The only person's life I'm worried about protecting is yours."

"You wouldn't need to if you'd have just left me alone. But you didn't, for some sick, twisted reason. You've been holding on to some archaic arranged marriage, forcing me into this life. Between you and whoever sent that woman, I'm not safe, Christian."

I get closer to her, my chest heaving. "Do you understand how fucking crazy I went just now? I don't give a shit about you not liking being here. You don't have to like my methods, but you're going to need to get used to them real damn quick. Don't go off without me again. Do you understand me?"

"Why do you care so much? You've done nothing but hurt me. You've lied, manipulated, berated, and abused me. Now all of a sudden, I matter to you. You need to protect me and keep me safe." She mocks me, her voice mimicking my own—accent and all. "Is it because only you can hurt me? You want to be the one to kill me when this is all over?"

I freeze in place, thrown off by her words. "You're the last person I would ever want to kill."

"Like you really care about me."

"Can't you see how insane you make me?"

The lift dings, alerting us that we've reached the penthouse level. Siân breaches the threshold, holding the doors apart with her hand.

"I don't make you insane. You do that all by yourself. But don't worry, I may not be safe from you, but I am safest with you. So you don't have to be concerned about me running."

With that, she drops her arm and turns the corner that leads to our room. Her words replay in my mind, and I fight the urge to smile. She isn't going to leave.

I follow her, watching her back and meeting her gaze when she glances back at me.

"And where are your shoes?"

I stare down at my bare feet, suck in a deep breath, then move forward. "Good question."

MONSTER

17

SIÂN

After his big blow-up in the breakfast area, Christian has had me glued to his side. If I go to the bathroom, he's at the door. If I'm in the middle of a shower, he watches me. It was only yesterday that he started to let up. I caused him to distrust me, and for some weird reason, it affected me. He's done horrible things, but seeing how afraid he was for me helps me see him in a different light. Especially now that he's softening around me.

For a few days, it's almost like being back in Florida again. Back at Christian's apartment, before I knew anything about the real him. When all I could see was what he wanted me to see. What I needed to see. His kindness, his attentiveness. His desire to give me everything I wanted.

His indulgence, too. We've streamed countless movies, all my favorites. He sits and watches them with me, cuddling with me. Nothing forced, though. He's left it up to me for once.

And for the first time since learning the truth, I want to be close to him. I need his nearness, the strength of his arms around me. Even when we're doing nothing more than watching an old romantic comedy, this silent protection of his embrace allows me to sink into the moment instead of always wondering in the back of my mind how much longer this can last.

It's enough to make me want to stay here forever. When we're away from his father, Christian can be the man I fell in love with. I don't feel so clueless or used now that I know I didn't imagine the way he used to be.

"What's next?" he asks as the credits roll on what has to be the twentieth movie we've watched since reaching the hotel.

"Maybe I'll take it easy on you. No romantic comedy this time. You can take a Sandra Bullock break."

"Thank God. I'm not sure how many more happy endings I can take."

"We could watch a bunch of weepy dramas, instead. Maybe you'd like that a little more. A movie where somebody dies tragically."

"Violently?" he asks, lifting an eyebrow.

"Not usually in the weepy movies, no. More like a tragic illness or something like that."

He screws his face up in disapproval. "How about something with a little action? Gunplay, jumping off tall buildings."

"Do you really think either of us needs to watch something like that right now?" Real life is action-packed enough. I'm trying to get away from reality, not have it thrown in my face.

"Maybe I want to live vicariously." He gets up from the sofa, stretching before emitting a long, deep groan. "As nice as this has been, I'm not used to spending days on end doing nothing but watching TV."

"I'm sorry you feel like you have to stay locked up here with me."

His arms fall to his sides as he turns my way. "You never have to apologize. I've told you before that nothing matters more than protecting what's mine." Normally, hearing him talk about me that way would turn my stomach. It would at least stir resentment in my heart.

I don't mind it so much now. Being his means being protected. I can't forget what brought us here and what's keeping us here, but I can sleep at night. And I can almost forget, for at least an hour or two at a time, that somebody out there wants me dead.

He walks over to the window. I don't have to see his face to sense his wistfulness. It's dangerous, softening my opinion of him like that. Thinking of him as human and having a heart. The conversation we had the first night here went a long way toward helping me understand him, even if the puzzle isn't yet complete. I do know some things. He's not a monster. He was trained to be one, perhaps from birth, but there's still something in him that's good. It's capable of feeling. Wanting, regretting. Maybe even loving.

Or am I only telling myself that? I always end up with more questions than answers when I start thinking too much.

"Do you think it would be safe for us to go out? Even if it's only for a walk? We could both use the exercise."

He tenses before shoving his hands into his pockets. "I wish I could say for sure."

"Only a few minutes. Nobody's going to try to assassinate me in the middle of a crowded street. I'm not that important."

"You are to me."

"You know what I mean," I press as gently as possible. "I haven't said it before now because I didn't want to be a problem, but I'm dying to get out of here for a little bit. I feel like I'll go crazy if I don't, I don't know, touch grass or something."

"Touch grass?" He looks back at me, smirking.

"Yes. And now I will deliberately seek out grass to touch."

That's enough to break through his stoic facade and get him smiling. It's easy to forget how beautiful he truly is. I've been a bit more interested in his behavior lately to let my thoughts wander to his looks. "I guess a walk wouldn't hurt anything." I practically jump up off the sofa, ready to get going. Never has a simple walk seemed like such a treat.

We take the elevator down to the lobby, which is a lot busier than it was when we first arrived. Then it was late enough that we were the only people at the front desk. Now, there are dozens of people spread out through the airy space. Now that we aren't in such a hurry, I can admire the beauty all around me. Sunlight streams through tall windows and makes the crystal dripping from overhead chandeliers sparkle brilliantly. I could stand here and watch the light prisms all day.

"Mr. Russo!"

I tug Christian's arm when I hear his name being called out by one of the clerks at the front desk. He turns to them, eyebrows raised.

"We have a message here for you, sir."

"I'll wait here," I offer, sitting on a leather chair. It's even nice to be around people again. I've been secluded for too long.

Christian goes over to the desk. I overhear the clerk apologizing, saying they have to find the message. He waves a hand, leaning against the counter to wait. When he looks back at me, I give him a little wave.

"*Signorina?*" Miss?

I realize the man standing over my shoulder is talking to me. I look up, expecting one of the hotel staff, ready to get up if I'm not allowed to sit here.

He isn't wearing one of the uniforms I've seen on other staff members since our arrival. He's dressed in black, wearing a ball cap with the brim pulled low over his eyes.

And he's carrying something in one hand. There's no time to put everything together before he jams that something up against my neck. At first, I think it's a gun, and this is it. This is where I'm going to die. But he pulls it away, muttering in Italian as he turns it around in his hand like it was supposed to work but didn't.

That's when I find my voice. "Christian!"

I scramble out of the chair, but the stranger wraps a hand around my bicep before I can get away. He hauls me in close to him and then starts dragging me away.

Gasps and muffled shouts sound out all around us, but that's not what matters. What matters is Christian barreling through the crowd, red-faced and snarling. I don't know if it's fear or the fact that he's been spotted that makes the attacker let go.

He shoves me at Christian before weaving his way through the crowd, knocking an older woman to the floor in his haste to escape.

"You're all right. You're fine." Christian wraps his arms around me, glaring at the exit. "The son of a bitch was carrying a stun gun."

"It didn't work."

"Thank fuck for that."

"You're not going after him?" I lean into his embrace, trying to catch my breath.

"He's gone already." He holds me almost painfully tight for a second before letting go. "That message was likely a ruse. He would have followed whoever delivered it up to the penthouse."

"I didn't think anybody knew we were here."

"Neither did I." His head swings back and forth like he's waiting for another attack. "Evidently, we were both wrong."

"We aren't going for a walk, are we?"

"I was thinking a helicopter ride might be more in line with our next steps." Even though my heart sinks, I know he's right. At least at his father's house, there are guards. Out here, it's only the two of us.

And there simply isn't a way to prepare for every situation. If that stun gun had worked, this might've ended a lot differently.

∽

"Whoever they are, they must have powerful connections." I watch from my spot on the bed as Christian paces in front of his bedroom window, occasionally glancing outside. What does he think he's going to find there besides the guards he ordered to patrol the grounds in constant shifts? "They paid off that doctor, which I'm sure couldn't have come cheaply. They found us at the hotel. A needle in a haystack."

"You used your last name."

"Do you know how many hotels and resorts there are in this country?" The sharpness in his question keeps me from pursuing the topic.

"I'm scared. That's all."

"You don't have to be scared anymore."

"How can you say that and sound so sure of yourself?"

"Because now, we know the monster who wants you dead is desperate enough to step out into the open. I have no doubt the fool he sent to the hotel was an errand boy, but if he's desperate enough to attempt a kidnapping in broad daylight, in a crowd of people, he's bound to make another mistake." His lips stretch in a vicious smile. "He might not know it, but he's shown his hand."

Wow. Is that supposed to make me feel better?

"Great," I say and draw my legs up onto the bed, wrapping my arms around them. "I'm living with a monster while another one is out there trying to kill me—along with a bunch of other people. And you thought bringing me to Italy would make me safe?"

His scowl is a reminder that certain thoughts shouldn't be voiced in his presence. "So far, you've managed to avoid getting killed. Maybe you should remember who's responsible for that."

My heart sinks as the truth of his words makes it through my awareness. He's always saved me, and there's not a doubt in my mind he would kill anyone who dares to try to kill me again. And they will. I don't doubt that, either. But he'll fight for me until his final breath. Whether or not I want him to, no matter how I fight him.

"Could you come here, please?"

He turns away from the window and quirks an eyebrow. "Why?"

"Please." I extend my hands, waiting for him to join me by the bed. He does, though his gait is a little slow at first, unsure. He takes my hands, and I pull him closer until his knees touch the mattress.

"What's this all about?"

Rather than respond verbally, I let go of him and take hold of his belt. My eyes remain locked on his while I unbuckle it, then unbutton his pants. "Why are you—?"

"Why are you asking questions?" The truth is, I'm not sure I could explain why if I tried. I'm not even certain it makes sense to me, and I'm the one now lowering Christian's pants and black boxer briefs so I can take him in my hand. He's already semi-hard and getting harder with every stroke.

Is it gratitude? Partly, I'm sure. He's saved my life more than once, even back before I knew him. He didn't have to spare me, but he did. And now his whole life is wrapped up in keeping me safe. How could I not feel grateful?

Besides, I want to be close to him. I crave his nearness, the sweet oblivion that comes when he touches me. I don't have to think of anyone or anything else. I only need to feel.

I take off my shirt and bra, tossing them aside. "Touch me?" I whisper. He takes my breasts in both hands and plays with them while I go back to stroking his now rigid member.

"Put it in your mouth," he growls, and I'm all too happy to do what he commands. It's different now, better without him forcing me into it. Like before, when all I knew was he was my boyfriend, and I loved him.

Someday, I'll get up the nerve to point out how much nicer it is when I'm a willing participant instead of merely somebody having things done to them.

I plunge my head down, then pull back slowly, maintaining tight pressure around his shaft. His deep groan encourages me, making me bold enough to run my tongue around his head before taking him deep again.

"Holy shit. That's incredible." He massages me, tweaking my nipples and spreading heat through my core. In moments my pussy is wet, aching for him to fill me. I need him inside me. I need him all over me. My head bobs in a steady rhythm, and I can't help but moan around him when I imagine his dick moving like this when he fucks me.

He uses one hand to cup the back of my head, but instead of shoving me down, he only strokes my hair. "So sweet. So good to my cock. Show me what you can do. And if you're good enough, you'll earn yourself a nice, deep fuck. I'll give you the honor of coming on my cock before I come inside you."

That shouldn't encourage me. The so-called honor of coming on his cock. Just the same, my head bobs faster, my eagerness only growing. My muscles clench in anticipation of what's to come, my excitement oozing from me and soaking my panties.

"I can almost smell you," he grunts, thumbing my nipple faster than ever while the fingers of his other hand tug at my hair. It's unreal, the sensations racing through me, making the hair on my arms stand up and sending goose bumps racing up my legs.

"Are you wet for me, Siân?" I moan out my response, and he groans. "Fuck yes, that's nice. Do that again." This time, I emit a long, deep moan that makes him growl like an animal and tense up all over.

He slips out of my mouth an instant later, glistening with my saliva. "Get on your knees on the bed." I catch sight of him fisting his cock before I turn my back to him, positioning myself the way he asked. He yanks my pants and panties down to my knees in one motion, not bothering to strip me all the way before sinking into my dripping tunnel. I rock forward from the force of his first thrust, gasping.

"You're already close. I can feel it." He takes me by the hips, pulling me in while driving himself hard, deep. "So fucking tight. Squeezing me. Are you almost ready to come?"

"Mmm, yes... yes, I am..." I lean down, one arm under my forehead, giving over to him. Letting him take control because I know in the end it'll be worth it. Craving the way his fingers dig into me so hard it might leave a bruise. Even craving that bruise because it will be a reminder of this. Forgetting everything for a little while in favor of pleasure.

"You get off on sucking my cock, Siân?" He hits me with a series of shallow, rapid thrusts that leave me squealing, the tension rising every time he hits my G-spot.

"Yes! Yes, so good, oh, fuck!"

"This is what you were made for." His balls slap against my clit with every thrust, and even that's good. Better than good. "You were made for me. To be fucked by me. Protected by me. Say it."

I can barely breathe, much less speak. "I was... made... for you..." I manage.

"And now you're going to come with my cock inside you."

"Yes!" I sob, desperate now. I need to come. I'll die if I don't. My muscles tighten, squeezing him, and I press my face to the mattress just in time to muffle a scream of pure ecstasy when the tension breaks, bliss rolling over me in waves and blocking out everything else.

Everything except Christian now pounding harder than ever. "You ready for my load? Because here it comes." One thrust, two, and he roars in time with his hot seed filling me. I'm still lost, shaking from the last remnants of my release, but I note the moment he leaves me and wish I didn't feel so empty afterward. I doubt he'd ever understand if I tried to explain.

Nothing needs to be explained right now. He crawls beside me and pulls me onto my side. Drawing me close, he wraps his body around mine like even now, he wants to protect me. For a long time, there's nothing but the sound of our heavy breathing and the warmth of his embrace.

Right now, that's all I need.

18

CHRISTIAN

*I*t's time. If last night taught me anything, it's that Siân wants me despite how hard she tries to fight against it. And after nearly losing her, I can't wait any longer. Marrying her has been the only thing I've wanted since the moment I heard those words slip past her mother's lips.

Completing this union won't stop the threats that loom over us, but at least it will prove to my father that I am serious. And all the teasing and taunting he's done, the dark, murderous glances he's given her will stop. He's never loved a woman, not that I've seen, but one tradition he's kept from generations before him is that if she's yours, under the eyes of God, she's off-limits to anyone in the family.

He makes his own rules and always has. But he also made me a promise at fourteen years old. The day he turned me into a killer, he told me I could have her if I proved myself. And while his word matters none to anyone else, he knew it was the one thing to secure my place in his army.

And now, after fifteen years of being without her and periodically watching from a distance, it's finally happening. She'll finally be mine by the end of the night. And she'll get to suck me dry like she did last night every fucking day for the rest of forever.

I shake my head and sit up in bed. Who would have ever thought that I would be this excited, this nervous even? I don't care about anything, and I certainly don't rattle—except where Siân is concerned.

Being with her, around her goodness, does something to me. It makes me feel more alive. Where pain is normally my love language, and yes, I love bringing her pain, but I'm learning I can handle a gentler touch as well. Last night was different, yet so much like our time in Florida.

When I was the opposite version of myself, I wasn't as ruthless with her. I took my time and allowed her to open up to me on my own time. But the moment it all came to light, that changed. I returned to my truest self, and she's been pulling away from me a little more each day.

Except for yesterday. Except for the entire time we were locked away, just the two of us in that penthouse. We moved like in the old days. It was peaceful, freeing even. It won't be like that always. Hell, probably never again, but I can do better. I can try to be better for her.

I meant it when I told her she doesn't have to hate it here. I can make sure of that. As long as she behaves and does what I say, we can be good together.

Staring down at a sleeping Siân, I suck in a breath and maneuver to retrieve my phone from my pants pocket on the floor. The bed shifts with my weight, and I glance back to be sure I haven't disturbed her. She needs her sleep because tonight is going to take a lot out of her.

With my phone in hand, I rest my back against the headboard. Quickly, I punch a number into the text message field, then shoot a message to Tony. He responds immediately.

Tony: *Adesso sono una wedding planner?* Now I'm a wedding planner?

I type my reply.

Me: *Trovami un prete per stasera. E chiedi a Helga di ordinare l'armadio. Due vestiti e uno smoking.* Just find me a priest for tonight. And have Helga order the wardrobe. Two dresses and a tux.

Tony: *Sono almeno l'uomo migliore?* Am I the best man at least?

Me: *Solo se questo si spegne senza intoppi. E porta il custode. Avrò bisogno che lei sia convincente.* Only if this goes off without a hitch. And bring the caretaker. I'm going to need her to be convincing.

Tony: *Qualsiasi altra cosa Vostra Altezza.* Anything else, your highness?

I don't bother sending a rebuttal and set the device on the nightstand. One thing about Tony is regardless of how much he pushes back, he'll do what I ask. He jokes about the best man thing, but I wouldn't want anyone else. He's the closest thing to a brother I've ever had, my only friend. He's a few years older than me and came into the family right around the same time I stepped up to claim my place. Samuele ordered him to my detail, and over the years, all the bickering, he's definitely someone I would want at my side on my wedding day. It's said to be the most sacred day of your life next to your birth and the arrival of a child. So why not have him there.

And no, we don't have to go all out, but Siân deserves the extravagance. This is the first and last time she'll ever be taken as a bride. It needs to be perfect for her.

Siân stirs, soft murmurs escaping from her pouty lips. I smile at the face she makes, remembering the first time I watched her sleep ages ago. She scrunches her upper lip toward her nose while turning her head side to side, only to roll over. It's cute—it's her. And she's mine. Finally. Always and forever.

Her chest rises, and my eyes trace her frame beneath the covers. She's still naked, the memory of how hungry she was for me replaying in my mind. Focusing on the curve of her hip, I reach out to touch her, softly tilting her body so that she is flat on her back. I need to taste her, return the favor from her swallowing me whole, and show her just what it will be like for the rest of our lives.

Just the thought of being able to devour her for eternity excites me. My dick is already tenting the thin sheet that acts as a shield from the temperature. Though hot out, it's a bit chilly indoors, set purposely to keep everyone alert. But now, it serves another purpose.

A quick look up, and I find Siân's nipples hard and peeking through the fabric. I pull the covering back, watching as it drags along her perfect flesh. Tiny bruises in various places on her body are visible, and I lean in to kiss each one. I did this to her. I marked her flawless skin with my aggression. It's beautiful, just like her.

Despite the nip in the air, she's warm. I grab her ankles and slide them apart while planting myself between her thighs. She stirs but doesn't wake. The residue of my dried cum stains the inside of her thighs, and a low groan bubbles in my throat.

I love fucking her, filling her tight little cunt with my seed. And I can't get enough. All I want is to fuck, suck, and lick her until she can't see straight. I want her writhing under me, on top of me, beside me—any which way, really. I just want her body. Over and over, and then some more after that.

One would say I should wait till tonight to commemorate our vows, and I will. Tonight I'll feed my cock into her hot pussy so deep she can taste my cum for days. But now, I want to eat her and make her scream my name.

Her lips, so pink and slightly swollen from last night, stare back at me. My mouth waters, and I lower myself onto my stomach, bringing my face to her sex. Her scent—our scent is intoxicating.

Slowly I run my thumb along her slit, but I don't part just yet. Instead, I enjoy the feel of her, my shaft stiffening with each subtle pet. She turns her head to the left and wiggles her hips, only to settle again. Her breathing is the same, and I know she's still in a deep sleep.

I shift on my elbows and use both thumbs to pull her lips apart, my mouth watering at the sight. I stroke her clit with the pad of my thumb in a short repetitive motion. One second after another, it starts to come to life, recognizing the signs of being pleased. When it starts to preen, her hood slips back, and her bud finally comes out to play.

Taking her into my mouth, I suck on her, then flick my tongue over her clit. Taking my time, I keep my rhythm steady. I watch her through my lashes, hoping and wanting her to wake up to fuck my face.

"Fanculo," I groan under my breath. *Fuck.* My topolina is so fucking sweet and perfect for me. She was worth the wait, worth me disobeying my father, worth me saving her—worth me breaking her.

When I dip my tongue into her channel, her sex squeezes me. A primal growl escapes me, and I lap her up, sucking her entire pussy into my mouth. Even asleep, her body bends for me, her pussy hungry for me.

"Mm," a soft moan slips past her mouth, but it's as if it hasn't quite registered what's happening yet.

It's when I slip my finger into her cunt that draws her awake. Her back arches, lifting off the mattress with her mouth agape.

"O-oh. Mm, Chris—"

I hook my finger, grazing it along her G-spot, essentially cutting her short and pulling a louder cry from her.

"Yes. God, that feels so good."

I crawl up on my knees but don't stop hitting her spot. Siân hasn't even opened her eyes yet, but she opens her body. Back arched, legs wide, and fist twisted in the sheets, she grinds against my hand.

By now, my cock is rock hard, begging to be inside her. I settle up to her, and she simultaneously drapes her thighs over mine.

"Open your eyes, topolina. I want to watch your face as you come."

She follows my command, locking eyes with me, and I swear I almost lose my shit. I fist my cock, tugging my length as Siân continues to fuck my hand. Unexpectantly, she twists herself into an awkward angle, one that allows her access to my dick.

Siân swats my hand away, replacing it with her own. I stare down at our connection, nearly coming undone at the sight of her tiny hand around my fat cock. And she does it so well, just as good as when she sucked me last night.

It's not lost on me that she's different and that when I'm not forcing her, she thrives. But it was my coercion that got her here. Before, she never would have spontaneously taken me into her mouth, not without a little coaxing. And now, she's taking charge of my orgasm the way I have hers all this time.

And I love every fucking bit of it. I can see the shell breaking whether she's ready or not. Whether she wants to or not. But it's true. This moment right here is evidence of that. Just a few days ago, she cried when I touched her, and now—look at her.

"You were made for me," I say around a moan as I pump my hips, allowing her to palm fuck me. "I can't wait till you're mine wholly. Then I'll get to dirty every inch of your gorgeous frame again and again."

I pick up speed, flicking my wrist in tune with her strokes on my dick, and together, we revel in it. She fucks me while I fuck her, and it's amazing, euphoric.

"What do you want, beautiful?"

Siân stares at me, barely able to speak. Once she catches her breath, she says, "Fuck me. Make me come on your cock."

"Gahh." Shaking my head, I keep fingering her, and she doesn't stop pleasing me, either. I love it when she owns what she wants.

"Please, Christian."

I stretch my hand so that I can play with her clit with my thumb and finger her slit at the same time. And she goes wild. Her breaths quicken, her hips move faster, and the hold she has on my dick tightens. That only brings me closer to finishing.

"Never beg." I move my hand along her slippery pussy at a rapid speed. "Do you hear me? You're a queen. *My* queen, and you never beg. You state what you want, and you take it if you have to. Understand?"

She nods with her face contorted in ecstasy.

"Fuck me." She huffs. "Now."

My dick pulses, and pressure builds in my balls. I'm going to come, and I want to be inside her when I do. But I won't fuck her, not fully. No, I'll save that for the wedding night. However, I will let her come on my dick.

I get my rhythm, and when I'm certain she's close, I slap her hand away, fist the base of my shaft, and slide inside. She's warm. She's tight. She's *home*. It only takes two, maybe three thrusts before we're both screaming each other's name, and I fill her cunt with my cum.

Maybe this will be the time I plant my seed.

Sated and spent, we stay like this for a moment until my member goes soft inside her. And when I do move, I pat her on the thigh.

"Let's take a shower. I have a surprise for you."

∼

WE'VE SPENT MORE time than intended in the shower, taking turns washing each other. The thing that matters most is how different it all seems, how seamless. Near-death experience changes things. They can bring you closer and make someone view life and the people around them differently. Some people even act another way.

That's how it appears with Siân. I guess after two incidents where her life was threatened, she's decided to trust me. To give in to this thing between us and to stop fighting. Aside from the spat over the breakfast bagel, I noticed it back at the hotel. The entire time we were there, we kind of blended together, moving about like we did in Florida.

Every so often, I catch her staring at me, and when I go to kiss her, she playfully pushes me away, only to steal the kiss for herself. I can get used to this. Not the cutesy flowers and rainbow shit, but her being with me, happy and content. That's how I know today is the perfect time to make it official.

Finally, we exit the shower and get dressed before finally being ready to leave the room.

"I like when we're like this. I've missed it," she admits, but I don't respond.

All I can give her is a smile because the truth is, I don't know if I can give her this level of me all the time. My life doesn't work that way, but I've told her I will try, and I meant it. Roughness, aggression, that's more my speed, but for Siân, I'll do what I can. I'll give her more of the gentler side if it means she smiles more.

"Come on," I encourage and take her hand in mine.

"What's this surprise you have?" she asks while stepping out into the hall, waiting for me to close the door behind us.

"Sii paziente, topolino." *Be patient, little mouse.*

"You're going to have to teach me Italian."

"Okay." I nod. "I can't believe you don't know it, though."

Siân shrugs. "I did, and I do understand some things. But when we got to the States, Cynthia made sure all we spoke was English. We had to blend in."

"She never should have let you forget your roots. You should be proud to be Italian. There is nothing else better in the world."

"We didn't have a choice, Christian. She did the best she could."

I huff and decide to leave well enough alone. We head to the first floor, the barrage of voices greeting us before we reach the bottom landing. The foyer is empty, so we walk toward the sounds. It's Tony's voice I recognize first, and then a stern female voice.

"Comportati bene, o sarò tentato di ricambiare il favore di quando mi hai sparato nella tua cucina." *Behave, or I'll be tempted to return the favor from when you shot me in your kitchen.*

"Avresti dovuto schivarti," she seethes. *You should have ducked.*

We turn the corner into the great room in time to stop Tony from stalking toward her. I fight the urge to laugh. He's pissed with me for not allowing him to harm her. She shot him and essentially has gotten away with it. If he had his way, she'd have been skinned alive a long time ago.

"Relax," I order.

Tony peers up at me at the same time as Cynthia turns in her seat. The moment she and Siân lay eyes on each other, they take off into each other's arms. Cynthia pulls her into a motherly embrace by tucking her into the crock of her neck with a hand at the back of her head.

She plants one kiss after another on Siân's face, hair, and forehead, then pulls her close again. They sway, and almost instinctively, they each begin to cry. Tony rolls his eyes, and I shoot him a look that tells him to cool it. She needs this. They both do.

When Cynthia backs away, she runs her palms down Siân's arms, proceeding to check her over for any sign of harm. The bruises around her throat have healed, and any marks that were of my doing are covered by her clothing.

"Has he hurt you? Are you okay? I'm so sorry I couldn't protect you," Cynthia rambles on.

Siân cups her cheeks. "Cyn. Cyn. I'm okay." She gives her a reassuring smile. "How are you?" Siân says softly.

There's a look in Cynthia's eyes, one full of concern and reservation. She stares at Siân a moment, then darts her gaze to me and back. I can see questions rolling in her mind with the way her face moves from a scared parent to a disturbed one. She knows the difference and saw it the second we walked in the room. The glow coming from Siân is just as evident.

The last time I allowed them to see each other, the vibe was different. Siân was different. Then she was flustered, agitated, in dire need of escape, but now, not so much. Now, she's smiling, and her body language is that of a woman who's just been fucked. Not one in need of rescue.

"I'm good...considering," Cynthia says hesitantly. "Are you okay?"

Siân shrugs and lets out a breath. "Considering someone tried to murder me, yes."

Cynthia's eyes grow wide. "You bastard," she snips in my direction, her sight boring into me like a dagger.

She lounges for me only to be dragged back by Tony. Siân jumps between us, holding up a hand to stop her. Meanwhile, I look on, watching as she goes through every emotion under the sun. She wanted to protect Siân, to keep her safe from monsters like me. I can appreciate that, and it's the only reason I didn't get rid of her the way I did everyone else.

"Cynthia. I'm okay, really. I am. Christian saved me."

Cynthia frowns. "What is happening?"

I step closer, taking my place beside my woman, then wrap my arm around her waist. "You can pull back the bulldog attitude. Siân's protection is the only thing that matters to me."

"You're the only reason she needs protection." Cynthia grabs Siân's wrist and yanks her behind her, separating us with her body as a shield.

Tony is about to intervene, but a mere shake of my head stops him. Instead, he positions himself behind Cynthia with his hand on his gun. I laugh internally, knowing how badly he wants to hurt her for shooting him. The shot was clean through, and he's mostly healed, but his resentment remains. I've had to put someone else on watch at the cabin because I was certain Tony would have tortured the old broad.

"I won't let you touch her."

"And you're supposed to be able to stop me?" I ask with a raised brow.

"With every fiber of my being."

I chuckle. "You know, I admire your bite, that's for sure. It's cute you think you have any control over this."

Siân darts her gaze at me, disapproval flashing in her eyes. I ignore her expression and step farther into the room. Walking around the large Victorian-style furnishing, I approach one of the many bars we have on the estate. I flip four tumblers onto their bottom, then fill them with two fingers of scotch.

Tony steps up to me, immediately taking one of the glasses while I take one for both Siân and Cynthia. Sauntering over to them, I watch the way Cynthia follows my movement while still holding her arms out as if she can really keep Siân away from me.

Cynthia flinches when I hold the tumbler out to her, but when she notices that I'm not threatening her, she reluctantly accepts it. Her grip is shaky even though her face says she's not affected by this at all. She has a great poker face, that's for damn certain.

After handing the other over to Siân, I head back to the bar to grab my own. "Have a seat," I say, turning back and using my chin to point toward the sofa.

Tony sits first, but Cynthia continues staring between us, refusing to sit. When Siân sits in the closest chair, Cynthia plants herself next to her with her hand on her shoulder—anything to keep her ward close. Who can blame her? It's been over a month since they've been able to be this close without someone trying to pull them apart.

I notice Siân taking Cynthia's hand. She needs to be just as close to her caretaker. A small part of me dislikes that I've done this to her and made her feel so deprived of something she clearly needs. But it's the only way to secure our future together. She will be my wife today and needs to know that if they want this type of time together, then they both will have to comply.

Turning my attention to Tony, I swallow down a large sip, and they all seem to follow my lead, though the women don't seem nearly as confident doing so.

"Did you get everything in order?" I ask while adjusting in my seat, my cock still semi-hard from my shower with Siân. I didn't fuck her like she begged this morning, and my dick won't be satisfied until it gets a taste.

Tony nods. "The priest will be here at five." He checks his watch. "In about three hours."

Damn, I hadn't realized how late we stayed in bed. Finishing off my drink, I stand to pour myself another.

"Priest? What are you talking about? A priest?" Cynthia asks. She and Siân are both on alert.

Siân's brows draw together as Cynthia tightens her grip on Siân's hand.

I stare for a beat. "You've got a lot to catch up on."

Just as I begin to tell them about my plans for the day, Helga enters the living room carrying two garment bags. With a look in her direction, I see confusion written all over their faces. I knew Siân would be thrown off by today's event, but she also knew this day was coming.

"Il tuo guardaroba per il matrimonio è qui. Preparerò tutto il resto." Helga leaves as soon as she finishes. *Your wedding wardrobe is here. I shall prepare everything else.*

"Wedding?" they say in unison.

"Yes. Today we're getting married."

"No. No," Cynthia voices, her words matching Siân's reaction.

"You've known this day was coming," I deadpan and drain my second drink before setting the empty glass on the coffee table.

"Yes, but you didn't say so soon," she retorts.

"So soon? I will never let you have her."

"Oh, Mommy dearest. I've already had her. And you know as well as I that you don't have a choice. You've never had a choice."

"You're going to have to kill me. I will not let this happen."

I huff, then push off the couch. Siân jumps to her feet, planting herself between Cynthia and me.

"Christian. No. Don't you touch her."

"I won't need to touch her. All you have to do is comply. You know the deal, and you've been so good. Don't ruin that now."

She shakes her head in rapid succession while maneuvering so that she and Cynthia are walking back toward the exit. They are so focused on me that they don't notice Tony as he stands and walks around the opposite side to position himself at the exit.

"No."

"Siân, don't test me. You know what happens when I get upset."

"You're not going to hurt me or kill me. You're obsessed with me."

"Maybe, maybe not." I tip my chin in Tony's direction.

He draws his weapon, but it's the sound of it cocking that draws their attention. Tony presses the barrel to the back of Cynthia's head, and she freezes.

"Stop it." Siân is at his side, tugging on his arm to lower the gun, but his stance is strong.

Over and over, she pulls and pounds on him, yet he doesn't flinch. It'll take a lot more for him to react, like a gunshot to the shoulder. I imagine this moment makes him happy, he's been wanting the chance to repay Cynthia, and all I would have to do is give the word.

"Christian, please. Make him stop."

"What have I told you about consequences?"

"You told me you wouldn't hurt her."

"And I won't. She'll go on to live out the rest of her life so long as you make it down the aisle today."

"Go to hell, you bastard," Cynthia blurts.

"Is this your surprise? All of the nice words, and gentle touching, were just you trying to control me? What happened to us being equal? Hm? Or was it all just a lie?"

"We'll be equal in marriage. I've been very clear. You behave, and Cynthia won't be badly harmed. But she's here today to ensure you make it to that altar."

"I'm so stupid. Here I was thinking you were changing, that maybe there was some good inside you, but you're just twisted and demented. Just like your father."

"And that's your problem, topolina. You spend so much of your time overlooking the things right in front of you. I'm the only person who's shown you their true self."

"You're a monster."

"I never denied that. But someone here has lied to you for your entire life."

Cynthia's back stiffens at my words, her eyes nearly bulging from her skull. It doesn't take a rocket scientist to see the truth. They're the spitting image of each other, from the same color eyes, the shape of their nose, the brown hair even with the strands of gray sprinkled along Cynthia's crown, their physical appearance though Siân's frame is slender from her youth.

The evidence is written in their features, yet somehow, Siân has missed that as she does everything else. When I make eye contact with Cynthia again, she's pleading with me.

"What is that supposed to mean?" Siân asks. She catches wind of the glances shared between her beloved caretaker and me.

There's a pregnant pause. Everyone stares at each other. Emotions are heightened, fear and frustration presenting their ugly heads.

Stepping close, I can feel the heat radiating from them. "Why don't you tell her who the fuck you really are?"

MONSTER

19

SIÂN

I stare at my reflection one piece at a time, applying makeup mechanically. I could be a painter swiping colors over a canvas, but no. An artist feels a connection to the work they are creating. I feel no connection to myself at this moment. I only see parts of my face rather than the whole. I can only take in so much at one time.

Is this the way it goes when your entire life has been blown apart? Everything I thought I could believe in and trust has been shattered. For all I know, this is my mind's way of trying to cope with the fallout. Narrowing my focus until I can only tackle one tiny thing at a time. Smooth on the foundation. Apply contour. Highlighter. Blend.

She lied to me. So did he. All of them, everyone, nothing but lies. And for what? My protection? If I hear that one more time, I'll burn the house down. I was never given a choice. I see it now as I swipe shadow over my eyelids, leaning in close to the mirror. When I'm this close, I can't see anyone around me. Including the biggest liar of all, hovering somewhere behind me in the room. Waiting to help put my dress on.

She's smart not to say anything. She hasn't breathed a word since Christian left us alone again so I could continue preparing for this nightmare of a ceremony.

"We must arrange your hair," one of the maids' murmurs.

I meet her eye in the mirror, finding her over my shoulder. "Another few minutes, please."

"We mustn't keep them waiting."

Until now, I've been meek. Grateful for even the slightest bit of kindness or communication from anyone in Samuele Russo's sprawling home. I've gone where I was supposed to go, when I was supposed to be there. The fear of retribution was enough to make me dance to everyone else's tune.

Today, that's changed. There's been a seismic shift inside me, and I see everything clearly now. Or maybe that's shock dulling my natural reaction. Either way, I couldn't care less about keeping anyone waiting.

"Another few minutes."

She lowers her gaze, and I wait a bit before going back to my work. If I'm going to be forced into marriage, I may as well look my best. I will at least have that much going for me.

My hand shakes. I have to stop what I'm doing for a second before I end up making a mess. *Focus. You can do this.* As heartbroken as Cynthia's lies have left me, I can't fail her. I have no doubt Christian is desperate enough to make good on his promise of what he'll do if I don't give him what he wants. Like it or not, Cynthia saved my life all those years ago.

Now, I understand why. I understand everything. As I apply my makeup, I think about it all as my thoughts fade into the distance.

"Tell her." Christian pulled his gun and held it to her head, unflinching. Unblinking. "Tell her, or I'll do it. And I suspect you'll make it sound a lot nicer than I will."

Cynthia's eyes crinkled at the corners like she was in pain while my mind raced in a dozen different directions, scrambling to figure out what she could possibly have to tell me. Whatever it was, it took having a gun to her head to get it out.

"I love you," she whispered. "From the day you were born, nothing in the world has mattered more than you. I need you to remember that. I would have agreed to anything, no matter the terms, so long as it meant keeping you safe."

"I don't understand," I whispered back.

"And I know this is going to hurt you," she continued. Her voice shook slightly, which was somehow the worst of all. If there was one thing I could count on from her, it was strength. Whenever we had to run, she always came up with a plan while I panicked and freaked out. Nothing could touch her. Nothing could shake her.

"Whatever it is, just tell me. I'll try to understand." I could barely string a sentence together with the gun's muzzle pressed against her temple so tight.

"Siân, your father and I were in love. We didn't mean for it to happen. I tried so hard to turn away from him. I know he did the same. But it was impossible."

I thought I could find a way to understand anything, but this? "You had an affair with my father?"

"Come on." Christian nudged her with the gun. "No half-truths. Tell her all of it."

"Why are you doing this?" I asked him, but he only snickered.

"I only want to provide context," he explained. "Trust me. It will motivate you."

"You're exactly the monster I knew you would be." Cynthia trembled, but I knew it wasn't from fear. I'd seen her enraged whenever my stalker—Christian—found me and announced his presence.

"Get on with it. There's a wedding to be performed."

"Tell me," I insisted. "Please. Get it out."

Our eyes met. Tears welled up in hers. "I am your mother. Your biological mother."

Immediately, everything in me pushed this away. "No," I whispered, even though my heart knew it was true. "That can't be. I would have known."

Christian sighed. "You know it's true. If there's one thing I would change about you, Siân, it's your inability to accept the truth when it stares you in the face. If you're ever going to survive, you need to stop wasting time denying what's so obvious."

No matter how I wanted to ignore him, there was no use. I saw the truth in Cynthia's eyes.

I shake my head, my vision blurring from the tears pooling along my lashline. "I don't understand. All this time. This—" *I glance from her to Christian and back.* "You've known all along that he would come to take me. How could you agree to give me to him?"

Christian huffs, but I don't acknowledge him. I need to hear this from Cynthia—my mother. How could she hide me away yet lie to my face day in and day out?

"All I wanted was to keep you safe. I've loved you your entire life. I'm so sorry I failed you."

"How did you fail me?"

"By letting you get involved with him."

Christian clicked his tongue. "Now, now. We both know this was how it was meant to be. She was always going to be mine. You couldn't take her away from me. You never had a choice."

Cynthia drops her head.

"What does that even mean?"

"Since she's leaving out details, allow me. Everything that happened, the promise of your hand in marriage, the death of your father, and the mother you knew, was all because of her. She didn't just have an affair. As she said, she loved him, and his wife, the woman who claimed you as hers, had to sit back and watch the man she loved choose another."

As Christian talks, I continue reading Cynthia's expression, and I can't make sense of it all.

"After you were born, Marco was supposed to get rid of Cynthia. But being the greedy man he is, he didn't. Instead, he kept her on staff, allowing her to be with you as your nanny while his beloved had to look his indiscretions in the face daily. He couldn't just let it get out that he had a bastard child, so he forced his wife to sign your birth certificate and tell society you belonged to her."

"No."

"I guess the hatred for you was deep-rooted because just shy of your tenth birthday, she approached my father. She'd resented Marco so much for what he'd done, for choosing Cynthia, for choosing you, that she made him a deal. Kill you all and take over Marco's territory. She didn't want any of it, just vengeance. She needed to make them pay for what she'd endured, and you were just collateral damage."

"How do you know all of this? You couldn't have been more than a child yourself."

"You know by now that I watch. Things people think are secrets aren't. I overheard the deal and needed to know for myself. And when I saw you, I knew you would be mine. Your family was going to die. My father was going to see to that no matter what. Only he wanted me to be the one to do it. I only agreed if I got to have you. Somewhere along the way, Marco learned the truth and called it off, threatening a war. You've met my father. He doesn't take too kindly to being threatened, and well, you know the rest. I allowed Cynthia to free you. I actually watched as you sprinted across the property, ducking into the nearest forest."

"Why did you let us go then?"

"The rules changed. Samuele wasn't going to give you to me. He'd decided all of you needed to burn, including Cynthia. But now you know the truth about who you would be losing if you don't go through with this arrangement. She isn't only your caregiver. She's your mother, your flesh and blood. Would you *sacrifice her because of your pride? Because you're so damn stubborn and refuse to accept that this is your life now?"*

His question echoes through my head as I finish my eye makeup and lean back from the mirror to check out my work. Anyone who looks at me will see a blushing bride. I guess I'm better at makeup than I thought I was because I feel like anything but.

It's almost a relief to sit and let somebody else take over. I don't much care what they're doing with my hair. It might as well not be mine—I'm that disconnected. Almost like I'm watching myself from outside my body. The women work quickly and efficiently, and none of them seem especially happy. Do they feel sorry for me? I'm sure they're only doing the job they were given. They know better than to drag their feet or ask why. They also know better than to look happy for me.

I'm supposed to be happy on my wedding day. My wedding. I'm getting married today. My life is happening to me without me making any decisions of my own. No matter how I grasp and stretch and struggle, control is still out of reach. Thinking about it is enough to make my heart race. Blood rushes in my ears, drowning out the murmurs from the maids as they ask to pass the hairpins and spray.

I almost wish Christian had killed me along with my parents. Why did he bother leaving me alive? To use me this way? Like a dress-up doll he could push around.

"You're beautiful," one of the women murmurs. I glance up at her, and she offers what I'm sure is meant to be an encouraging smile. I can't muster up one in return, though I wish I could. It's not her fault.

"I have the dress." Cynthia's voice almost sounds foreign. She's fighting back emotion. What must this be like for her? I can't believe I'm even asking myself that. Why should I care what this is doing to her? She could have told me so many times who she really is. I might have had time to process the shock.

The woman I always thought of as my mother—what did this do to her? Having to raise another woman's child as her own? I can't remember her ever letting on, though now the memories I have of Dad and Cynthia together make more sense. Like that day in the plaza that I remembered when Christian took me shopping. Context is everything, as he said.

And now I remember how happy Dad seemed. Happier than he ever was when we were together as a family at home. More relaxed, natural, carefree. I finally understand. He was with the woman he really loved and their child. I don't know if I should feel sorry for them or if I should hate them. Maybe a little of both.

Because I do love her. It isn't like she hasn't been a mother to me all these years. Now, it's official. And just like Christian always was who he was before I knew the truth about him, the same is true for Cynthia. She was always my mother. Nothing about the past changes just because I know the truth now. I have to get right with it. I only wish I knew how.

Almost as much as I wish I knew how to stop loving Christian.

I don't say a word to Cynthia as she helps me into the dress. It's chic, clingy, and probably costs thousands of dollars for all its simplicity. White lace over flesh-colored satin, it almost molds itself around my body as Cynthia, and one of the maids, work on the seemingly endless row of buttons that runs up the back. It has a short train that swishes around my feet when I turn slowly, looking at myself in the full-length mirror.

"For what it's worth," Cynthia murmurs behind me, "you're the most beautiful bride I've ever seen. I know that's probably cold comfort right now, and I'm probably the last person you want to hear it from, but that doesn't make it any less true."

My throat's too tight to speak. I can't even look at her in the reflection in the mirror. Not when my love for her is just as strong as my sense of betrayal. Not when I'm embarrassed with myself. Christian had a gun to her head. I have no doubt he would've killed her to get his way. How can I love him? An irredeemable psycho. There must be something deeply broken inside me if I'm able to love him in spite of all of that. Everything he's done to me.

The maids leave us alone. Cynthia adjusts my train and inserts a few extra pins in my hair where it seems like it's falling loose. She's gentle, as always, and when she finishes, she rests a hand on my shoulder. At first, her touch is featherlight, as if she expects me to shrug her off. When I don't, her grip firms. "I don't know if it's strength or shock getting you through this. I'm proud of you either way. I thought you should know that."

Strength? Shock? Try helplessness. He's finally broken me down. I know there's no hope of getting out of this, so why bother trying? All fighting does is make things worse. And even if she did lie to me all my life, she also loved me. She still does. If this means saving her life, I'll do it. She's already sacrificed so much of hers for me, after all.

Because she had no choice, did she? She accepted the way things were and did everything she could to survive. She didn't waste time crying and whining and asking what she did to deserve the hand fate dealt her. She simply adjusted and moved on. Can I do that?

I meet my gaze in the mirror, and there's a hardness in my expression that brings Christian to mind. I've seen him like this. Hard and cold, impenetrable. Now I understand why he had to build walls around himself and why he learned to disconnect emotion from his actions. It's easier than breaking down.

It's time I started behaving that way. Right now. If this is what my life is, I need to accept it instead of causing myself more pain by fighting it.

My chin lifts. My shoulders roll back. I'm about to become a Russo. Now's the time to start behaving like one.

I glance at Cynthia, and her brow lifts. She doesn't say a word, though I see from the way her posture changes she knows something is different.

She sees it in me, and why not? No one in the world knows me better than she does. Not even Christian, who delivers a single knock against the door before pushing it open.

There's no need to do the whole *you can't see the bride before the wedding* thing, so I don't bother. Instead, I watch his mouth fall open, his eyes almost bulging. It isn't often he's rendered speechless. "You are just as stunning as I imagined." He extends a single white rose. "For you."

I accept it without saying a word. It's perfect, pure.

"Cynthia, I need a moment alone with my husband-to-be." I gaze down at the rose, rotating the stem between my fingers.

"We don't have much time," he reminds me. I only stare at the flower while Cynthia's footsteps ring out, eventually ending up in the hall. "What's this about? Don't think you can get away with—"

"I'm not trying to get away with anything." I raise my head, locking eyes with him. He looks incredible in his own right, wearing a dark suit I'm sure was custom-made. "But I do want to get a few things straight with you before we exchange vows."

He tilts his head, his lips twitching like he's waiting for the punchline. "Go ahead."

"It occurs to me I've been approaching this all wrong. It's about time I step into the role I was born to play. I am my father's daughter. A Guiliani. I was always intended to be your wife and stand by your side at the head of the Russo family. And I intend to take my place."

"That's all I wanted to hear."

"You aren't talking now. I am." He blinks rapidly, and I push forward. "If I'm going to be your wife, I'm going to be the equal you promised I would be. I have to thank you now for taking the time to toughen me up over these past months. I understand now why you needed to do it. The life I'm about to step into, it isn't for the weak. I appreciate that now. I'm ready to be the wife you need me to be, but in turn, you're going to be the husband I need. No more treating me like a doormat. No more degrading or humiliating me, no matter how much it gets you off. I won't accept it. Do you understand me?"

Either he anticipated this, or he's too surprised to laugh. "I do."

"Good. Because I'm sure I can find ways to make your life just as miserable as you've made mine."

"I never wanted to make you miserable. All I want is for us to be together. That's all I've ever wanted."

"You'll get that, but I'm going to get something in return. If you love me, if you want me to be happy and take my place at your side, there's something I'm going to need you to do for me."

"Anything. Name it."

MONSTER

20

CHRISTIAN

I've been waiting for this moment since I was fourteen years old. At the time, I didn't understand the significance. All I knew was that I needed her as mine. I've heard the tales of men growing emotional the moment they see their brides, and for the longest time, I saw it as nonsense.

Love and marriage, in the traditional sense, aren't like that for us. Those who do get married do so as a transaction. Love isn't a factor. It can't be. All that mattered was the needs that the union would satisfy.

But now, standing at the altar in front of a bunch of people who ultimately mean nothing to me, I get it. Siân's gorgeous, and I saw that when I was in her room just a few moments ago. Now though, it feels more prevalent. After all this time, she will finally be mine forever. Something shifts in me, a display of emotions I've never experienced before. It shouldn't surprise me that everything is different with her.

I've spent all this time molding her to fit the queen I need, but she's been doing that with me. Before her, I didn't feel remorse or care about whether or not my actions had gone too far. I don't second-guess myself or ask to be given a chance to prove myself. I don't feel, I don't care. Yet with Siân, I've done all of those things.

Music fades into the back of my mind with each step she takes. It's a slow descent, and the stiffness in her shoulders reminds me that while she looks graceful, while she is making her way to the altar to take me as her husband, she didn't want this. A good man would see the pain and free her. We discovered a long time ago that that man isn't me.

She'll grow to love me, and I'll learn to give her all the things she's been asking me for. All we have to do is get past this moment, complete this ceremony and cement our place in each other's lives.

Then I think back to her request, her words vibrating through me. I haven't given her an answer. It's not that I'm torn over killing my father but more so that she's the one who ordered it. The irony of the whole thing looming over us. From the moment I laid eyes on her, she has been the only thing that mattered, and everything I've done up till this point was just me going through the motions.

It was me playing the part of the loyal son, living in the shadow of a man who I'm sure would kill me if it benefited him. He's never been a father, not in ways that matter to most. Family over everything is the motto he beat into me, and for the first time, I think I get it. Siân is my family, and I will protect her at all costs. So if that means killing the man who raised me to prove that to her, then so be it.

I blink away my thoughts, and at the same time, I realize the wetness on my face. A single tear trails my left cheek, and I quickly wipe it away. The closer Siân gets, the more comfortable I get with the decision.

If anyone is going to take out my father, should it be an enemy? Should I allow his legacy to be forever tainted? To give anyone outside the family the opportunity to claim that victory? No. They don't deserve it. He is my father at the end of the day, and it would be better that I am the one to end him and not someone else.

A sacrifice is what this will be. My entire upbringing has been a sacrifice for the family. The harsh parenting and lessons in murder and mayhem were all for the family, even down to ordering me to kill a man before I'd even grown a hair on my chest. He sacrificed my innocence for his gain, and Samuele's death will be the sacrifice for my future.

With a renewed look on life, I push my shoulders back and step off the makeshift platform to meet my bride. She's stunning. Even when she's visibly nervous, she manages to hold her head high. And I know that is partly because of Cynthia. After everything she's learned today, she is going through with our nuptials to protect the woman who raised her. But a part of her is also torn with herself. She loved me once, and I'm inclined to believe that hasn't completely gone away.

Siân turns to Cynthia, who smiles despite everything that has happened to her as well. Their relationship will be forever changed after the events of today, but every mother longs to see the day their daughter is married. At least, that's what I've heard. I've never had a mother, so I wouldn't know what that looks like.

The two hug in a long embrace, tears falling from their eyes. After a while, they break apart, only for Cynthia to take Siân by the hands.

"I am so sorry you're doing this to keep me safe. But—"

Siân shakes her head. "It's okay. You've protected me my entire life, and while you may have kept the truth from me, nothing changes how much I love you. It's my turn to worry about your safety."

Cynthia sighs, then gives Siân a nod, silently agreeing to the terms of our newest agreement. I want to feel sorry for forcing her hand and threatening to kill the only loved one she has left to get her to this point, but I can't. Siân is mine, and I will secure that by any means necessary.

After saying their piece, Cynthia turns and saunters over to her seat next to Tony. He sits upright, his resentment for her still brewing at the surface. I ignore the brief interaction between them and hold my hand out to Siân. Hesitantly she accepts after glancing around at all the faces of those here to witness this.

It looks like any other wedding, except the people in the crowd, are equipped with more weapons than in a war zone. Every member of my father's organization is here this evening, something I'm actually happy about. We still haven't figured out who ordered the attack on Siân or the hit on the other families. So having them here in case the motherfucker tries again is for the best.

Siân grabs the train of her dress, and for the first time since this all started, I take in the elegance. Helga did an amazing job pulling this all together so quickly. Tony too. One would think this has been planned for months, down to the color scheme, flowers, and décor. There isn't a stone unturned.

I give her a smile, and she returns the gesture. It's a lazy one at best, but a smile nonetheless. As she steps up on the platform and takes her place beside me, I'm hit with a sudden rush of nerves. Sucking in a breath, I pull myself together and signal for the priest to begin.

"Today, we've come together to witness the union of these two individuals. Christian Russo and Siân Giuliani," Father Frances says through a thick Italian accent.

As he performs the ceremony, marrying me to my beloved for eternity, everything else ceases to exist.

∽

AFTER THE CEREMONY, we all gather out on the patio for a traditional reception. Music blares loudly from the speakers, mixing in with the different voices. Loud cheers and jabs are thrown about, all in the name of a good time.

Aldo has outdone himself as usual. Tonight's spread is complete with every traditional Italian dish you can think of. Alcohol is served in rapid succession, and everyone seems to be enjoying themselves. Everyone except Samuele and my beautiful bride.

Every so often, I catch resentful glances from my father, but he hasn't outright said anything. But what's most obvious is the nerves racing through every fiber of Siân's body. She did well at the wedding by keeping her head high and not letting anyone see her flustered. Right now, though, while sitting between Cynthia and me, not so much.

When she reaches for the champagne flute in front of her, her hand trembles. I place my palm over hers to steady her nerves. She makes eye contact with me, and I see the fear and uncertainty in her eyes. Neither of us speaks, but words aren't necessary. In the short time we've been together, even with all of our differences, I know this woman, including what it takes to relax her.

Siân nods softly, mimicking the deep breaths I emulate. One. Two. Three deep inhales before she's able to compose herself. I know what this is about, and it has nothing to do with the fact that she's a new bride. In fact, it has everything to do with the promise I made to her.

A life for a life.

Her father died at my hand, and now, even though she hasn't said those words, she wants it to be me who avenges the first man she ever loved.

Cynthia notices the change in Siân as well. She reaches for her, pulling her close to whisper in her ear. Siân doesn't seem interested by the way she pulls away, shaking her head. It's funny how things can change in a matter of seconds.

Before, she was dying to be near Cynthia, but now that she knows the truth, she's barely been able to look at her. Even at the wedding, when they shared their moment, Siân was slightly closed off. I guess I have myself to thank for that.

They'll find their way back to how they were. At the end of the day, Cynthia is her mother and the only parent she has left. That means something to her, more than it will ever mean to me.

The sound of silverware against glass draws everyone's attention to the table in the center of the courtyard. Samuele stands to his feet while rubbing an old, callous hand over his Brioni suit. Instantly, Siân squirms in her seat, her nerves beginning to win at the battle she's been fighting from the second we sat down.

Samuele stares in our direction as the rest of the crowd watches him. With a hand over Siân's, I silently encourage her to keep it together and never show my father he gets to her. She's struggling. I can see it, and if all eyes were on her, they would see it too.

Leaning to whisper into her ear, I say. "Keep it together, topolina."

Siân swallows, the tension in her posture so loud I can hear her heart beating. She's flushed, her skin growing slick with sweat that glistens along her collarbone.

"Everyone, thank you for celebrating this special day with my son and his beautiful bride." He narrows his sights on us, the hint of a sarcastic grin threatening to peek through his otherwise pensive stare. "You know. I remember the first time Christian laid eyes on her, and he begged me to let him have her. It was a long time ago, back when her father and I were—"

Before he can finish spewing whatever deliberate lie he's about to tell, Siân springs to her feet, her chair flying backward and clinking against the pavement beneath us. I join her at the same time as Cynthia, neither of us fazed by the glances thrown our way.

Siân pulls her hands away, dodging our advances, and stammers back, taking off toward the house. Cynthia attempts to follow her, but I stop her, instructing her to return to her seat with the tip of my head.

"I'm going to check on my child," she combats.

"Sit," I snap. My stare is more pensive than the one my father wears. "Give her a minute. She'll pull it together."

It takes a moment for her to contemplate whether or not she wants to test me, and luckily for her, she doesn't. I return to my seat after she does, and when I look forward again, Samuele is grinning from ear to fucking ear.

Fucking bastard—and now more than ever, I can't wait to deliver on my promise.

I was wrong. I thought I could do this, but I was wrong. Nobody could sit there in front of all those people and pretend to be happy when they wanted no part of this in the first place. It's one thing to make the best out of a shitty situation, but another to pretend to be happy about it. So many eyes on me, so many expectations.

What am I supposed to do? Thank them for bearing witness to the happiest day of my life? It's obscene, all of it. It's evil. Taking something that's supposed to be beautiful and sacred and turning it into this ugly, twisted thing.

I wet a towel under the cold tap and press it against the back of my neck, hoping to cool myself off. I'm flushed, burning up inside, only it's not a fever that has me acting this way. I'm not sick. Not physically.

How is this my life? That's what I can't wrap my head around. I can tell myself all I want to that it's all a matter of accepting what is and moving on, but it turns out, things aren't that easy. I only thought they could be. Yet another way for me to run from the truth. And what is the truth?

I raise my head, looking at myself in the mirror. A blushing bride, I am not. More like a heartsick mess.

But the truth is, no matter how wicked and depraved Christian behaves, I'll still love him. There's no way to convince my heart otherwise. How am I supposed to pretend there's anything normal about that? How can I love somebody who'd so callously take a life?

How could I order him to kill his father?

That's not who I am, is it? I certainly felt like it when I issued the order. It wasn't even difficult. I felt no twinge of guilt.

The sounds of feasting and revelry going on outside the bathroom. Everybody's partying it up while I fight like hell to hold back the tears. Who am I? I hardly recognize the girl in the mirror even though she wears the face I've looked at every day. I wish I could pretend this isn't the real me. I would give anything to disassociate the way Christian does. Now I understand why he needs to do that. Why he pretends to have no conscience. It's the only way he can live with himself.

No matter how I've fought against humanizing him, I can't ignore the truth. No more pretending. He's just as human as I am, even if he acts like the devil himself.

After all, I proved to myself earlier that I'm capable of evil, too. Ordering him to murder Samuele.

My stomach churns at the thought of it, clenching until I'm sure the little bit of food I managed to choke down for the sake of appearances is about to come back up. I swing around and crouch in front of the toilet in preparation and hope nothing gets on my dress. Even now, I want to make sure I still look decent in front of the guests. I might be a raging wreck inside, but I don't need to look like one.

The nausea passes before anything comes up. I still wait, afraid to move in case I stir my stomach around too much. Once I'm sure I'll be okay, I sit down on a small chair that seems completely out of place but is a godsend right now. I have to sit down. My head is spinning.

Do not cry. Be strong. I grit my teeth, growling at myself in my head. *You're better than this. Don't let them see what this is doing to you. Don't let him see.* For once, it's Samuele I'm thinking more of, not Christian. He disapproves of this marriage. That much is obvious. At first, it struck me as odd. Didn't he agree to the marriage years ago?

The answer is obvious. Christian basically gave me the answer back at the hotel when we were hiding. His father had no intention of going through with the match. It was something Christian said when he described the way his father did business. He would clap somebody on the back and call them a friend when he had no intention of following through. He would say whatever needed to be said at the moment to get what he wanted.

Which has to be at least part of the reason he wanted me dead, along with my parents. Even though my mother wasn't really my mother. How am I ever going to make sense of all of this? It's like being lost in a dark maze. The walls are higher than my head, making it impossible to see over the top. No matter how I turn, I only end up hitting a wall. It's enough to make me dizzy and disoriented.

Thinking back to the deal Samuele made with my father has served a very good purpose, though. It makes me feel a little less horrible for telling Christian to kill him. It's what he deserves. He's had it coming for a long time.

And wouldn't it be ironic for his death to come at the hands of his son? Ordered by the girl who was never supposed to survive the hit he ordered? I'm sure if given a moment to think it over, he might see the dark, twisted humor in the situation.

But I've seen how Christian operates. I doubt he'll give the man a moment to think anything over.

Dear God, what am I thinking? Who have I become?

This time, when my throat tightens, and a familiar stinging sensation rises behind my eyes, I can't fight what's coming. I can only be so strong. It isn't long before a tear drips from my eyes, then another. I use a tissue to blot it as gently as I can, keenly aware of the effect on the makeup I tried so hard to get right.

I don't want to lose myself. How am I supposed to exist in this ugly world without erasing who I am?

It's no use trying to hold back the tears. Maybe this is what I need. I need to cry and let it out. After a few minutes, a glance in the mirror reveals a blotchy, swollen, tear-stained mess. So much for the beautiful bride. Nothing about this day has been the way it's supposed to be, though, so I shouldn't expect anything else.

A sudden knock on the door startles me. My heart jumps, and I drop the tissue I was using. "Give me a minute," I call out.

I stand, leaning over the sink, forcing myself to take deep breaths. I can't stay in here forever. Somebody was bound to find me. *Get it together. Don't show them what you're feeling.*

Another knock sounds, more insistent this time. Are there any other bathrooms in this place? There has to be. "Please, give me a minute." They try the doorknob, and I realize the instant it begins to turn that I forgot to lock the door when I came in. I reach for it, but it's too late. It's already swinging open.

It's only Christian.

In the grand scheme of things, it could be worse.

"Please, can I at least have a minute to myself? Is that too much to ask?" I bend back over the sink, dipping my fingers under cold water and patting my cheeks.

He doesn't say a word. He only stands behind me, his back to the wall, arms folded. I can see him out of the corner of my eye. "The silent treatment?" I ask with a sigh. "Don't take this the wrong way, but between the two of us, I feel like I'm the one who has more of a reason to be upset right now."

He's still silent. Funny how that used to scare me. I would go through all sorts of ugly scenarios in my head, trying to explain to myself why he was acting that way. What it meant for me. Now, though, instead of inspiring fear, all I feel is disgust.

"You know, now isn't the time to try to intimidate me," I warn. "I'm not in the mood to be who you need me to be. So if you're waiting for me to tremble and beg, you're going to be disappointed. Maybe it would be better to go back out to the guests. I'll be out there in a minute or two."

He still won't respond.

I grip the edge of the sink with both hands and look up at him in the mirror. "When did you change your clothes?" I ask.

He's dressed in a pair of black slacks and a dark-gray T-shirt. It's a little informal for a wedding reception. "You know, if we're going to be married, you need to learn how to communicate a little better. I can't spend the rest of my life asking questions and never getting answers."

The hair on the back of my neck starts to rise when our eyes meet again. It's the way he's looking at me, staring coldly. Like we're strangers. I've seen him wearing that expression before. Like with the doctor, the way he glared at her. Like she was nothing, nobody, lower than dirt.

"What did I do this time?" I whisper. A lot of the fight has left my voice, but I don't care. This isn't the time to pretend to be stronger than I feel. "Would you at least tell me? Otherwise, we need to get back out there."

Stony, impenetrable silence. There's not so much as a twitch in his muscles to give away the fact that he's more than a statue. All of a sudden, getting out of here seems like a very good idea.

Yet when I reach for the knob, ready to get away from him, even if it means facing my joyful guests, his arm shoots out. He takes hold of me, almost brutal, when he yanks my hand away from the knob.

"What are you doing?" I demand while he takes hold of my other arm and shoves me against the wall. "Stop it. This isn't the time!"

He only chuckles. It's a grim, cold sound that sends an icy finger running down my back.

"I'm serious. There are all those people waiting for us. Can this wait until later?"

I look up at him, ready to spit in his face if that's what it comes to—until I really take a look at his face for the first time since he entered the room. He looks exactly like Christian. The same features, the same eyes, the curve of his jaw, even the same ears.

But there's something different. I can't put my finger on it, but I know for sure that while he looks exactly like my husband, I've never met him before.

The breath catches in my throat when I realize it. "You're not Christian."

He lets go of one of my arms, grinning, before drawing a pistol from his waistband and hitting me over the head. Before I can scream, everything goes black.

MONSTER

22

CHRISTIAN

I lose track of how long Siân has been gone. My father finished his little speech, and everyone proceeded with the festivities as one normally would. Now, people are talking amongst themselves, and more food, drinks, and desserts circulate from table to table.

Two courses have been swapped out when I pull myself from my thoughts and stare at the empty seat beside me. Cynthia's eyes are focused on the crowd, her body rigid with unease. Nothing less than expected. She doesn't want to be here any more than I want her to be.

Throwing my gaze around, I crane my neck to look over everyone to get a better view of the back of the house. A tingle pricks through my fingers, and I inadvertently fist the arm of my chair.

Where the fuck is she?

I catch a glimpse of my father's expression when I settle back into my seat. He's staring at me. Leaned back in his chair, with his legs wide and discriminatingly smug. A chill settles in my bones, and the hairs at the nape of my neck rise. I can feel the cool, tingling sensation of nerves making their way through my body.

Why is he looking like that? His eyes are boring into me as if he's trying to get a read on me. Almost as if he knows that there is a shift in the air. As if somewhere deep within, he knows Siân and I have conspired against him.

I roll my shoulders back, putting the thought to the back of my mind. He doesn't know shit. This is what he does. Use his presence in an attempt to intimidate. It's useless, and he knows it. One thing he's hated about having me as a son is that while I may follow his orders, he's never been able to instill fear in me.

I stay in line out of respect for the hierarchy. The dark glares didn't affect me as a child, and they certainly won't affect me now. Especially when I know that today will be his last night breathing.

He's disrespected Siân for the last time. She's my bride now, which means that from this point on, she's my world—my everything. And she wants him gone. So I'll make it happen if it means making her happy.

A server cuts across my view, blocking me from my father for just a second. That's all I need to clear my mind and hold my head high. When the coast is clear, Samuele catches me staring this time, my scowl more menacing. I know my father, and when he gets this look in his eyes, he's up to something. For a moment too long, we share a silent disagreement.

From the corner of my eye, I see another one of the servants strolling by and reach out to grab his arm without breaking my gaze from Samuele. Something tells me that I need to keep an eye on him.

Siân has been gone way too long, and all of a sudden, I feel as if dear ole Dad has been watching me for a reason. I tug the man down so that I can whisper in his ear.

"Trovala." *Find her.*

He needs no other explanation and rushes off with a curt nod. With one eye on him and the other on Samuele, I somehow manage to watch them both. When the servant disappears inside the house, I focus solely on Samuele again.

Until Cynthia leans over and taps me on the shoulder. "I'm worried. Siân has been gone a long time."

I don't look in her direction. "It's fine. She'll be down in a moment."

Cynthia doesn't settle back into her personal space. "I'm serious, Christian. My spirit is telling me that she's not okay."

"I said it's fine."

Even though my sight is straight ahead, I can see the disappointment seeping from her; I practically feel it radiating. And it's loud and clear. Cynthia pushes back her seat, but I grip her wrist before she can get all the way up and force her back into her chair.

"Sit the fuck down," I seethe and release her with a jerk.

It isn't lost on me that Cynthia's mother's intuition must have kicked in. I'm sure it's no coincidence that she gets worried at the same time as I have an uneasy feeling.

Always follow your gut, is what he's taught me, and right now, that motherfucker is churning. Needing to know right now that Cynthia's intuition is wrong, I jump to my feet and step around my chair, buttoning my tuxedo jacket as I do.

I saunter behind Cynthia and let my hand rest on her shoulder. "I'll bring her down," I announce in a tone that only she can hear.

I'm gone before she can respond, dodging running into someone along the way. There's a slap to my back, and I give an empty tilt of my head and return the pat on the person's shoulder. Siân is the only thing I care about that I go into tunnel vision, not even registering the face of whoever it is.

The closer I get to the house, the faster my steps grow as the soles of my shoes scrape against the blades of grass. I stalk up the stairs that lead into the kitchen entrance. Suddenly, I hear the slap of heels against the concrete stairs behind me, but I don't bother turning to see.

It doesn't surprise me that Cynthia didn't listen. Like mother like daughter, I guess. We storm through the kitchen, past the dining room and grand living room, past the study, and past the ridiculously large paintings of twin pit bulls.

As we approach the guest bathroom, we spot the servant up ahead. His back is to us, and he's whispering with Helga. Helga glances over his head, her back stiffening and her eyes bulging when she sees me.

He catches the expression she wears and slowly turns to peer back at me. I can see the larger gulp he takes and know immediately that Cynthia was right. We both were.

"Dov'è Siân?" *Where is Siân?*

He shrugs with a pained look on his pathetic mug while shaking his head from left to right. Rage starts to work its way through me, burning me up from the inside out. In the blink of an eye, I wrap my hand around his throat and slam him into the wall. The pictures on the wall rattle, but I don't care.

Helga screams, and Cynthia claws at my back, yelling for me to let him go.

"Non lo so, signore." *I don't know, Sir.* He tries to slip his hand between my grasp and his throat, but it's useless. "Sono venuto a trovarla come avevi chiesto ma non era qui," he struggles to get out, gasping between words. *I came to find her as you asked, but she wasn't here.*

I release him, and he huddles over, fighting to catch his breath. I storm into the bathroom, and he's right—Siân isn't here. The bathroom is cold and stale. The water is still running, and when I turn to face the door, my shoe slicks across something slippery. Cynthia and I glance down simultaneously.

My body stills, back steeled, fists balled at my sides so tight I break the skin. My palm stings as warm sticky blood drips between my fingers.

"Fucking find her!" I yell and push out of the bathroom.

I see red, pushing Helga out of the way, but Cynthia catches her in her arms. Reaching for the closest painting, I rip it from the wall and toss it down the hall. It smashes against the tall decorative vase, sending glass everywhere.

But I won't stop. I spin in the opposite direction, stalking my way to the security room. Someone took her from right under my fucking nose. While we were all out there, she was in here being attacked.

I replay the faces of everyone in my head, searching my memory to be sure nothing or no one was out of place or missing. But I come up short. Tony was still at the table when I left, and so was Samuele. No-one else here would have dared to cross me like this, so that leaves just one person. Whoever sent that doctor and tried to kidnap her at the hotel.

It has to be the person taking out the different families. But why Siân? Why would they set their sights on her when there is a room full of men from our organization? Something tells me this is personal.

How did they know I was ordering a fertility doctor? How did they know where to find us when I was deliberately careful not to leave a trace? And how would they know exactly when to strike?

They had to have been here all along, just waiting for the perfect moment to get her alone. People enter the house. I can hear them in the distance as I force the door open and step into the cold room.

Fifteen security screens showing footage stare back at me. I slam my palm over the mouse, clicking from one screen to the next seeking a shot of Siân.

"Christian," Tony's hushed voice calls out from the doorway.

I tilt my head in his direction for a brief second, only to focus on the screens again. I catch movement on the camera on the top right.

"There." I point at the screen when I see Siân draped lifelessly over a dark figure's shoulder.

He's dressed in all black and seems to know the property intimately. He tucks his head, using Siân's body to hide his face from the camera.

"Christian," Tony calls out. "He was pretending to be one of the workers."

I peer at the discarded vest that's bunched in his hand.

I draw back, then jam my fist into the closest screen. It sputters, then fizzles to black.

"Who the fuck is he?" I demand to know. "How the fuck did he get past security?"

"We'll find her," he promises, already punching numbers into his phone.

As he puts the receiver to his ear, I remember my own phone and the tracker I had embedded into her engagement ring. I told her not to take it off for a reason. Initially, it was to keep her from getting away, but now it's probably going to help me save her life.

I dig my cell from my inside jacket pocket and unsteadily scroll through my phone until I locate the tracking app I installed when I got the ring. It loads painfully slowly, every millisecond feeling like an eternity. The bright screen screams at me, and a second later, the page fills with a map. I zone in on the blinking red dot, my heart shattering into a million pieces as I watch it rapidly move across the screen.

23

SIÂN

For the second time in months, I wake up wondering what the hell happened to me. And once again, my head throbs when I so much as flinch.

It's a different kind of pain this time. Sharper, more intense, radiating from one central point. And unlike last time, I don't have to think hard once the fog of unconsciousness begins to clear.

He's Christian, but he's not Christian. A twin? He never mentioned having a brother, much less a twin brother. How could he have kept that from me? Was I never going to find out? If he had been honest, I would have known I was dealing with a stranger in that bathroom. How stupid was I, worrying about cleaning the tear stains off my cheeks while he stood there, ready to do this?

I'm sitting in a wooden chair with my hands tied behind my back. Whatever he used to bind me, he did a solid job. Thanks to how tightly I'm bound, my fingers are starting to go numb. It's the same for my feet, which he also tied tight. My neck aches, and I wonder how long I've been sitting with my head hanging forward.

When I try to raise it, there's no helping a groan of agony. I might even have a concussion. He hit me so hard. Every beat of my heart is a throb at my temple, sending ripples of pain radiating through my entire head.

I open my eyes slowly, gingerly, and at first, I'm horrified by how difficult it is to lift my eyelids. Did he tape them shut? No, the reality is more gruesome than that. Blood must have run into them when my head hung forward. I can hardly see, and I can't wipe anything away because I can't use my hands.

I need to think. Panicking isn't going to help anything, especially when any change in my heart rate means increased pain in my head. I'm not going to get through this if I panic. How would Christian handle a situation like this? How far have I fallen that I'm now looking to him as an example of how to conduct myself?

First, where am I? Second, where is he? I don't even know who he is. I don't have a name to use when I'm thinking about him. Am I alone? Is he waiting somewhere, ready to jump out and threaten me some more?

I close my eyes again, deciding the first thing to do is calm myself down. I tried meditation in the past, back when Kyla decided we needed to become healthier and more Zen. Maybe one day, I'll be able to think about her without experiencing searing pain in my heart, but I can't worry about that right now. Right now, I'm trying to save my own life. And that means calling on every trick at my disposal.

Like meditating, I was never very good at it. My thoughts always kept wandering, which frustrated me and pulled me out of practice. I don't have to be perfect now. I only need to get my blood pumping more slowly so I can manage the pain.

I take a deep breath on the count of four, then hold it for another four count. While I do, I imagine the beauty surrounding the hotel where Christian and I went into hiding. The lights dance on the water. Sailboats float in the harbor, gently bobbing. Villas dot the hillside, lights burning bright inside, Like sparks of life in the darkness. It was so beautiful, so peaceful. I imagine it down to the last detail, even the feel of the chair by the window. Not the chair I'm in now, but a plush, silk-covered armchair. That's what I'm sitting in. That's where I am. And there's not a worry or care in the world. Breathe in... breathe out. I can almost smell the herbal tea sitting beside me.

By the time I let go of the image, the stabbing pain has weakened to a dull throb. When I tentatively lift my head, the world swims a little, but the pain doesn't increase. I'm in control of that.

Now, where am I? It looks like a warehouse or a factory. There are holes in the roof, letting moonlight trickle in. That's the only light I can see by. I'm pretty sure I can make out the outline of heavy machinery several yards in front of me, but I can't tell what it is.

I do know the floor is dusty. It tickles my nose, and I have to fight back the urge to sneeze. That's the last thing I need to do. I just know I'd have to start the whole meditation thing over again because it would kick off the pain in my head. And I wouldn't be able to wipe my nose, either.

I breathe softly, straining my ears for any sounds. What I think might be the skittering of rodents makes me shudder. I hope they leave me alone, wherever they are. Whatever they are.

That's all I hear, though. No footsteps, no voices. No heavy breathing. I think I'm alone. He left me here alone. I have no doubt he'll come back at some point, though. Or maybe he won't. Maybe the idea is to leave me here so I'll starve to death while Christian...

While Christian what? He'll look for me, no doubt. He might even already be looking as I sit here trying to put my thoughts together. He has to know by now that I'm missing. How long will it take him to track me down? How will he even know where to start? Did he know his twin was in attendance? Does he know his twin is even crazier than he is?

"Help." My mouth is so dry, my throat hoarse. "Help!" I shout anyway, even over the rising pain in my head. There must be somebody around here. Someone close by, someone who would hear my cries echoing. I try to move my feet, but all that gets me is chafed skin. The same goes with my wrists, but I have to try. I wonder if I could stand—while my feet are bound together, they aren't tied to the chair. There's no rope around my waist, either. If I move fast enough, I might be able to stand without having to use my arms.

Before I have the chance to try, unfortunately, a cold laugh cuts through the air. "That's right," someone encourages. "You keep trying. Maybe somebody will come and save you."

He's been here all along, watching. Yes, he and Christian are definitely related. It's exactly something he would do.

He steps beneath a pool of moonlight, and again, I'm taken aback at how much he looks like Christian. But even in his worst moments, Christian never looked at me the way this man does. With such cold, bitter hatred. I can't help but tremble under his gaze as he approaches.

"My apologies."

My God, he sounds just like him, too. It's surreal.

"It seems I ruined your wedding day. How thoughtless of me." He scrunches up his face a little before grimacing. "Then again, let's not pretend you were very happy. Unless I mistook the tears I witnessed in the bathroom. You didn't seem particularly happy, but then I don't have much experience with happiness. I'm not certain I would recognize it if I saw it." He speaks with a thick Italian accent, telling me he's probably lived here all his life. Not like Christian, who spent so much time in the States.

"You have nothing to say to me? Too bad." He shakes his head in what I know is mock sadness. "I wanted so much for us to get to know each other. After all, you're a part of the family now. My sister." How does he manage to make it sound so ugly? My skin crawls, even more so as he advances on me. I tense all over, prepared for him to hurt me. Why he would want to, I don't know, but then I don't understand anything about this family.

"You don't want to talk to your new brother?" He walks around the chair in a slow circle. He's having fun with this. That much is obvious. I'm nothing but an animal in a trap, something for him to play with.

"I suppose you aren't the talkative type. Honestly, I prefer it that way. I hate a bitch who rambles on and on like she expects me to care about anything in her head besides the tongue she'll use to lick my balls." He's behind me now, where he pauses his circling to run a finger over the back of my neck. I shudder in revulsion, unable to help myself. "There are plenty of other ways for us to get to know each other that have nothing to do with talking."

"Don't you touch me," I warn through gritted teeth.

"There she is. The feisty little hellcat. You weren't so feisty back at the house, were you? You couldn't even tell you weren't speaking to your husband. Then again, I'm sure you didn't know I existed until today."

"Why didn't Christian tell me about you?" My voice isn't shaking yet, but it will be there soon.

"You would have to ask him. Unfortunately, I don't think you'll have the opportunity." He takes a few slow steps, stopping in front of me. I force myself to lift my head and stare straight at him. I'm not going to cower and weep the way he so clearly wishes.

Not even when he reaches out and runs his fingers over my cheek, my chin. I grit my teeth, forcing myself to stay still and not give away the screaming panic in my head. What's he going to do to me? His hand travels lower, fingers dancing along my throat.

"My brother's lucky," he tells me in a soft, almost gentle voice before cupping one of my breasts. "I get why he would risk everything for you. Why he would fight so hard to keep you alive."

Suddenly, his hand clamps down, taking me beyond the point of pain, but then I've felt pain before. I've been humiliated, used, degraded. I can stand this. I have to. He wants to break me before killing me?

My mind reaches for something else to think about and lands on something he just said about Christian fighting hard to keep me alive. "It was you, wasn't it?"

The pressure eases, and I can almost weep with relief when he takes a backward step. "What was me?" he asks, almost playful.

"You're the one who tried to kill me."

He gives me a slow golf clap. "Bravo. There's more to you than a tight, sexy little body, I see. The things I could do to you. You would forget my brother exists." His laughter is cold, bordering on the edge of insanity. "The way he did with me."

So Christian doesn't know he has a twin? That makes no sense, but then why should any of this start making sense now?

"Oh, yes." He looks me up and down, licking his lips. "I would start with that mouth. By the time I got done fucking your face and filling that nasty little mouth with my cum, you wouldn't be able to smart off."

He taps his chin, tipping his head to the side. "What would I take next? Your cunt? Or your asshole? Tell me." He leans down, grinning. "Has he taken your asshole yet? Or have you been saving it for me all along? I would love to be your first time. Stretching you, leaving you gaping open so I could watch my cum dripping from you. Just the thought of it is getting me hard." He lowers a hand to rub his crotch, and sure enough, there's a telltale bulge beginning to stir.

"It's enough to make me want to get you off that chair and put you on the floor so we can get started." He comes to me, taking the back of my head in his hand, and I can't help but whimper when he pulls my hair. "I might get started now, come to think of it. I could force-feed you my cock. How much of it do you think you could take before you began to weep?" He pulls my head forward, making my shoulders and arms scream with pain so he can rub his erection over my face. I try to turn my head away while I groan in disgust, but he pulls my hair harder and forces me to submit.

"So many things we could do together. I could split you in two with this cock." He wiggles his hips, grinding himself against my face before finally letting go so I can gasp and cough. "And who says I'd have to use my cock? There's nothing like cold steel in a hot, wet cunt."

Moonlight gleams off the barrel of his pistol, and I whimper again. "Why are you doing this?"

"I told you. I only want to get to know my sister-in-law. To find out why you're so important to brother dearest that he would go to all the trouble to keep you alive."

"So you sent the doctor to the house?"

He taps a finger on his nose. "Of course. If you were going to be my brother's wife, you would have to be proven fertile. Otherwise, he would have no use for you. There would be no furthering the family bloodline."

"At the hotel. That was you, too?"

"It was only a matter of time before you showed yourselves." His lips curl in a snarl. "The damn worthless idiot botched it at the last moment. As they say, if you want a job done right, you have to do it yourself."

"You still haven't told me why."

"You'll find out soon enough. I do hate repeating myself." I can breathe easier when he tucks the gun away again. There's no forgetting it's there, but if it's not in his hand, there's less of a chance of him suddenly blowing up and using it.

"What do you mean?"

"I mean, once my dear brother swoops in to save his precious topolina once again, I intend to explain myself once and for all." He cups my cheek almost tenderly, stroking it with his thumb. "And then, I'll kill you both."

And I thought Christian was a monster. He's ten times worse.

Christian. He must be looking for me. Before now, I might rack my brain trying to come up with ways he could find me. Now, I'm not sure I want him to. It would be better for him if he didn't.

Because this time, saving my life will mean losing his own. And I don't want him to die for me. If I have to die, I want to do it knowing he's still alive. Until this very minute, I didn't know how much he meant to me. It's the cold certainty in his twin's voice, the absolute assuredness that he's going to murder my husband, that's suddenly cast a spotlight on my true feelings. I can't ignore them. I can't avoid them. It doesn't matter if it's wrong. I love Christian. I'm going to stand by that now, for as long as I live.

Though if this maniac gets his way, it won't be much longer.

24

CHRISTIAN

"What are you going to do?" Cynthia follows me, hot on my tail.

"Do you know who took her?" Tony questions.

I stalk toward the gun room, ignoring their questions, my focus on Siân and Siân alone. Bursting through the doors, I'm unbothered by the loud slap it makes when it knocks against the wall. Quickly, I punch in the passcode to the lockbox, impatiently waiting for the cases to spring open.

When they do, I grab three extra clips for the gun I keep tucked in my waist. Then I snatch an assault rifle from the rack along with a double-edged blade. Cynthia is spewing question after question at me, but I ignore them.

I storm past her but can see from the corner of my eye that she is still following me closely. "Christian," she calls out.

"Find her. I'm going to bring her home," I snip.

"Then I'm coming with you."

I crane my neck and push a deep breath from my lungs. "No."

"Yes." Cynthia grabs my arm and forces me to look at her. "She is my daughter, and I have kept her safe until you found us," she spits with her nostrils flared and tears brimming in her eyes. "You don't get to disrupt our lives and then make me sit back and wait."

I see her pain, and surprisingly, I get it. It hurts. Siân's been taken, and I know it's because of me. Not many people know who she is, and we've been careful not to tell anyone before today that she is the last surviving member of the Giuliani family. I can't help but feel like Cynthia's words are factual. I didn't have to take Siân, and if I didn't, she would be safe right now.

If she's hurt, this will be on me. But you better believe that if a hair on her perfect head is unkempt, there will be consequences.

"You will stay here."

"N—"

"Cynthia. I don't have time for this," I snap while gripping her by the shoulders.

She stares at me, eyes wide and breaths uneven. "She's my daughter."

I soften my hold on her and steady my own nerves before responding. "And she's my wife. I will bring her back—for us both. But I can't save her if I'm worried about you too."

"So you do have a heart?" she adds sarcastically.

"You mean a lot to Siân, so if I can help it, I won't let you get hurt."

"I can take care of myself," she adds.

Releasing her, I scratch my brow. "That's never been a question. But you're staying here. Tony."

"I'm not a fucking babysitter," he butts in.

"And I'm not a child," Cynthia retorts.

"You're going to stay with her," I order.

He shakes his head. "And what about you? We don't know who had her or how many men there are."

"I don't care."

"You should. I don't know what's gotten into you, Christian, but you're being reckless."

I take a moment, unsure if I should tell either of them what's really going on in my mind. The truth is, he's right, but considering the circumstances surrounding it all, I have my suspicions. Tony has been in my corner for years, and while he technically works for my father, I know I can trust him, and Cynthia—well, I might not be able to trust her, but when it pertains to Siân's safety, we see eye to eye.

"I'll be fine. Something tells me that whoever took her wants me."

"And what tells you that?" He fights.

I stare at Cynthia for a moment, not wanting to set her off more than she already is. Then I take Tony by the arm and pull him out of earshot.

"I need you to stay here and keep an eye on Samuele."

He frowns. "He's been weird lately. Siân's presence has upset him more than it needs to, and something tells me he might be behind this. No one knows who she is except for us, yet someone has come after her three times. I need you to stay put and make sure he doesn't leave."

"And what are you going to do? How are you supposed to find her and be sure it's not all a setup?"

I bring my phone to his face and show him the tracking app. "The engagement ring I gave her has a tracker embedded in it. Whoever took her has only come after her. Even with what's been happening with all the dead mafia family members, the only person they came after is Siân. Not me, not Samuele, hell, not even you. He's gone out of his way to make it known that he is bothered by her presence."

"What are you saying?"

"Think about it. Everyone this mystery killer went after is someone who is in rivalry with my father. The doctor who attacked Siân, only *we* knew she was here. And only *we* knew about the hotel I took her to. And only *we* knew about the wedding?"

"You think it's an inside job."

"I think there is more to the story my father has shared with us."

"He wouldn't do that."

"You don't know him as well as I do, Tony. He's a master at manipulating and deceiving. So I need you, the only person I trust aside from myself, to stay here. I will be okay. If I'm right, this isn't an ambush."

"You don't know that."

"Trust me." I turn on my heels while ripping my tux jacket from my body and dropping it to the floor. Quickly I prepare myself, stuffing all extra clips and slipping my holster on my body.

Not caring about anything else, I shove the device into my pocket, ensuring that I have all of my weapons, including the one I keep tucked in my ankle holster, just in case. They are still on my tail, followed by the slew of other people here to enjoy the festivities.

I ignore them all, storming toward my Ferrari with a mission in mind. I'm going to find my woman, and if it turns out that my father really has something to do with it, killing him will be the least of the torturous things I want to do to him.

Once I'm behind the wheel, I pull up the GPS to the blinking location where Siân is and floor it. In my rearview mirror, I see Tony, Cynthia, and even Samuele lining up in the driveway. I push them to the back of my mind and focus on the road.

According to the app, they are on the outskirts of the village in an abandoned area located right off the docks. It's been years since the civilians of the surrounding villas have used the place, leaving it open to all sorts of riffraff.

My engine roars loudly as I hit the curve at a one-hundred and twenty miles an hour. I need to get to her before it's too late. If I'm right, they aren't really after Siân. Had that been the case, they would have killed her already. Instead, they tried to take her from the hotel and again tonight.

No, there's a reason behind all of this. Whomever this is, it's me they are after, and I'm prepared to give them exactly what they want. And soon enough, they'll learn they've fucked with the wrong person. There is one thing I hate more than being tested, and that's fucking with what's mine.

They'll die—every last one of them.

The ride to the secluded location is dreadful and feels longer than it actually is. It's pitched black out, and thankfully there aren't many cars on the road. I coast down the single dirt road, hitting my headlights along the way. The last thing I need is to alert them that I am coming.

Tony was right about one thing, I have no idea how many men I'm up against. So if I'm going to get Siân and me out of there alive, then all I have is the element of surprise.

The path is rocky and uneven, and it's not until my eyes adjust to the change in lighting that I can see where I'm going. With only the moon to guide the way, I slow my speed and stay close to the edge to be safe.

Up ahead, a tall, dark structure comes into view. It's quiet for miles, the only sound coming from birds and waves against the dock in the distance. I pull over to the side of the road, snatching my weapons on the way out of the car.

Using the app, I follow the blinking red dot. According to this, Siân is being held inside the building about a thousand feet ahead of me. I throw my gaze around, taking in as much of my surroundings as I can with it being so dark out. The closer I get, the more I can see. There is a light on in the building, and parked in front is a run-down car. I don't bother to register the make and model as I duck behind the nearest bush to survey the place.

After several seconds of no movement, I inch forward, keeping low with my pistol drawn. Once I approach the building, I duck behind the car, then rush toward the door and press my back against the steel structure.

I listen for a moment, hoping to hear anything to give me an idea of what's going on inside. A chill runs through me, and every hair on my body stands at the sound of her voice. So weak and strained.

"Please. Why are you doing this?" Siân groans out, but her plea goes unanswered.

Peeking through the slit in the door, I spot her in the center of the room, and she's tied to a chair. From what I can tell, she's alone—not a soul in sight. I'd be stupid to assume whoever took her is not lurking, but I can't think about that. Not when she's visibly hurt.

Blood lines her forehead, part of it caked along her eye. My blood boils, red flashing across my vision for the fact that she's hurt. She's alone, afraid, and bleeding, and I fucking hate it.

I sneak inside, being careful to keep the door from squeaking. Approaching Siân, I dart my gaze around but don't see anyone. It appears to be just us, but there is a vibe in the air. I can't quite put my finger on it. It's a familiar sense but strange because I couldn't even begin to explain what it is. Similarly, when you know eyes are on you, even if you can't see anyone, like some sixth sense that sends waves of nerves and unease running through you.

"Topolina," I whisper while crouching down in front of her.

Siân jumps with her eyes wide and pushes her back into the chair to get away from me.

I frown, unable to make sense of her reaction, but I manage to get it together. "Baby. Relax, it's me."

"No, don't touch me. Christian is going to find me."

"Siân?" She's delusional. That must be it with the amount of blood she's lost.

She thrashes around, and I have to hold her still. "Stop it. You're going to hurt yourself. It's me, little mouse. I'm going to take you home." I inch around, pulling my knife from my pocket to slice at the ropes that bind her.

Before I can succeed, there is movement behind me, and I spin with my finger on the trigger, ready to unload the clip. But I freeze. Like a deer in headlights, I stare at the person in front of me, a face that matches my own that's slightly hidden behind the barrel of a gun. Confusion rolls through me, and for a second, I think I'm starting to grow delusional as well. Then he speaks, and I know that I am indeed lucid.

"Ciao, fratello." *Hello, brother.*

My stomach is knotted tight, confusion seeping through me as I stare back at eyes that mirror mine. His features, down to the sideways grin, are all the same. This can't be right.

Brother? He called me brother. I would know if that were true—wouldn't I? All these years, there is no way possible that the person standing in front of me is indeed who he says he is.

But I've always believed what I can see with my eyes. Sight doesn't lie. Words, actions, emotions, and even smell can deceive, but it's hard to dismiss the things right in front of you.

"Who are you?" I ask after a beat, my mind going a hundred miles a minute.

He huffs and paces to the right. I go left, being sure to keep distance between him and Siân. We stare at one another, but he's not nearly as thrown off as I am. This tells me that while this is the first time I'm ever seeing him, he's extremely familiar with me.

"Oh, come." He tilts his head with a click of his tongue. "Isn't it obvious who I am?"

I don't respond, so he continues.

"I'm you—well, a part of you. But I see dear ole Dad kept that from you."

I shake my head. "Why don't you fill me in?" I spit.

"You know, I don't know whether to be offended that you haven't a clue about me or excited to finally be face-to-face with the infamous Christian Russo...my long-lost twin brother."

"Yeah, well, the feeling isn't mutual. What do you want?"

"Your bride here asked me the same thing."

"It was you? You've been the one after her?"

He grins. "Ding. Ding. Ding. Uno per il mio caro fratello." *Ding. Ding. Ding. One for my dear brother.*

I growl under my breath and continue to block Siân from him as he moves about the space. Neither of us drops our weapons, and we seem to move in sync with each other.

"And the families. You've been taking them out too?"

"And to think Dad said you were an incompetent idiot."

I see red flashing across my vision. "He set this up?"

He stops moving but never takes his eyes off me, the gun still pointed in my direction. "Something tells me you already know the answer to that."

"Why?"

"That's a question for him. If I'm being honest, I've wondered that myself."

"No. Why am I just now finding out about you? Where have you been?"

"Oh, brother. We don't have nearly that amount of time."

"Find the time. You're here now and will die one way or another, so you might as well spill it."

He laughs. A deep, guttural chuckle echoes off the walls of the empty warehouse.

"Fair enough." He smirks. "What have you been told about your mother—our mother?"

I roll my shoulders uncomfortably but don't answer him. The truth is, I know nothing. From my earliest memory, it's just been Samuele and me —no mother and no brother. He's never even mentioned it, and now that I think of it, I never questioned it.

"She was the daughter of a rival family. Apparently, she and Samuele weren't supposed to be together, but he went after her anyway. And when he was done with her, he discarded her like yesterday's trash. But she couldn't just return home. She was pregnant by the enemy, and her family would never accept her or us. She managed on her own for a while, but eventually went to him for help, demanding that he take us in or she would go back to her family and tell them everything they wanted to know. But you know his temper, and he didn't take too well to being threatened."

I listen intently, hanging on word for word. It doesn't make sense, but rarely does anything make sense when it comes to my father. We do what he says because it's the order of things. He's the Don, our boss. Besides, how can one miss what they've never had? No brother. No mother. He's just a man with my face, sharing a tale that is hard to wrap my mind around.

"He killed her," I interrupt, some weird feeling spreading through my chest.

"Yeah. And tried to get rid of me right along with her." He lifts his shirt, showcasing the gunshot wound in his abdomen. "Only he failed when it came to me. He shot us both, her in the head, killing her instantly.

The bastard didn't even have the decency to make sure I didn't suffer. He left us on the side of the road, bleeding out. It was hours before someone found us."

"When was this?"

"We were four."

I shake my head. "That doesn't make sense. I don't remember any of that."

"Why would you? You were the chosen one. For some reason, he spared you, kept you safe while he drove our mother and me away, and executed us. They say I was lucky because, by the time I was found, I was on the brink of death."

"Where have you been all this time?"

"The people who found me took me in, nursed me back to health, and raised me. Ironically enough, it was our true family. They found me lying in a pool of blood next to our decomposed mother. It's still unknown if Samuele deliberately dumped us near her family's estate, but lucky me because I wouldn't be alive otherwise. They shared what they knew when I was older, but they could fill in only so many blanks. It was all speculation, really, because it had been years since she'd run away. But over the years, I've managed to piece together enough."

"And what? Now you're here to enact your revenge?"

"Revenge, vengeance—take your pick," he says nonchalantly.

"Something tells me you know my reputation. You're pretty fucking stupid to come after me."

"You've seen my work, brother. We're more alike than you think."

"We're nothing alike," I spit.

He huffs. "Oh, yeah. Who do you think put all of this into motion?"

I frown, glancing back at Siân, who stares between us dumbfounded.

"While you were chasing your pretty new bride in Florida, I found our father. I had every intention of ending him, but he made me a deal."

"And what was that?"

"He would tell me everything I needed to know, even give me your place if I did one thing for him."

I stare, and when I don't respond, he continues.

He grins. "Take out his rivals, and when I'm done, end you."

"And why would he do that? You said it yourself. I'm the chosen one."

"You were, but then you started to rebel, and well, you know how he is with those who disobey."

"And that's why you've been after Siân?"

"She's just collateral damage. Just a means to get to you, and if she has to die in the process, so be it."

I storm toward him, my teeth bared, and pull the trigger, but he's quick. He jumps out of the way, his laughter growing louder.

"We really are alike. When I asked Samuele about why he picked you over me, he said it's because he could see early on that you were unhinged, and he could use that. He needed a soldier he could mold into the warrior he needed. We shared the same face—you and I—but I clung to our mother while you did not. You were more interested in the guns on his table than anything else. But then he made that deal to give you her, and you've been off the rails. Well, not at first, but eventually he found out she was alive but figured there would come a time when knowing that would be useful."

"And now you'll fill that role," I deadpan.

"Eh." He shrugs. "I'm simply playing a role until I have his trust, then I'll put one through his skull the same way he did our mother. You may not remember any of our past, but I, on the other hand, remember every minute of it. And he will pay for what he's done right after I get rid of you."

I raise my pistol again, staring him in the eye as he does the same.

"What's your name?" I ask, my chest heaving.

"Why?"

"So I know who I'm killing."

He pauses for a minute, completely unfazed. "Enzo."

I nod, tightening my grip on the handle, but something clicks, something I've never felt before. I want to end him, make him pay for touching Siân, for thinking he can touch me, but I can't. As I stare in eyes—my eyes—my twin's eyes, I can't, and for the first time in as long as I can remember, I don't pull the trigger.

MONSTER

25

SIÂN

I don't know what's more unbelievable: watching Christian stare down the barrel of a gun or how much I need him to get out of this unharmed. I'd do anything he wants if that's what it comes to. I'll even be the wife Christian wants. Anything. *Please, God, don't let him die tonight. I need him to live. He has to get out of this. What am I going to do without him?*

I'm not afraid for myself. I know that much in the middle of panic worse than any I've ever experienced. Even if he dies and I die, too, it's his life I care about. He has to live.

What I feel must be love if I care more about his life than I do about mine. Until now, I knew what I felt but couldn't fully accept it because of who he is and what I've seen him do. None of that matters now. I need him. I love him.

One thing is obvious. Even if Christian is a quicker shot than his brother, somebody will die here. And why? For what? Call it the benefit of being a third party, but it seems I see everything much clearer than them. "Neither of you has to do this. You realize that, right?"

Enzo snickers, his eyes never leaving Christian. "Don't waste your breath. What, you think begging for your husband's life will change anything?"

"But why are you doing this? I mean, really? Who really harmed you? Was it Christian?"

"Siân," Christian warns. Like his brother, he's laser-focused and unmoving. He hardly even moves his lips to speak.

"No, enough of that. You're not going to tell me I can't speak."

Enzo blurts out a harsh laugh. "What a shame you'll both have to die today. She might have been just what you needed."

"And what would that be? What do I need?"

"Somebody to call you on your stupidity, for starters. She would keep you on your toes."

"Correction. She will keep me on my toes because I'm walking out of here with her once this is done."

"You know, you could both try to listen to me." I wish I could do something, anything but sit here in this damn chair. I'm sick of being helpless. There's nothing I can use but reason. I have to get through to at least one, if not both of them, and fast. Enzo is too wild, far more unpredictable than I thought even Christian could ever be. Like handling a live grenade.

"Both of you. Think about this for a minute." I turn my attention to Enzo. "Your father tried to kill you. And Christian." I look his way next. "Now you know he wants you dead, too. Do you find that hard to believe? Because I don't. I don't think your brother is lying."

"She's right, you know," Enzo agrees. "That is part of the deal. As much as I want to kill you for personal reasons, I'm about to carry out his orders."

"So you see? Who does he actually care about? Who is the only person Samuele Russo has ever given a shit about in his entire life? Christian, don't pretend you don't know the answer. You told me already, remember? It's him, first and foremost, only him."

Christian grunts. "She's right about that," he mutters. "You haven't spent all these years with him. I've seen it time and again."

"Enzo, think about it. You came back into the picture after such a long time of being away. He thought you were dead. And what did your father want from you when he found you alive? Did he encourage you to get to know your twin? Did he bring you into the fold or teach you the ways of the family business like he did to Christian?"

"Of course not," he snarls. "Why would he? He decided I wasn't good enough a long time ago before I was old enough to prove myself. I was too young to even know I was being sized up. I never had a choice, dammit. Because of you." He bares his teeth in a snarl, glaring at Christian.

I might have taken that a little too far, too fast. I need to dial it back. "I'm so sorry your father did that to you. He's a cruel and stupid man. I think we can all agree on that. He might run a big family and have a ton of money, but he's stupid when it comes to people."

He's breathing hard, but at least his finger isn't tightening around the trigger. "We can agree on that."

"What Samuele did to you had nothing to do with Christian. It had to do with him. You are a tool for him. You've systematically eliminated all his competition. All his foes, or friends who he was only using until they stopped being useful to him."

"Listen to her," Christian urges.

"Shut the fuck up," Enzo barks back.

I have to raise my voice to be heard over them. "Please, I know it's hard to hear, but you seem like a logical person. You're smart. Now think about what your father has made you do. Think about what it means to get Christian and me out of the way next." I glance at Christian and hope he manages to keep quiet while I handle this. All he's going to do is exacerbate the situation.

"It means I get what's been mine all along!"

"It means he'll find a way to get rid of you, too," I murmur. I actually feel sorry for him because I'm not making any of this up. None of this is much of a stretch, considering who I'm talking about. What would it be like, knowing my father wanted me dead? Not only that, but he went out of his way to arrange it? It's enough to make me want to cry for this lost, twisted soul who never had a chance.

"That's not true," he grunts out. "You don't know what you're saying."

"He wants to protect what's his," I remind him. "Do you think he would give it to you? I don't think so. It has nothing to do with you. I'm speaking historically. All this time, Christian thought it would go to him. And Christian has only ever done what his father wanted him to do."

"Except for one very important thing." Enzo lifts his chin, gazing at Christian over his nose. "Isn't that right? You let him down by putting your feelings over his wishes."

"And do you think there will never come a time when you won't make a mistake like that? Eventually, he's going to want you to do something that you can't do for one reason or another—and even if that never happens, he'll make up something. He's a wicked, cruel man. And he's greedy. He wants, and he wants, and it doesn't matter who he has to get rid of. He's a black hole sucking the life out of everything around him. No matter how much he sucks up, it'll never be enough. Do you really want to be just another one of his tools?"

This time, he doesn't have a quick little answer. He doesn't even tell me to shut up. Still, he doesn't lower the gun.

"Listen to me." I jerk my chin toward Christian. "Your brother never had a chance to figure out anything he wanted from life. Your father trained him to be a killer from day one. He never had a childhood. He had no friends, no hope of becoming anything other than what he is right now. And the one and only time he tried to do the right thing, look where it got him. He wasn't even allowed to save my life. I was ten years old. I hadn't done anything to deserve what your father wanted. And because Christian has a conscience, your father hates him. That's what it's all about. He couldn't break him. He couldn't turn him into some mindless weapon. And now he's turned you against each other. Why would you fight for what he wants when you can fight for what you want? Both of you, together?"

Enzo's eyes don't have that hard look in them anymore. I'm almost afraid to believe I got through to him. I don't want to get my hopes up. I think it's fair to imagine he's starting to listen. I grasp that idea and hold it tight.

"He never gave you a chance at living a real life," I remind him. "And I understand why you would want to do anything it takes to be part of his life now. If my dad was still alive, I'd do anything to build a relationship with him. But this isn't the way. You two should be working together against him because he pitted you against each other. That's not what a father does."

My throat's almost too tight to speak, but I can't fail now. I'm so close to getting through. "Christian's your twin. I have to admit, I don't understand that bond, but I'm sure it has to be there for both of you."

"Try again." His jaw tightens, and my heart sinks with it. I was so close. "There is no bond here. He took away everything that was supposed to belong to me, and he acted like I don't exist."

A snarl bursts from Christian. "I told you, we were young. I don't remember. What do you think that does to a child? He never talked about you. Dad pretended you never existed. When you're a kid, you believe in adults. That's the best way I can explain it."

For the first time, Christian looks at me rather than at his brother. "And she's right. The chance for us to be true brothers was taken from us. Neither of us had a say in what happened. It's not each other we should be fighting now. It's him." His face crumples like he's pained. "I don't want to kill you. You're my brother. The man who pitted us against each other should be worrying about it now."

"You can work together," I whisper. *Please, please, listen. Don't let him do this to you.*

"How do I know you won't try to kill me once we stop him?"

Christian lifts a shoulder. "It's a fair question. I would ask it myself. All I can say is, I'm willing to put the past behind us if you are. I understand why you acted as you did. I've done things for him, as well."

Yes, like murdering my family, I think. Samuele has been destroying lives for so long. It's enough to make Enzo lower the gun, and after a beat, Christian drops his as well.

I'm almost glad my hands are tied behind my back since they're the only thing keeping me upright. "Christian, please." My head drops forward, my whole body going slack. Now that it seems tragedy has been averted, I don't have the strength to hold myself upright.

He drops to one knee beside me, taking my face in his hands. "Siân, stay with me."

"I'm just... wiped out, I guess."

"You've been running on adrenaline all this time." He works at untying me, and before long, he lifts me from the chair and holds me close to his chest. Now it's real. Now I can rest. I wrap my arms around his neck, my head nestled against his shoulder while he carries me out to the car.

"Rest here now. I'll get you home soon." He doesn't get behind the wheel right away after placing me in the passenger seat, though. I watch through the window where he and his brother stand a few paces from the car. I hear their voices, but as hard as I try, I can't make out what they're saying.

When he gets into the car and doesn't say a word before pulling away from the old building, it's clear that it wasn't a pleasant conversation. I wouldn't expect it to be. If it wasn't for the intense energy radiating off him, I might tell him again what a relief it is, knowing he's safe. How scared I was for him. How I want nothing more than for us to be together, forever.

Instead, I don't say a word. It isn't that he's acting particularly aggressive or angry. That, I have experience with. It's his calm that has my nerves on edge all over again. He's absolutely even, steady. He doesn't even drive very fast, steering with one hand while clutching his gun with the other. It rests in his lap, and I have to wonder what he thinks he's going to do with it. Some questions are best left unasked.

The energy in the car is eerie. The only reason I can sit here and silently deal with it is because I know it's not directed at me. And unlike the situation back at the old factory, I don't feel compelled to beg for Samuele's life. I'd be more inclined to give him the go-ahead to do whatever he needs to do.

Still, it's chilling. He's completely checked out. I would have expected him to fuss over me a little bit, but he hardly looks my way. He's that focused on whatever it is he's about to do. Deep in the back of my mind, I have to ask myself what he's capable of in this mood. Has he snapped? Once a person snaps, there's no telling what they're capable of. That's usually when people end up dying in mass murders. Wild, terrible things like that.

I feel nothing but relief when we reach the mansion—strange, considering how I normally feel about the place. Countless cars are still parked around the property, so the party hasn't ended. Not that there would be any partying now. Not after I'm sure Christian tore out of there, determined to get to me. I doubt they're here to comfort Samuele, either. They only want to see how this plays out.

And by all appearances, they're happy to see me when Christian leads me from the car. I don't have it in me to get into a conversation, and I'm sure one look at the dried blood on my face is enough to keep most of them away from me.

Except for Cynthia. "My God." She runs to me the second I'm inside. Her arms are out, hands reaching for me. It only makes sense to lean into her embrace. "I thought I lost you."

"It's not as bad as it looks," I murmur before flinching back when she raises her hand to my head. "But maybe let's not touch it, you know?"

Christian marches past us, past everyone. He doesn't say a word. He acknowledges none of the questions, none of the attempts to shake his hand as if to congratulate him on a job well done. The house might as well be empty for all he notices. I can only watch along with everyone else as he storms up the stairs, presumably in search of his father. I know that's exactly who I would want to talk to before anyone else.

"My God!"

"What is this? A joke?"

"Who the hell—?"

The confusion now blooming near the entrance pulls my attention from the back of Christian's head. Even Cynthia gasps, clutching my arm. "Who is that? It can't be!"

But it is. And now that Enzo has strolled into the house like he belongs here, everybody else knows it, too.

othing else matters. Not the glances or loud gasps coming from everyone the moment I return with my bride or the shock I hear when they undoubtedly meet my brother, my twin—Enzo.

It's a hell of a lot to wrap your mind around, that's for damn sure. But the only thing I care about is answers. He says this was my father's doing. All of it. And now, I need to hear it from the horse's mouth. Samuele is a ruthless bastard, and none of this should surprise me. It does, and I fucking hate it.

To think, I questioned whether or not I could go through with it and kill him as Siân asked. For her, I would have, and after everything I learned tonight, there isn't a doubt left in my mind. He's never going to stop, especially once he learns that I know the truth about everything.

Heat creeps up the nape of my neck, my vision blurs, and before I realize it, I'm living outside myself. Watching down as I angrily search for my father.

"Dov'è?" *Where is he?* I snap, my anger now directed at Aldo.

He stares at me, uncertainty etched into his features, but he knows better than to deny me. "Nel suo ufficio, signore." *In his office, sir.*

I stalk through the house and up the stairs toward my father's office. Flashes of the night replay in my mind, images of Siân bonded and strapped to that chair, blood staining her beautiful face. My blood boils at the memory, and I fist my hands at my side.

Finally, I reach the entryway of his office. The door is ajar, and behind the oversized desk is the man who raised me. With a cigar in his hand and a drink sitting next to the stack of papers he's reading, he is completely unaware that his plan failed.

Pushing open the door, it creaks, drawing his attention. He stares up at me, his cigar hanging between his lips. Samuele reaches for his drink, slowly bringing it to his lips, then settles back in his seat.

"It's inhospitable to run away from your own wedding reception. Where have you been?" he asks nonchalantly.

I'm fuming. "You know exactly where I've been. But I guess you expected I'd be dead by now," I quip.

"And why would you think that?"

"Why don't you tell me about Enzo?" I direct with a tilt of my chin.

My father locks his fingers together, bringing them to his face while he rests his chin against his knuckles. The bastard. He sits there, void of any expression on his hideous mug.

It takes everything in me not to jump across that fucking desk and put a bullet between his eyes. To finally put an end to this once and for all. If what Enzo told me is true, good riddance. But I need to hear it for myself.

I shouldn't care about the truth. My entire life, it's just been him, me, and this business. There were no feelings, no emotions, no time to mourn, crave, or desire a maternal touch. But hearing the words that came from Enzo's mouth, the inhuman nature in which he killed her. I didn't even know her, and I felt my heart rip from my chest as the words left Enzo's lips.

All this time. All the lies. All the years I've spent living under his thumb, and he just decided to get rid of me. Is that what it was like with them? He was bored with her, so he killed her and tried to kill Enzo. But what if I wasn't drawn to the darkness? Would he have killed me too?

I need to know.

"You sent him to kill me, right? That was your plan, wasn't it? To introduce me to the brother you never told me about as I stare down the barrel of his gun?"

"What difference does it make? You survived, standing in that very spot."

"That's what you have to say? I survived. Why?"

"Why not?"

I stand stunned, briefly caught off guard by his rebuttal.

"You stand there as if your presence is going to stir something in me. As if you want some sort of an apology. You're mistaken if you think you're getting that. Enzo—your brother, as you so quickly claimed, was a means to an end."

"Even as a child?"

He doesn't answer.

"Was he a means to an end when you raised your pistol to the chest of a four-year-old? Was she—the mother you stole from me? If they were just a means to an end, why did you choose me?"

"You could have easily been a means to an end as well. You're looking for remorse, and you should know better than anyone that it's a fool's errand. You want an I'm sorry and—"

"I want to hear it from your mouth. For years, you failed to mention a mother or a brother as if never speaking of their existence would keep it hidden."

"Surely you didn't expect me to explain the laws of reproduction, Christian. I mean, has it not been your mission to knock up that…"

He stops short, a smile brimming on his lips when he looks past me.

"Little bitch." His grin widens.

"Christian," Siân's soft voice sounds off behind me.

I glance back over my shoulder, recognizing the fear and panic on her face. It's the same expression she had at that warehouse tonight. She's worried about me. But it's not just that. This is about what she's asked of me. I saw it tonight at the reception as she sat disembodied next to me. She meant it at the moment. Hate and passion would do that to you. But as the day went on, as she stewed with her stance, she realized she regretted ever having the thought.

"Siân, leave," I demand while turning my attention back to Samuele.

"Still protecting her. Haven't you figured out that she's been the root of all of this? You and this incessant desire to have her. She's ruined you."

"I'm your son and have done every fucking thing you've ever asked of me. And now you try to end me?"

"And that's supposed to mean something?"

"I forgot. You have no problem killing a son. You chose me over Enzo, but now you want me dead?"

"I would have settled for just her. But you had to interfere. You're worthless to me now. Enzo was a means to an end, and now he can be a means of replacement. Maybe finally, your little bitch will die when I order it and stay that way."

Before I realize what's happening, I move around his desk, reaching for his throat. He slaps my hands away, immediately reaching for the gun under his desk at the same time as I pull mine from behind my back. But I'm quicker and press the barrel into his neck, surely pushing against an artery.

"Christian," Siân screams. "Don't," she pleads. But I know it's more about her not wanting to see any more death than it is about saving his life.

I glance over at her, taking in the shock and desperation in his eyes.

She shakes her head. "Don't do it. He's not worth it."

She means well, and it's cute that she still thinks there is some way to save my conscience. That ship sailed long before I ever had a choice in my life. And in this world, every threat is worth it. If I don't kill him tonight, he'll never stop coming after her or me now that his plan has been revealed. There is truth to her statement, though.

His actions ultimately led me to her, no matter how twisted the union may be. And despite his demented ideology toward his own bloodline, Enzo earned this honor the most.

"I promised my new wife a life for a life," I seethe, and he stares at me.

He's unbothered, a man afraid of nothing, even with my gun pressed to his throat.

"You made me kill her father, and I was going to let her watch me kill you, but I think someone else is more deserving," I continue.

He laughs. It's low at first but slowly grows into a fit of hysteria. "Her? Like she has it in her. Look at you. You can't even do it yourself. Before, you never would have hesitated. She's made you weak," he taunts, digging deep with his insults.

"Sono abbastanza sicuro che si riferisca a me." *I'm pretty sure he means me.* Enzo's deep voice and accent comes from behind me.

From the corner of my eye, I notice him entering the room. Samuele strains to see, his eyes growing wide when he finally realizes that his plan has backfired.

"Sembra che l'unica persona che viene sostituita qui sei tu. E mentre il tuo freddo cadavere marcisce sottoterra, io rivendicherò tutto ciò che hai costruito," I whisper. *It seems the only person being replaced here is you. And while your cold dead body rots underground, I'll be laying claim to everything you've built.*

He laughs again. "You'll never live up to my name. I made this fucking family. I made you."

"You're right about one thing. You did make me, which is exactly why I'm going to enjoy watching him put a bullet through your skull."

Releasing him with a jerk, I walk backward, giving Enzo the signal to claim his life for himself. He denied him, leaving him for dead at the tender age of four. Samuele deserves to die today, and Enzo is owed the most.

A smile creeps onto my brother's face, and something inside me tingles out of familiarity. I guess we're more alike than Samuele gave us credit for. Samuele tries again to reach for his gun.

"Don't be foolish," Enzo taunts.

"Let me guess. You want revenge for me shooting you?" Samuele asks Enzo.

He shakes his head. "That would be pointless. I'm very much alive. But if you like, call it vengeance."

And with that, Enzo puts two slugs through his chest. Two holes, dripping blood in a spot identical to where Samuele shot him. Karma is a bitch, and Samuele's has finally caught up with him. He lets out a deep cry, his body thrashing in pain. Enzo watches for a moment, almost as if he's savoring the image of our father fighting for his last breaths. And just when I think we can't be any more alike, Enzo walks around the desk, stepping closer, then brings the tip of the Glock flush against his head. Without blinking or even taking a breath, he pulls the trigger, grinning as the life drains from Samuele's eyes.

Siân screams, her legs giving out on her. Quickly, I manage to catch her, keeping her up with one arm around her waist. Her mouth is wide open, only no sound is coming out. She's stunned, her fear stuck in her throat. She holds on to me, fighting to let air into her lungs.

"You're okay. Just breathe. It's all over now," I encourage, then peek over my shoulder at the scene.

We started the night on a different note, but in the end, Siân was right for what she said to us. Enzo is not my enemy. Samuele pitted us against each other. He lied to me, raised me to be like him, only to betray me. He discarded Enzo, made him an orphan, and left him to die. Samuele is who needed to pay, and now he has.

But one fact still remains. Our father might have orchestrated this whole thing, but Enzo played his part.

"Fratello?" I call out. *Brother?*

Enzo lowers his gun and slowly turns in my direction. When he does, I lift my weapon and let off a shot on his shoulder. He grunts, immediately gripping his wound to control the blood already gushing out.

"Touch my wife again, and the next bullet will be between your eyes." I turn to see the hall full of people. Every member of our organization bears witness to their boss slain at the hand of his own.

And like loyal soldiers they are, they step aside, silently welcoming me into my new role. No longer the Underboss, and not a soul here is prepared to challenge that.

With my gun in my hand, I pull a frantic Siân close to me and lead her past the crowd.

MONSTER

27

SIÂN

The only thing keeping me on my feet is Christian. He leads me to his room rather than to the practically empty cell I've been locked in all this time. I'm glad I have him to steer me around because otherwise, I'm not sure what would happen. I can't wrap my head around anything I've witnessed tonight.

It's all starting to catch up with me. The pressure in my head builds with every step I take. Images overlap memories of what I saw earlier. What I felt. Enzo overpowered me in the bathroom. I was already in such a terrible place before he ever entered the room. It was already carrying the weight of marriage. Being trapped. Knowing this is my life and wondering how I'm supposed to live every day for the rest of it as a Russo. Horrified at myself for ordering a hit. A murder.

Fear for my life. Fear for Christian's life. The pain, the uncertainty of being Enzo's captive. That's the closest I've ever come to death. Closer than the night, Christian decided not to murder me along with my parents. Closer than the doctor, the hotel, all of it. Within moments, if I hadn't said the right thing at the right time. What if I messed up?

All of it. It's all happening too fast, too much at once. And the cherry on top: witnessing yet another man lose his life. Even if it was only

Samuele, and even if he deserved it, I still watched another man's life get extinguished tonight.

Nobody could take this and feel anything but horror.

Nobody but the man I'm married to. I cling to him while stumbling into the bedroom, afraid I'll hit the floor otherwise. "You're safe now. It's all over," he reminds me in a quiet voice.

"Is it?" I ask.

"Do you still doubt me?" He sets me down on the chest at the foot of the bed, and I understand why. I wouldn't want to sit on the bed in this dirty dress, a dress that was so beautiful when I first put it on. Now it's grimy, caked in dust, the train filthy with old grease from the factory floor.

I shake my head. "No. I mean, how do you know? What if something happens tomorrow? Or next week? Will we ever really know for sure we're safe?"

"So long as you have me, you don't need to worry."

Right. But I also watched with my heart in my throat as he and his twin brother locked in a face-off. His life hung by a thread, and I had to sit and witness it.

"I thought I could handle this." I'm not talking to Christian. I don't know who I'm talking to. The air around us? The dresser across from me? My dead father? Am I losing my mind?

"Thought you could handle what?" Christian rubs my hands briskly like he's trying to warm me up. But I'm not cold. No, I feel hot and flushed inside. Like there's a fire burning in my belly. The dress is too tight, and I'm sweating again. I'm losing it. This is where I finally break for good.

My lips move for a while with no sound coming out. Finally, I find my voice. "I thought I could be strong. I thought I could live with myself, telling you to kill him. But that's not who I am. I can't become a monster to fit into this life. That's not me, and I don't want it to be. I want to still be able to feel things."

"There's no reason you can't."

"If it means feeling like this? Right now?" Even to my ears, my laughter is sharp and unsettling. "Now I see why you disassociate. I couldn't do the things you do and live with myself. I don't even know if I can live with myself now."

"You can. You did nothing wrong."

"I told you to kill somebody."

"To protect yourself. And as an act of vengeance. Don't get yourself so hung up on words and meanings. What you did, you felt you had to do."

"But who does it make me?"

"Siân. Only Siân." He reaches for me, ready to touch my face, but I flinch before he can make contact. His eyes darken, and I know I've hurt him, but I couldn't help it.

I only thought I could handle this. I was so wrong.

I touch a hand to my stomach when it clenches. My head starts to spin again, worse this time, and all of a sudden, I feel very, very sick. The hurt in Christian's eyes turns to concern, and he reaches for me again, but this time, I push him away before stumbling for the bathroom. He's behind me, trying to encourage me. I'm going to be okay, but what does he know? He's not the one with a hand clamped over his mouth to catch what's about to burst forth.

I almost don't make it to the toilet, vomit splashing upward from the force with which my body ejects it. Again and again, I heave my head halfway into the bowl.

His hand is on my back when the worst of it passes, rubbing in slow circles. "It's okay. You'll be fine. Take deep breaths." All I manage to do is shake my head before another round of heaving comes over me. I guess it was bound to happen after all this stress. The wedding alone was enough to make me feel sick, and so much has happened even in the past few hours.

The second round passes. I lift my head, hoping to catch my breath, and Christian meets me with a damp cloth. "There, there." He mops my brow, and I can't deny how good the cool cloth feels against my flushed skin. "You've been through so much. It's understandable, getting sick. But it will pass." He's almost unbearably tender, like he's taking care of a child.

I open my mouth to thank him, but unfortunately, all that comes out is more vomit. This time, some of it gets on him before I hover over the bowl again. When is it going to end?

Minutes pass while I hug the bowl, breathing as slowly and evenly as possible. He's right. This will pass. And it seems to be—my stomach doesn't feel as tight anymore like it's trying to expel its contents. I'm sure I've thrown everything up by now, anyway. My ribs and back hurt from the force, and my throat feels like I took sandpaper to it.

Christian gets up, rinses out the cloth, then returns to wipe my face. I don't have the strength to do it myself or to tell him to stop. And it does feel nice, almost as nice as being cared for. He takes the task very seriously, his brow furrowed in concentration as he cleans every last bit of mess off my face.

He notices me watching him, and the ghost of a smile plays over his lips. "You're beautiful, you know. You're so beautiful."

"You can't mean that right now."

He only laughs indulgently while helping me to my feet. I'm understandably unsteady, swaying a little. But there's no more nausea.

"I do." He turns me around, and without a word, he begins unbuttoning my dress. "You're the most beautiful thing I've ever seen."

"My face is a mess, my makeup is ruined, and there's probably still dried blood in my hair." I haven't checked my reflection. I didn't even want to look at myself while we were in the car for fear of what I'd see. "I'm pretty sure I puked on you a little, too."

"A little." He says it with all the care of somebody commenting on the weather. "I won't hold it against you."

When I undress, the ruined gown pools at my feet, and I step out of the circle of fabric. Christian turns on the shower, then extends a hand to me. I'm still a little woozy, so I accept the help without complaint. The warm water is comforting, and the idea of being able to wash this terrible night off me makes it feel even better.

I'm leaning against the wall, enjoying the feeling of water against my skin, when to my surprise Christian kicks off his shoes and joins me while still in his suit. "What are you doing?"

"Washing you. I'm not sure I trust you alone in the shower, the way you're swaying back and forth."

"Am I?"

"You are. But that's what I'm here for. Remember? I'm your husband." He gently but firmly positions me under the showerhead. At first, the feeling of water against my head makes me wince, but soon the discomfort eases. Once my hair is soaked, he shampoos it, taking care with the bump his brother gave me.

"Can I ask you something?" With my eyes closed like they are, I find it easier to voice the question weighing heavy on my heart.

"Go right ahead."

"How can you be so calm now? Your brother killed your father right in front of you, and you shot him for what he did to me. And not even tonight, either. I've watched you kill other people. You hardly reacted at all. Almost like it never happened, even though I watched it. How can you do that?"

He pulls the showerhead from its mount, tipping my head back to rinse out the shampoo. It feels so good. Under any other circumstances, I would love this. Being taken care of, cherished. Not to mention how good it feels physically. Having my hair washed has always been my favorite part of going to the salon for a cut.

When he speaks, his voice is surprisingly soft in contrast with his words. "Life, in general, doesn't mean much to me. I don't know if that's how I was born or how I was trained to think. Regardless of the reason, that's how I manage it. One life out of so many others. What difference does it make?"

Once he finishes rinsing my hair, he replaces the showerhead before reaching for a loofah. I wish I had it in me to laugh at how silly he looks, drenched from head to toe, his suit clinging to him. He might even be sexy under the right circumstances, but these are not those circumstances.

"Besides," he continues while soaping up my back. "You said it yourself. He wasn't much of a father. The man I am now is who he created. Consciously, at that. He knew what he wanted from a son. When I didn't deliver, he decided I was disposable. I doubt anyone would blame me for neglecting to shed a tear over his death."

I see the truth in this, and I completely understand why he'd feel that way. After everything his father's done, he has every right to feel nothing now that he's dead.

Still, this is the man I'm now bound to for the rest of my life, whether I like it or not. "What's bothering you?" he asks when I shudder.

"It's just..." I turn slowly, and not because the front of my body needs washing, too. "What happens if you get tired of me?"

"That would never happen."

"You can say that now. Nobody ever plans on getting tired of someone. How do I know that will really be the case with us? Five, ten years from now, will you kill me?"

He's not amused anymore. Setting the loofah aside, he places his hands on either side of my face. "Siân. I need you to understand this because I will only say it once. Nothing in this entire world matters but you. I would walk away from this house and the land it sits on and the country in which that land is located, never to return. I could walk away from everyone I've ever known. I could give up every penny and start fresh. It doesn't matter. I am tied to nothing."

He leans in. "Nothing except you. And if you told me to walk away from everything and everyone I've ever known this minute, I would turn off that water, put on some dry clothes, and walk away with your hand in mine. Always with you. You are the only thing I need in life and all I've ever wanted. You are the one good, true thing that exists. Nothing and no one will ever take your place because you are the only person who's ever made me feel anything more than boredom or, worse, emptiness."

He presses a hand to the small of my back, pulling me close until I'm flush with his ruined suit. It's not the suit I'm thinking of. It's his warmth, his solidness, the strength. The strength I need so desperately now when I've never felt so weak and lost. "I would lay down my life for you. I would destroy anyone who stands in the way of your happiness, your health, and your safety. No question. You're all I live for. You're all I will ever need. I could as soon live without my heart as I could live without you."

I want to believe that. I want it so much. And when he looks at me like he is and touches me the way he's begun to do, his hands sliding over my wet skin, I feel how much he wants me. I know the intensity of his desire. But is that enough? I can only hope it is. Because my heart belongs to him, and only him. And that scares me more than anything.

I feel him stirring against me and look down to find him growing erect.

"You see the evidence of what you do to me," he observes with a chuckle. "To show you how sincere I am, I'll take it easy on you tonight. No need to consummate our marriage just yet."

That does nothing to satisfy the hunger growing in me. It comes as no surprise, wanting him after everything we've been through tonight. It's the effect he has on me. There's nothing I can do about it.

I take his lapels in my fists, straining against him. "I just want to be close to you. I need you."

"What do you want me to do?" His lips are so close to mine, almost brushing against them. Anticipation is enough to make my fists tighten and my toes curl.

"Make me come, please. I need it."

He responds by closing his arm around my back, then leaning me against the wall before running his other hand from my throat to my stomach. When he probes my lips, I part my thighs, gasping at the touch of his fingers against my sensitive folds. It's a relief to connect this way. Getting back to the basics, where nothing matters but the two of us at this moment. It's enough to bring tears to my eyes, and they mix with the water still raining down on us.

"My beautiful Siân." His lips land on my throat, placing warm, wet kisses. "My beautiful wife. My everything, my all."

I close my eyes and melt against him, desire taking over everything else. There is no pain, no confusion, no questions.

"I love the way you respond to my touch," he whispers against my throat, breathing hard. "How wet you get without me having to try. You were made for me." He lifts his head. "Tell me. Tell me you were made for me."

"I was made for you."

And I was. How else can I explain what he does to me? Even when I hated him, when he made me feel dirty and used and scared as hell, I couldn't help the way he lit me up.

I wrap a leg around him, spreading wider, giving him encouragement to slide a finger inside me while his thumb works my clit. He rubs my

G-spot in time with his external strokes, and I have to press my face to his shoulder to keep from deafening us. It's never been this intense, the shocks radiating from where he's touching me.

I'm hanging on for dear life, riding out the full-body shocks rocking me. "That's right. Let yourself go. Let it all out."

His teeth sink into my neck just hard enough to hurt, and for some reason, that's enough to take me just a little higher. High enough for it to feel like my head's going to explode and like fireworks are exploding behind my eyelids. I shudder again and again from the force, sobbing out my release. It's almost scary how strong I'm coming. Stronger than ever before.

Even Christian notices. "Remind me to do it that way more often. There's nothing like hearing you come that way."

I can only nod. That's all I can manage. But if I could, I'd tell him I think it had to do with almost losing him tonight. Losing us.

The sun is out, sitting high in the sky, its rays shining in through the window. We're in bed, and Siân is sleeping peacefully. I stayed with her last night, catering to her in every way possible and monitoring her for any signs of discomfort. For a good chunk of the night, she was in and out of the bathroom. It wasn't until about four hours ago that she finally stayed asleep.

As I watch her, the clearer things become for me. She's worth it. Everything I've done has been to get us to this moment. Gentleness isn't something I do very well, but I'd be lying if I said it wasn't a nice change of pace. It's almost as if the moment Samuele's judging eye was no longer a factor in my life, the pressure shifted. The pressure I didn't really notice at first. This is my life—darkness and chaos—disappointment, betrayal. It was all something I've seen again and again.

But now that he is gone, I can see things for what they were. Not that I think I would be a different person if he was indeed a different father. But the question does linger in my mind. If my upbringing was different, maybe I wouldn't be as disassociated as Siân pointed out. The thought sounds good, but the truth is, I am who I am.

I continue to watch her sleep. She tosses a bit, settling her face close to mine. Her mouth is wide open, and the puffiness that plagued her features yesterday has faded. She's perfect. So precious—so innocent—so mine.

I lean down, planting a kiss on her forehead while letting my hand rest against her stomach. "I love you," I whisper.

For the first time in my entire life, I utter those words, and something builds in my chest. Heat creeps up my cheek, a tingling sensation spreading through me like wildflowers. It's her. It's always been her. I asked myself once if she could change me, help me feel something other than the world around me, and now I have my answer. We can make each other stronger. I can teach her to be bold, proud—a leader. And she can teach me what it means to be human—as she's so often put it.

Siân stirs but doesn't wake just yet. I smile at the pout of her lips. I think back on everything, trying to come to terms with how a mother could betray her. I thought mothers, biological or not, were natural nurturers and protectors. How could she not love Siân?

But then again, people do unthinkable things when they feel they've been pushed beyond their limits. Siân was a constant reminder of Marco's infidelity with Cynthia. Hell has no fury like a woman scorned. I get that now. Siân might have changed her mind about killing my father, but she'd been scorned too many times to count.

She'll never have to worry about that again. I'll keep her safe, teach her how to protect herself, and finally get her to pay closer attention to the things and people around her. I huff at that thought. Here I am, going on about her lack of attention when I, too, missed things right in front of me.

The knock on the door pulls me back to the present. Being careful not to wake her, I slip out of bed and walk barefoot to answer it. I don't need to ask who it is because I already know.

Yesterday took a toll on her. From the wedding, learning that Cynthia is her biological mother, ordering me to kill Samuele, and being kidnapped. One thing after another piled up until her body couldn't take anymore. At first, I just thought it was her body reacting to the trauma she experienced, but after about the fourth trip to the toilet, I realized it was something else entirely.

For the better part of the morning, I continue to watch her as if I'll magically see any sign that solidifies my suspicion. The only way to know for sure would be to test. I've never used protection with her, and it's been my goal to plant my seed inside her.

Fuck, she'd look so fucking gorgeous carrying my baby. I can't wait to see her round and swollen with the evidence of how fucking perfect we are together.

I swing the door open to Helga standing on the opposite side.

"Buongiorno, signor Russo. Ho le cose che hai richiesto." *Good morning, Mr. Russo. I have the things you've requested.* She holds a steel tray out toward me, bowing her head until I accept it.

"Grazie Helga." *Thank you, Helga.*

She nods and scurries away. Once she's out of sight, I quietly close the door and make my way back over to the bed. The scent of a hot breakfast fills the room, stirring Siân from her sleep. She groans and twists beneath the sheets before finally opening her eyes.

When she notices me, she smiles gingerly and stretches out her muscles. "Good morning," she grunts.

"Buongiorno, topolina." *Good morning, little mouse.*

"What time is it?" Siân wipes her eyes with the backs of her hands and sits up in bed.

"Just after seven."

"Really? I feel like I haven't slept a wink."

Approaching her, I set the tray on the mattress next to her. "That's because you didn't. You were up and down all night."

"Eww. I'm sorry," she whines.

"About?"

"I ruined the night. It was our honeymoon, and I spent the entirety of it hugging the toilet."

I smirk. "We've got nothing but time to commemorate our marriage. All that matters now is that you get something in your stomach."

"I don't know what happened. I must have eaten something bad, or my anxiety got to me."

"I have other thoughts." I settle in next to her.

She peers up at me for a moment while gripping the handle on the lid at the same time. As she lifts it off, she says. "And what's that?"

Siân glances down at the tray with wide eyes and her mouth open when she gets her answers. She shakes her head, her hands beginning to tremble a little. She's visibly nervous, sweat preening along her skin, and the pasty-pale complexion she wore as she vomited returns.

"No. It was everything that happened yesterday."

I pick up the test and rip open the packaging, then place the test in her hand. Siân doesn't move. She only stares at the stick, her chest heaving. After everything that's happened in the past few months, this is the best of them all. And once we know for sure, I'll have it all—my bride and unborn child.

"Get up. Go take the test," I encourage.

It takes her a beat, almost as if it took a while for my words to make their way to her ears. She's shocked, and I get that. Being pregnant is the furthest thing from her mind. But they say when a person dies, new life is born. While technically there hasn't been a birth yet, learning that she is indeed with child would be as close to that as I can get.

Reluctantly, Siân climbs out of bed and slowly trots over to the attached bathroom. She stares back at me every few seconds with fear and trepidation in her eyes. She crosses the threshold, and I hop to my feet, strolling across the space to join her.

The bathroom feels brighter, colder than usual, and I wonder if it's because we've just woken up or if the unknown is getting to me also. I stand against the sink with my arms folded over my chest as Siân rolls her panties down and lowers herself onto the toilet.

She frowns at me.

"What?"

"You're just going to watch? That's weird."

I chuckle. "Oh, little mouse. You don't even know the things I've watched you do."

Her brow furrows. "What is that supposed to mean?"

"It means you're sexy as fuck when you're fingering yourself. Now, piss."

Siân gawks at me. "W-Wha?"

I don't answer, but something tells me she doesn't expect me to. Without another word, Siân empties her bladder onto the stick, and as she's wiping herself, I take the stick from her hand.

"W-Wait," she attempts to get out before I have my fingers wrapped around the test. "My pee is on it."

Unfazed, I turn my back away from her, my sights focused on the reader. Siân flushes and washes her hand, the sound of her moving about behind me fading into the distance. The dial seems to taunt me, the results staggering like a video buffering.

"What does it say?" Siân asks as she steps in front of me.

"Nothing yet."

"Should it take this long? Maybe it's defective?"

"Shhh," I whisper when the first blue line dances on the screen.

I place the test on the counter, and we hover over it. There is an eerie silence in the room, only the sound of our breathing emulating through the air. Everything goes still at the plus sign staring back at us.

Siân is frozen in place with one hand on the counter for balance and the other resting on her cheek. She doesn't speak and has even stopped breathing.

A grin stretches across my face, and I drop to my knees to plant kisses all over her stomach. This is what I've wanted—her and our baby growing inside her. One day soon, it won't be just her and me. In nearly no time at all, there will be a little girl with her gorgeous face or a miniature version of me.

I've thought about this moment from the second I found her in America, but now that it's finally here, it hits me harder than I expected. Before, it was about claiming her, making her mine through and through, but this is so much more. Warmth floods my insides lifting her nightshirt up and over her hips, I grip her waist and pull her close to me. Her skin is soft against mine, her scent intoxicating. I don't care that there are bits of dried vomit on the fabric or that she's trying desperately to make me stand.

I stare at her flesh for a moment, running my gaze along her belly, locking every single hair to memory. Bringing my mouth to her stomach, I kiss her there. Over and over, I plant tiny love marks all over her belly.

She's going to bear my child, and from this moment forward, I vow to be a better man to her and a better father than mine ever was. When I finally get over the initial reaction to learning that we're having a kid, I peer up at Siân.

She's tense, uncertain. I can tell by the way her shoulders are hiked up around her ears. She is holding onto the counter with one hand, and the other is over her mouth. I rise to my full height and pull her into my arms.

"Hey. What are you thinking?" I ask.

Siân shakes her head, unable to find words. I kiss her forehead, then her cheek, and the other while pressing our bodies together. She melds into me, tucking her head in my chest, her breathing growing more erratic by the second.

She's panicking, a full-on anxiety attack wrecking its way through her. Her arms are shaking, everything is trembling, and I try to distract her. Anything to take her mind off things. But nothing seems enough.

"A mom?" she says more as a question. "I'm not ready to be someone's mom. You aren't exactly father material either, Christian. No. Let's take another one." Her words come out hushed and in rapid succession.

Cupping her cheeks, I force her to look me in the eye. "Siân. Breathe. The test is accurate."

"How do we know? Can't they be false sometimes?"

"I'm pretty sure you're thinking about a false negative. A positive is a positive, topolina."

"How do you know? How many girls have you done this with?"

"None," I deadpan. "The only woman I've ever wanted to bear my child is you."

"You can't possibly think that we're equipped for this. You were raised by a killer—you are a killer, for Christ's sake. And I—well, I don't know who I am anymore."

"You're my wife and soon to be the mother of our healthy baby. And we'll learn. For the sake of this child, we will figure it out together. I may be a murderous monster, but I would never hurt them."

"This is too much. I'm still trying to wrap my mind around being married to you, finding out about the lies Cynthia has told me my entire life, and now this. No. No. No." She pushes away, swiping at my hands when I attempt to pull her close again.

"Siân," I call out, fighting the urge to force her still. The asshole in me wants to sit her down and force her to hear me, but I won't do that. I promised her that I could be softer, so I'll use my words even though force is more my speed.

"Siân. Relax."

She continues to pace while rambling off all the reasons this will turn out to be a bad thing. "We don't know the first thing about being parents. How are we supposed to keep them safe when there are weapons all over the place and people coming after us?"

"Topolina."

This time when she doesn't answer, I step in her path, but it's as if she's zoned out. Lost in a sea of thoughts and scenarios. Waving a hand in front of her face doesn't get her attention, and neither does my touch. I watch her for a moment, finally realizing that if I'm going to snap her out of this trance, then I need to give her something else to think about.

Quickly I scoop her up, set her on the bathroom counter, and inch her legs apart. She's positioned at the perfect height, her sex nearly aligned with my crotch. My dick twitches as I try to figure out why it's taking so long for me to take her this way.

The skin on her inner thighs is soft against my waist, her center warm and inviting. And finally, when I reach under her nightgown to hook my fingers into the waistband of her panties and slip them from her body, she snaps back to reality.

The rambling stops almost immediately, and whether she realizes it or not, she's already reacting to me. It's no surprise. She always does. Even when she claimed to hate me, her body always came to life at my touch.

And I fucking love it. I love every little thing about her, that dimpled smile, the little snort she has after laughing too hard, the way she sleeps, the softness of her touch, the sound of my name on her tongue, and this tight little pussy.

I let my thumb brush against her lips, and a soft moan escapes her. Having her like this takes me back to the first time I tasted her. We were in the kitchen of my loft in Florida, and she'd told me what she wanted the first time.

"You're so fucking perfect for me," I say in a hushed tone. "We have the rest of our lives to figure it all out, so no more thinking today. You understand me?"

She nods, parting her legs a little farther. I continue to run my thumb over her slit, but I don't part her yet.

"We still have a marriage to consummate."

She swallows, and I lick my lips at the bob of her throat. I want to kiss, suck, and lick her there to taste her flesh, savor every inch of her.

"You'd like that, wouldn't you, little one?"

She nods again, timid and meek. Just as I knew it would, the worry in her eyes starts to disappear and what is left is unadulterated lust. I don't mean to take away from the concerns she has, but the fact of the matter is, they're pointless.

She will have my baby and look fucking amazing doing it. And when the child comes, I'm going to knock her up again and again. And she's going to like it. Once the initial shock subsides, she'll love our life together. I'm going to make sure of it.

"What do you want?" I ask.

Siân's eyes light up because she remembers the meaning of my question just as much as I do. But unlike that day all those months ago, she isn't shy or too afraid to tell me what's on her mind.

Leaning back against the mirror and planting her hands on the cold surface for balance, she stares at me, eyes hooded and mouth slightly ajar. "I want you to fuck me, Christian. And then I need you to promise me that from this moment on, you'll keep me safe and stick to the agreement we made before our wedding. No more lies. No more secrets. I know it would be foolish to think you'll stop this lifestyle, even if you truly wanted to. I'm sure your father has made more enemies than you know. And now that he's gone, I don't doubt they won't come after you. But if I'm going to do this, be your wife, protect this child growing inside me, you have to keep me informed."

"I can do that."

"Good because that is what I want. But right now, at this very moment, I just need you to make me come."

I fiddle with the waist of my pajama bottoms, but she stops me with a hand on my wrist.

"Gently. Like before—like you love me."

I freeze in place, my heart beginning to pound in my chest. With a firm grip on her waist, I pull her hips forward, and she crashes into me with a huff. Her arms find their way around my neck as we stare into each other's eyes.

"I do love you, and I always have."

Siân searches my features, her eyes roaming over my face for signs that I'm being truthful. I've deceived her, so her surprise in my confession is warranted. I realize that I could have done things differently, should have done them differently. But somehow, after it all, she's mine, and I'm hers. And I'm going to spend the next fifty-plus years giving her everything she's asked for.

"I'll need you to be patient with me, topolina. Show me how to love you."

Siân nods while cupping my face. Tears form in her eyes, but I devour her mouth before they have a chance to fall. She kisses me back, a soft moan slipping past our lips. Suddenly the seriousness that was once present fades into pure lust.

Her hands roam my bare arms, over my chest, and back up to my neck. As she touches me, her fingers lighting a trail of fire across my skin, I jerk my pants down, freeing my rock-hard erection. It never takes much to get me ready for her, and today is no different.

Taking her request to heart, I softly guide her back, positioning her so that she is flat against the counter with her pussy toward the edge of it. For the first time, the obnoxiously-sized countertop has a purpose.

Siân squirms to remove her shirt, tossing it somewhere in the distance. Her back lifts off the counter from the cold, a low hissing sound coming from her. It's quickly drowned out by a cry of pleasure when I slide my middle finger into her tight cunt.

"Mm," she moans and grinds against my hand.

Siân seems to come alive, touching herself all over. First, her breast, where she squeezes and tweaks her nipples, then along her stomach until finally, she's rubbing tight circles around her clit.

"Fuck, topolina," I groan while continuing to finger her pussy. "You look so goddamn perfect touching yourself like that."

"Ah...mmm, Christian."

My words must encourage her because she quickens her movements, bucking her hips in unison. Soon we build up a rhythm of her riding my finger and petting herself, and it's the sexiest shit I've ever seen.

"A fucking goddess," I say in a near roar, then take my free hand to stroke myself.

Gripping myself at the base to start, I then tug on my length, squeezing my cock the way I like, the tip swollen and ready to play inside her. I scoot closer, remove my finger from her pussy, and use her arousal to coat the head. A mixture of Siân's juices and my precum is nearly enough to send me over the edge.

Sizing myself up to her entrance, I press against her hole, using my thumb to guide me in. And just as she was meant to, she stretches around my fat head, her mouth falling open from just the tip alone.

Little by little, I inch deeper, watching as I sheath myself inside her. Siân spreads her legs wider, and my dick twitches at the sight. Proud and turned on, I rub her clit with my other hand while still gripping myself at the base.

"That's my girl. Open that sweet pussy for me," I praise while teasing her bud and fucking into her.

When she constricts around me, I have to stop myself from slamming into her and taking her hard and fast. She asked for gentle, for me to claim her body like a man in love. And I give her that. Slow, long, steady strokes are all it takes to have her writhing on the countertop.

I hover over her, smashing her full breast with my weight to taste her lips again. Siân grips my neck, keeping me in place, taking from me what she wants. As she tongue fucks my mouth, she grinds herself on my dick, her pussy squeezing me with each thrust.

We're in sync, she and I. Good and evil. Yin and yang. Light and dark, and we fit. I knew it all those years ago, and finally, she sees it too. She's opening up to me, and I don't just mean her body but her heart and mind. Months ago, she couldn't wait for the opportunity to escape me, but now, I get the sense that she wants to be here as much as I want her to be.

She deserves the world, and I vow to give it to her. I can't change—not completely, but for her, I will fight every day to make her see that she means the world. She once said I was the perfect villain. Maybe with time, she can be my beautiful monster.

"Shit, Christian," she whines through clenched teeth.

Her moan pulls me from my thoughts. I lift up off her, and when my vision focuses on her, a guttural groan builds in my throat because her release is written all over her face. She's close, hanging on the edge of ecstasy, falling apart at the seams.

"Fuck, Siân. You're so tight. Your pretty little cunt so hungry for me."

"Ohhhhh. Yeah. Yeah. Right there."

I grunt while gripping her waist and pounding into her, my rhythm never wavering. Over and over, I hit the same spot, and her body thanks me for it by gripping my cock and convulsing around me.

Leaning down, I plant a kiss on her belly. "I love you, topolina."

The moment those four words leave my mouth, she explodes around me, thrashing and riding the wave of her orgasm.

"Oh, fuuuck," she screams.

"Good girl, soak my dick," I demand while thrusting into her one final time before filling her with my load.

∽

Enzo's book is coming next. Check out Cruel Beast now!

EPILOGUE - SIÂN

"You were so excited about getting your surprise today, but now you're taking your time." Christian's voice floats my way from where he's waiting outside. It's cute seeing him this enthusiastic. He's not the hard, cold mafia boss. He's not the heartless assassin, either.

He's been my husband for the past seven months, and it's moments like this that prove to me he's a child at heart.

It's a pleasure, even a privilege, the chance to see him like this. Nobody who doesn't know him the way I do would ever believe he's capable of such sweetness and thoughtfulness. Playfulness, too. It's easy to forget sometimes who I'm really living with.

Of course, that part of him is never far from the forefront. Business concerns tend to pop up constantly, but they don't seem to carry the same weight as before. I'll never forget Samuele's cold, imposing way of conducting his life. He was a bully, violent and hateful. With him out of the picture, the bloodshed has ceased. At least for now, much to my surprise.

"Don't forget, things can change on a dime." Christian has reminded me of that more than once—most recently, a few nights ago, while we were lying in bed watching the baby kick me until I was sure they broke something. He placed a hand on my belly, laughing in approval when his child delivered a hearty kick in response to his touch. "But now, with a family to protect, I'll be less inclined to respond with violence. I would rather keep the peace for your sake than display a trophy case full of severed heads."

While the image he conjured wasn't exactly charming, I understood the point, and it means the world to me. We mean that much to him. He's not power-hungry or greedy the way his father was. He's not a pushover —he won't give up what's his—but he's not inclined to reach for more, no matter what the price.

"Siân! We still have to pick up Cynthia. She'll be waiting."

"I don't move as fast as I used to, or have you forgotten?" That's an understatement. I'm practically waddling now, only a handful of weeks from my due date. I didn't think it would be possible for my body to get this big and swollen. It's almost supernatural. If we hadn't already gotten confirmation from the doctor, I would swear there's more than one baby in here. With Christian being a twin, it wouldn't be outside the realm of possibility. I guess the only explanation is I'm going to give birth to a linebacker, then.

"I guess Grandma can't be annoyed if that's why we're running late." Over these last seven months, Christian and Cynthia's relationship has improved to the point where he can refer to her as the baby's grandmother without rolling his eyes or gritting his teeth, or otherwise demonstrating bitterness or hostility. He doesn't want the baby to know the kind of tension and strife he did when he was little. If it means getting past what's already come between them, he's willing to do it.

So is Cynthia, which comes as an even bigger surprise. If ever anyone could hold a grudge, it's her. Now I understand the reason for the grudge she held against the Russos, at least. That makes the civil, if not exactly warm, relationship she and Christian now enjoy that much more precious in my eyes. I'm sure with time, things will warm up even more.

I manage to wait until I'm in the car before peppering him with questions. "Will you at least tell me where we're going? Is it a place, or are we going to pick up something? Will it fit in the car? Is it for the baby?"

He starts the car, doing his best to fight off a smile. He's not doing a very good job of it. "No. You'll see when we get there."

"You know I don't like surprises."

"That's not true. You don't like not knowing what's coming next. There's a difference."

"Can you blame me? Honestly."

"No, I can't," he admits. "But don't you know by now you can trust me? I'm not setting you up for a letdown." His fingers tap against the steering wheel, and unless my ears deceive me, he even starts humming to himself as he drives to the house Cynthia has been renting since the wedding. I invited her to come live with us, but she decided she wanted her own space. I have a feeling it had more to do with the mixed feelings between her and Christian, not to mention everything Samuele put her through. He's been dead all this time, but he still looms large. There are moments when I almost expect to see him coming around the corner wearing that cold, imperious expression he managed to perfect somehow.

As always, Cynthia's first questions are about the baby. "How are you feeling? Did you get any sleep?" She slides into the back seat before leaning forward to kiss my cheek.

"I just talked to you on the phone this morning, remember?"

"I thought you said you were going to try to take a nap."

"I swear, you're no better than he is." I jerk my chin in my husband's direction.

"Far be it for me to care whether my wife is healthy and getting all the rest she needs." He rolls his eyes, but his grin gives him away. Whatever he's taking me to, he's ridiculously excited about it. I can't help but feed off that energy. It must be something really good if he feels this strongly about it.

"Are you kidding me? I'm surprised you let me do anything at all, Mr. Protective."

Cynthia lets out a knowing laugh. "Like you don't love it. We both know it makes you feel good to have others fawn over the way you are, so don't pretend otherwise."

It's times like this I wonder why it ever seemed like such a good idea for the two of them to be friends. All they seem to want to do is gang up on me.

"Do you have any idea where we're going?" I ask her, craning my neck to see over my shoulder. I can always tell when she's lying by the defensive hunch of her shoulders.

There's no hunch this time. "Do you think he would tell me?"

"Only because I know you would want to tell her."

She snorts, rolling her eyes. "I think we all know I'm experienced when it comes to keeping things to myself."

"That's not the kind of secret I'm talking about, which you know very well." I have to say, he's learning to control his reactions. As recently as our wedding day, I would never have imagined him capable of avoiding an outburst when someone contradicts him. "Happier secrets are more difficult to contain."

"So it's a happy secret?" I ask, nudging him.

"No, I'm taking you to a sewage plant. I thought you would enjoy the smell since everything seems to set you off nowadays."

He's not wrong about that. Things that never used to bother me suddenly turn my stomach. Even the smell of coffee. Cynthia swears that's perfectly normal, and everything I've read online backs that up, but I can't wait until things go back to normal.

Considering I'm going to get a baby out of the whole thing, it's not that much of a sacrifice.

So this is what it's like, being part of a family. It's been so long since the last time I felt like I had one. I hardly remember those days, and I've tried. Ever since the wedding, since learning where I really came from, I've combed through my memories and tried to deepen them. Being here in Italy, I thought the process might be easier. Seeing familiar places, that sort of thing. And it's helped a little. Just not enough to help me remember little moments from when I was a kid and the people I knew as my parents were still breathing.

This is the next best thing. Joking around with my mom and my husband while my baby sleeps soundly. Of course they are, now that I'm not trying to fall asleep. The dance party usually starts up after dinner. I don't mind that, either, even if I miss sleeping. I get the feeling I should get used to going without as much as I want. Things aren't going to get easier once the baby arrives.

"Just a few minutes more." His left leg bounces up and down now. The closer we get, the more excited he is.

I've never seen him like this. This has to be better than good, whatever it is.

He slows the car before turning onto a narrow road which soon opens onto a gravel driveway. Now he drops the speed further until we're almost crawling. Something about this is vaguely familiar.

"Have I been here before?" I look at him, then at Cynthia. She has a funny look on her face.

"No... Not here, though it does look familiar." She stares out the window, frowning. "Uncanny."

"What is this? Tell me. No joking." I'm speaking to Christian but staring out the windshield. Every roll of the wheels makes me more convinced I've been here in the past. When I was little, of course.

"You tell me."

He nods, and I follow the direction he's looking in. Now I can't believe my eyes. Now I know what I'm looking at—at least, what I think I'm looking at. It can't be, though.

"Christian!" Cynthia places her hands against the window. I turn my head to watch her. She looks like she's on the verge of a meltdown, but in a good way. If there is such a thing. "How did you do this? Is this the surprise?"

"You're looking at your new home if you'd be so inclined to share it with us. There's plenty of space. You should know that."

"Siân." Her hand grips my shoulder now, hard enough to make me wince. "Do you know what it is? Do you recognize it?"

"If… I had to guess," I venture, "it's the house I lived in when I was little."

"Close. It's a replica of your childhood home." He takes us the rest of the way up a winding driveway before pulling to a stop in the circular courtyard. Cynthia weeps softly in the back seat while I stare up at the stucco walls, the tile roof, and the lush landscaping.

He turns in his seat to look at both of us. "I located the plans for the original house. I wanted you, Siân, to live somewhere that reminds you of how life was before my father stepped in and destroyed it."

"But we didn't need a new house." Why that's the first thing that comes to mind, I don't know. My brain's not moving in a linear fashion right now.

"No, but you can't pretend being in my father's home doesn't remind you of everything he did. I don't want to put you through that. You deserve a new home where you can build new memories. With our family."

He looks at Cynthia next. "I meant what I said a minute ago. I would be happy to have you living here with us. You'd have all the time you want with this grandchild and the others who come after them. You and Siân would have the opportunity to be together, too. You deserve that."

My heart's too full to speak. I look back at Cynthia, waiting for her to respond.

Instead of saying it in words, she bursts out of the car and runs around to the driver's door. Christian opens it and barely manages to get on his feet before she throws her arms around him. "Thank you. Thank you." He pats her back and murmurs about it being his pleasure.

She leans in a little. "You coming in to look around?"

I'm sure I've never seen her this happy, except maybe when she learned about the baby.

"Give me a minute. I need to take it all in." I open the door, and Christian is quick to hurry over to help me. Under any other conditions, I'd wave him off, but right now, I need all the help I can get.

"What gave you this idea?" I ask once I'm on my feet. "And how the hell did you keep it a secret?"

He's glowing from his cleverness and pride. "I made sure the contractors and landscapers knew their asses were entirely mine if they so much as whispered to their girlfriends about this project. Word spreads fast. They signed agreements to keep it confidential."

"Smart."

"As for myself..." He grins, shrugging. "I told myself it would be worth watching you when we arrived. Are you happy?"

"Happy?" It seems like such a needless question. Don't I look it? "I've never been so happy in my whole life."

"Then it was all worth it." He pulls me in for a hug, kissing the top of my head. "Every bit. I can't wait to watch you make it a home. You have everything you want at your fingertips. The sky's the limit."

Yes, for once, I don't mind the idea of spending a ton of money. It's the fortune Samuele amassed, minus the chunk Christian gave Enzo. It was only fair. He's a Russo, too. While I doubt he'll come around for every holiday and family event, he did promise to attend the baby's christening. Small steps in the right direction.

He leans down, his lips brushing my ear. "And while this is a replica of your childhood home, where you were once young and innocent, make no mistake about it. I intend to degrade you in every single room, in every way possible."

"I'd be worried if that wasn't on your mind."

We exchange a knowing smile before starting toward the house. I can't wait to explore. I can't wait to raise a family here.

With my husband at my side, always.

About J.L. Beck

J.L. Beck is a **USA TODAY** and international bestselling author and one half of the author duo Beck & Hallman.

When she isn't writing you can find her sitting with a cup of coffee, in a comfy chair, with a book in hand. She's a mom (both kids and pups), wife, and introvert.

Learn more about her books on her website

www.bleedingheartromance.com

About S. Rena

S. RENA (SADE RENA) IS A *USA TODAY* BESTSELLING AUTHOR OF DARK CONTEMPORARY AND DARK PARANORMAL ROMANCE.

AS WITH HER CONTEMPORARY TITLES, SADE ENJOYS SPINNING TALES THAT ARE ANGSTY, EMOTIONAL, AND SEXY. BUT BECAUSE SHE LOVES A VILLAIN JUST AS MUCH AS SHE LOVES A HERO, SHE ALSO WRITES DARK, DIVERSE CHARACTERS WHO ARE FLAWED AND MORALLY GREY.

VISIT WWW.SADERENA.COM

Printed in Great Britain
by Amazon